ABOUT THIS BOOK

A witch, an angel, and a psychic face off with a supernatural force terrorizing their hometown—with its eyes set on the world.

Addie Beaumont, witch and future coven leader, loves her hometown of Havenwood Falls and would do anything to protect it. So when the supernatural village is threatened by a mysterious entity only known as the Collector, she's the natural choice to lead a task force to identify and stop him.

With little information about the Collector, Addie recruits psychic Harper Sinclair, who channels demons, and angel Micah Westbrook, protector of a teenaged oracle. But Harper's messages from Hell reveal only doom and gloom, and Micah refuses to contact the Divine, which could invite something much more dangerous to town.

But then people are attacked. Harper vanishes. And Micah's young ward is targeted next.

Micah must learn to trust Addie and this town to help protect his charge. Harper must embrace the darkness within her and control the demons before they control her. And Addie must face the fact that not everyone will go as far as she will to defend their home. But if she and the others fail in battle, the Collector will not only overtake Havenwood Falls, but will move on to the rest of the world. For this enigmatic entity has only just awakened.

HAVENWOOD FALLS BOOKS

Forever Loyal by E.J. Fechenda

Fate's Demand by Emily Cyr

The Wu & the Wand by T.V. Hahn

A Demon's Redemption by JD Nelson

Also try the YA line, Havenwood Falls High; the historical paranormal line, Legends of Havenwood Falls; the darker, sexier side of town, Havenwood Falls Sin & Silk; and the local supernatural college, Sun & Moon Academy.

Stay up to date at www.HavenwoodFalls.com

THE COLLECTOR: AWAKENING
A HAVENWOOD FALLS NOVEL

KRISTIE COOK   R.K. RYALS   BELINDA BORING

NADIRAH FOXX

To the Havenwood Falls Collective
We Make a Good Team

PROLOGUE

*W*ind whipping at her hair and cloak, Camellia carefully climbed the snow-dusted, rough-hewn stone steps up the side of Mount Mae, in the southeast corner of the box canyon known as Havenwood Falls. The town spread out far below, the buildings' roofs no more than tiny squares and rectangles still noticeable among the budding trees. In another month or so, many of those roofs would be camouflaged by greenery. Camellia couldn't really see much, however, because she was in the clouds. Quite literally. Way up here, above the tree line and near the top of one of the highest peaks in the state of Colorado, the snow swirled thickly around her, and the small village below seemed to belong to a different world.

She paused to glance around, peering into the near white-out for the monolithic-like stone that marked her destination. Pinpointing it slightly ahead and to her right, she realized she had almost passed by it and likely would have wandered in circles in what were quickly becoming blizzard-like conditions. For the Collector's estate would have never shown itself if she hadn't found that stone. Bracing herself against the wind once more, she tightened her hand around her cloak, pulling it close, and pushed her way upward to the landmark. As soon as her palm pressed on it, magical energy coursed through her, and the cloud of snow cleared, revealing a large estate. The structure—all glass,

1

wood beams, and stone—seemed to crawl up and into the stony peak as though a natural part of it.

A dark, cloaked shape stood at the top of the steps, in front of the massive wooden door. Seeing that Camellia had arrived, the figure stepped backward, disappearing through the entryway. Camellia followed, hurrying into the warmth of the mansion. Although all of the glass should have let in plenty of natural light, she plunged into darkness upon entering. She was expecting it, though. The Collector was not exactly forthcoming with his—or her or its—identity. Camellia only knew what she *needed* to know—that this entity was one powerful son of a bitch. She hadn't lived as long as she had by being stupid, so she never questioned, never protested, never demanded to know more. She obeyed, and she was rewarded for it. Handsomely.

Movement ahead led her into a large dark room furnished with several seating areas. Camellia hurried to the one near the fire on the far wall. The firelight barely reached the nearest chair, but its warmth beckoned her. She sensed more than saw the Collector take a seat in a high-backed chair angled just right so she could see nothing more than the cloaked shape.

Although she couldn't see the Collector's face, she could feel the intense gaze on her, appreciating her new form. New compared to the last time they met, anyway. "You look exactly like her."

"You sound surprised. This is what you wanted, yes?"

The head bobbed once. "Yes, of course. What news do you have for me about our beloved little town?"

Camellia wasn't sure, but she thought she heard a hint of sarcasm drop on the word *beloved*. She certainly held no sentiments for the town of Havenwood Falls, but she hadn't quite been able to discern the Collector's true feelings for it. The Collector was a complete enigma, one whose secrets would only be revealed by peeling back layer after layer—and she had a feeling there were thousands of layers. She may never know much about this entity before her. Although intrigued, she wasn't sure if she really cared to. She knew the Collector was a powerful being, more powerful than anything else in this canyon, which was saying a lot. She was certain she didn't want to be around when that power was finally unleashed.

"News," the Collector repeated, more a demand now than a question.

Camellia cleared her throat before announcing, "Michaela Petran is indeed back in Havenwood Falls. The inn's ownership has been transferred to her."

"Excellent. And the curse on her and the Roca bloodlines?"

"The Luna Coven has contained it to the eldest Roca boy, just as you expected they would do."

"Excellent, excellent." Quiet appreciation could be heard in the Collector's voice, deep and raspy with both feminine and masculine properties, making it impossible to discern the Collector's gender simply from aural cues. "If he doesn't cooperate, we can use that in our favor. We'll help him turn strigoi, and the Court will eliminate him for us."

"I think he will cooperate, though. He seems to feel remorse for his actions."

The Collector nodded, long fingers tapping against the chair's arm. "Good, good. Then our plan should work, especially with Adelaide's assistance. She has a soft spot for both the Petrans and the Rocas. She'll encourage him to do the right thing—support the Petrans and help restore the inn to the glorious place it once was. And while they're at it, we need him to find the Eye of Valerian. The magic it holds . . ."

The voice drifted off with a sound of reverence, making Camellia wonder just how much magic the artifact held for the Collector to want it so badly. Or perhaps quantity wasn't the point. Maybe it was the type of magic that was coveted—the dark type.

"May I offer him a bonus for it?" she asked.

"Of course." The Collector tsked. "These people and their money . . . They have no idea what's truly valuable. Speaking of, do you have the list?"

Camellia fished in her cloak's pocket and pulled out her phone. "Yes, here."

"You broke into the Tomb under the Academy?" The Collector

sounded mildly impressed. Sun and Moon Academy was magically warded, and only those in the Order of Castor, a secret society, knew about the Tomb below the library.

"You hired me for my shape-shifting abilities. It's not difficult to sneak in when you look exactly like someone who belongs there."

"I suppose so." The Collector muttered something about troubles and Loki. A leather-gloved hand flipped out of the shadows. "Let me see what the Court thinks they're hiding from me."

Camellia flipped through the images on the phone, then handed it over. "This is a list of all the artifacts in their possession, and if you slide to the next picture, another list, of those they seek."

The Collector gazed at the screen, perusing the first image. "I know exactly where the Blue Dragon Dagger is. It is safe where it's being hidden—for now. The Lantern of Tír na nÓg would be useful, and now that Akeel has passed, it should be easier to attain. We'll work on that later. Many of these are not what they think they are, and I know there are others in that town and surrounding it that they undervalue." With a swipe of the finger, the screen changed. "Ah! There it is. The Elan Chain. They apparently don't know there is already at least one link in the canyon. I believe more are headed this way, if they hire that Egyptian woman as the high school history teacher. We need those links. They are of utmost importance. Even more than the Eye of Valerian. If Hermod finds them . . . I *will* not let him win again!" The Collector banged a bony fist on the arm of the chair.

"I'm sorry—who?" Camellia asked, bemused.

"Nothing," the Collector growled quietly. "My concern. Not yours."

Camellia dipped her chin. "I'll see what I can find out about the Elan Chain."

The Collector gave a dismissive wave. "No, not your concern, either. I have other sources. I need you to keep your focus on obtaining the moroi artifact. I also need you to reach out to Rachelle. With what's coming . . . I need her as my eyes and ears again. It's time she returns to Havenwood Falls and infiltrates the town. She did well in gathering intelligence last time. She did so much for us then, and I have a sneaking suspicion she'll be happy to resume her efforts. Her feelings toward the town and its people are not exactly warm."

"Do I keep this appearance?" Camellia currently wore the skin of Magda, a witch and a member of the town's precious Luna Coven. A former member, anyway. Now she was wanted. "The Court searches for her."

"Not in town, then. You will have to arrange to meet with Mr. Roca outside of town. He's familiar with that appearance, comfortable with it. He'll be more apt to trust Magda and cooperate. Otherwise, when you're in town, be someone new. Unassuming. A frumpy, middle-aged man or something."

Camellia nodded. "I know just the shape."

"Then you know what must be done. And Camellia? You understand the consequences of exposing me." It was not a question, but a reminder.

Camellia averted her gaze, ducking her face in a near bow. "Completely."

"Go on, then. Find Rachelle. And bring me the Eye of Valerian. Your stipend has already been added to your account."

Camellia dipped her head once more, hiding the small smirk on her lips. She'd continue working for the Collector for as long as it proved beneficial—and the money waiting in her account was very beneficial. But when that was no longer the case, she'd just been armed with a wealth of information, and she knew full well that information was power.

Which was exactly why she hadn't disclosed everything she knew to the Collector.

CHAPTER 1

ADDIE

The wind howled through the box canyon, blowing snow sideways, the sharp edges of its frozen teeth slicing through my parka and biting into my skin. I usually wasn't bothered much by the cold. Up until a few months ago, I'd chalked it up to the fact that I'd grown up in this small town in the Colorado Rockies, where winter was a way of life. Now I knew there was another reason my body stayed warmer than others'. Something I didn't want to think about now—or ever. I was a witch, damn it, and highly trained and naturally powerful at that. Nothing else mattered.

I pulled my coat tighter against me, not even bothering to spell myself against the cold—it'd be a witchy thing to do, but I was glad to feel the chill of one of our coldest nights yet this winter. It meant I *was* more witch and less . . . other. The thing I didn't want to think about.

Peering through the blowing snow, I eyed the looming shape of City Hall, a dark shadow on the far side of Town Square Park. I'd had to remove my glasses for this trek because they were pretty useless in any kind of precipitation anyway. I refused to consider that it seemed a little easier to see as far as I could—that my eyesight might have improved recently.

That was another thing I didn't want to think about, because it would loop me back to the first thing.

I blinked against the snowflakes catching in my bangs and eyelashes, looking for other signs of life. Although the snow and clouds reflected the streetlights of town, everything seemed so dark and lifeless now compared to a month ago. All the holiday lights and decorations had come down a couple of weeks ago, after the Festival of Lights on January eighth, plunging us into what I called the dark days of winter. Although our town was normally booked solid with festivals and special events, January only had two. The next one wasn't until the end of the month—the Winter Carnival. If it weren't for skiing and snowboarding, the first month of the year would be pure suckage here in Havenwood Falls. Thank Goddess for the slopes.

Not that I would have much time for them this season. I had a few things on my plate. Well, one big thing. I was hoping tonight's meeting of the Court of the Sun and the Moon, the governing body of the supernatural residents in our town—Who was I kidding? They were the true rulers of all the town: supe, human, and anything else that moved. Anyway, I hoped they'd give me permission tonight to focus solely on one particular task—saving a certain Asshole Extraordinaire I couldn't seem to quit and my best friend's parents, all of whom were trapped within the same curse, though in different ways. A curse they trusted me to figure out how to break, supposedly with the Eye of Valerian, an old dark artifact trapped in its protective cage and tucked safely away in a lockbox at home.

"Ah, there you are!" Speak of the devil. As I passed the fountain at the center of the square, my best friend since kindergarten, Michaela Petran, rushed up, falling into step next to me. If I hadn't recognized her voice, I might not have recognized her at all. She was so bundled up in her parka, knit hat, scarf, and gloves, that I could barely see anything of her except her green-gray eyes, the eyes of the moroi vampires. Moroi meant she was mortal, which also meant she was not impervious to the cold, unlike some of the other vampires in town. "What a ridiculous night for a Court meeting."

Michaela had claimed the Petran seat on the Court a few months ago to represent her family and the other local vampires. The seat had been left vacant by her parents and then her aunt, who'd all died in recent years. Their final deaths were all part of said curse I was determined to break.

I was the Court's business manager, a position I'd been given shortly after high school graduation as part of my grooming to take the Beaumont seat sometime in the future, after both my grandmother and my mother died. That could be centuries, though. Thanks to our magic, we lived quite a bit longer than the average human. So yeah, I probably had centuries of this job to look forward to. Having Michaela on the Court now made it a little more bearable. At least now when things happened that nobody else in town could know about, I had someone to talk about it with. Not that I was a gossip or anything. But in our town, crazy shit happened, and on a pretty regular basis. Sometimes a person just needed to talk about it.

"Do you need me to warm you?" I offered, already pulling my hands out of my pockets.

Michaela pushed in closer to me. "You're the best!"

With a few murmured words and a twist of my fingers, we were cocooned in a bubble of warm air. The spell was such a tiny blip of energy, I didn't worry about anyone noticing or caring.

"I was at the bookstore today, and Sedona's ordering me a bunch of bridal magazines," Michaela said, rambling on with excitement. "Of course, I'm not bothering Xandru with it, and you don't have to worry, either. I won't really get serious about planning until this whole thing with Tase and . . . everyone . . . is cleared up, but when we started looking at all the different ones she could order, I got a little . . . enthused. Sorry."

"No worries. I'm glad at least one of us has a distraction." I hadn't missed how she'd stammered over the issue with Tase and her parents, not even bringing them up specifically. Anybody who didn't know Michaela might have thought she dismissed their dire situation because she was more concerned about her wedding than the fact that they were cursed to a special part of Hell called the Infernum. Those of us who did know her would see right through her efforts to pretend like it didn't bother her as much as it really did. Looking at bridal books truly was a necessary distraction for her.

Michaela was a bit of a control freak. It made her good at her job —owning and managing Whisper Falls Inn and organizing all of its special events—as well as taking care of her teenage sister and brother, though she was only twenty-five herself. It did not make her good at waiting and sitting on the sidelines, having to rely on others to solve her problems. I'd rather have her oohing and ahhing over wedding dresses than hounding me every day about my progress. I got enough of that from the Rocas.

After crossing Stuart Street, we turned to go around to the back of City Hall, where there was a lone, quite innocuous-looking metal door with a moon logo embossed into it. My grandmother Saundra and eternal dickhead Roman Bishop had just slipped through the door as we rounded the corner. Michaela and I picked up our pace, knowing if Roman had arrived, the meeting was close to starting. He was usually the last to join the rest of the Court, not to be bothered with waiting on anyone else.

Entering the door and heading down the steps to the basement, we quickly caught up to Saundra and Roman, who strode down the long hallway in silence. Both of them had obviously used a warming charm, because neither was dressed appropriately for the weather. Saundra had exchanged her normal skirt suit for dress pants, but her coat was not nearly thick enough to do much good against the cold. And Roman wore his usual thousand-dollar dress pants (I hated to admit how nicely he filled them out) and a leather coat—again, not heavy enough for tonight's storm. They both wore expensive Italian leather shoes better suited for the Mediterranean coastline than the mountains of Colorado.

They were always jumping down supes' throats for doing stupid things, like riding motorcycles in the winter, not because of the cold or potential danger, but because no normal human would dare such a feat, and it would look suspicious. But here they were, dressed for a party in the tropics during our worst blizzard of the season. Hypocrites. I wondered what the members of SIN, our local motorcycle club, would think about that, but thinking of them led me down a different path of thought I preferred to avoid. So I was grateful when we reached the double wooden doors at the end of the hall that opened up to the Court's meeting space.

The room was large, with a dais on the opposite wall, where there was a table and several chairs lined up behind it. Most of those chairs were already occupied with the other members of the Court. Michaela hurried up to her seat, while Saundra strode with deliberation up the center aisle and Roman sauntered his way in that direction. Below the dais, spread out through most of the rest of the room, were rows of chairs, furnished for a large audience. There rarely ever was one, including tonight. So those chairs were all empty—until I took a seat in the front row. I usually sat at my desk back in the corner and took notes from there, but I knew I'd be put front and center tonight, so I may as well take the position now.

While everyone settled, I produced a notebook and pen in my lap and began jotting down the members in attendance, all of them leaders of their respective Old Families: Lawrence Mills, aka Old Man Mills, frost dragon shifter (he probably delighted in tonight's weather); Elsmed Fairchild, fae of the Seelie Court; Michaela, moroi vampire; Saundra Beaumont, witch and High Priestess of the Luna Coven; Mathilde Augustine, witch and High Priestess of the Luna Coven; Roman Bishop, warlock and High Priest of the Luna Coven; Lilith Blackstone, witch hunter; and Mayor Barbara Stuart, human (the only one on the Court). I also noted that Siobhan McFeeny (Spring Court fae) and Odette Alverson (siren) were absent, and Mayor Barbie said she'd be their proxy for any votes tonight.

Sheriff Ric Kasun, wolf shifter, sat at the end of the table, too. He didn't have voting privileges, but he'd been in this canyon long before any of the Old Families had arrived, and he was head of our local law enforcement. For those reasons, he was present at the meetings and gave input on many matters.

There was no real leader of the Court—they all had equal votes—but Saundra often took the lead of the meetings, as she did tonight. After calling the meeting to order, she tilted her head toward me, her gray hair in its usual twist, her forehead wrinkling above brown eyes very similar to my own.

"Do you have any news on the situation regarding Atanase Roca and Irina and Mihail Petran?" she asked me, her voice formal.

"Not much more to report since last time," I replied, referring to the emergency meeting called after Harper Sinclair had channeled the Petrans from their entrapment in the Infernum for the second time.

Harper, a psychic scribe who was still learning how to use and control her powers, had inadvertently contacted the Petrans on New Year's Day the first time. Their information had led me to find and obtain the Eye of Valerian, which had wreaked havoc in the lives of those I cared about greatly—the Petrans and the Rocas.

"No news about the skinwalker who had been trying to steal the Eye of Valerian," I added. The creature had taken the shape of a former member of my coven and claimed that she worked for someone called the Collector.

"You mean the shapeshifter," Mathilde clarified, and several heads turned toward her. "Madame Luiza called it a skinwalker, but it is not of the same ilk as those of Native American origins. This one did not behave in the same way, and the skin it left behind did not have the same properties. We've tested it. It's the same creature who'd been at the inn last summer, but it's not a skinwalker. We shouldn't call it that."

"No news about the shapeshifter," I said, correcting myself.

"And the Collector she mentioned?" Old Man Mills asked. "Anything more about him?"

Michaela's eyes caught mine momentarily as my gaze traveled to the old man. After the events of that night, she and I had speculated if Mills himself was the person the shapeshifter had blamed, since dragons liked treasure and he owned the local pawn shop. But we didn't even know if the Collector was real or if the shapeshifter had simply been trying to distract us with a made-up story before it escaped.

"No, nothing," I said. "If anybody knows anything, they're keeping an impossible secret."

"The people in this town are used to keeping impossible secrets," Saundra said pointedly.

"Then we must work harder in discovering who this Collector is," Elsmed said, thumping his fist on the table. "He could be anyone in this town, and a danger to us all."

"Or he could be no one," Roman drawled, his dark blue eyes sliding over each of the other Court members as if in challenge. Michaela and I looked at each other again. "And he's done nothing to threaten anybody yet."

"I'm sorry, but what about the Petran boy?" Mathilde demanded. "And Atanase? All of our vampires could have been destroyed—or do the destroying, affected by that Eye of Valerian the Collector wanted so badly. Look what's happened to all the Petrans and the Rocas already!"

"I assume someone has questioned Atanase about the Collector," Old Man Mills said. "It seems he got himself tied up with this person. He probably has information."

I peered at the old dragon, wondering if he thought we were dumb enough to not start with Tase or if he was trying to throw us off his scent.

"Addie and I have both questioned him," Sheriff Kasun said.

Old Man Mills pulled back. "In Elsmed's presence?"

"Yes, in my presence," Elsmed, a mind reader, said. "Tase thought he was working with Magda the whole time. If he knows anything about the Collector, he has a good way of hiding those thoughts from me."

He and Old Man Mills both turned their frosty gazes on me. It was no secret I carried an amulet that protected my thoughts from Elsmed's intrusion. Many of us who knew about him did.

"If he does, he didn't get it from me," I said, holding up my hands in innocence. "But I'm fairly certain he knows nothing about this Collector person. He's so anxious to break the curse on himself that he's pretty much giving in to my every request. I think he would have told me by now, so I could focus all my energy on the Eye of Valerian. And I'm honestly hoping you will decide tonight that I may do just that."

"I agree with Lawrence, though. This Collector could be a real threat," Mayor Barbie said, running her hand up the back of her fluffy pink bouffant.

Michaela piped up. "Look, all of us who were in the cave with the shapeshifter that night have already told you what we think—that Faux-Magda seemed to throw the idea of the Collector out as a last-ditch effort to take the heat off of herself. Until we have some other kind of proof, we don't even know if the Collector exists. In the meantime, Addie could be wasting her time tracking down a fictional character instead of focusing on the Eye of Valerian and breaking the curse on Tase and . . . my parents."

Knowing her as well as I did, I could hear the very slight tremor in her voice as she said those last two words. She sat back, staring at the far wall, her chest lifting as she inhaled deeply. I knew she was fighting either tears or an angry outburst. The mention of her parents, who had been close friends with nearly everybody on the Court, quieted them for a moment.

"Michaela is right." Roman broke the silence. Michaela and I exchanged another look, this one of surprise. Roman never agreed with her or me. In fact, he seemed to enjoy making our lives as difficult as possible. He was the last person I'd expect to do anything that would lighten my load. "With no further proof of this person's existence, we have little choice but to accept Michaela and Adelaide's theory that the shapeshifter mentioned the Collector as a scapegoat. A falsity to distract us. I, for one, don't believe in wasting my time on lies. Adelaide needs to focus on the Eye of Valerian and breaking the curse to protect our town from Tase." He paused, then seemed to add as an afterthought, "And to free the Petrans, of course."

Then I understood. Roman, along with his brother Ronan and their company Bishop Enterprises, had business dealings with Tase. The curse on Tase might have been a strain on Roman's bottom line. Either that, or Roman was the one doing the distracting—downplaying the truth of the Collector because he himself knew more about him.

Or because he actually *was* the Collector.

That had been another theory Michaela and I had briefly discussed the other day, after Harper had channeled the Petrans a second time—the day we'd learned that the Eye of Valerian was the secret to breaking their curse and I was the one to do it.

By the time the Court meeting concluded, I'd been ordered to focus my time and energy on the dark artifact and breaking the curse, the shapeshifter's story about the Collector dismissed and quickly forgotten.

CHAPTER 2

SENORA

*S*now crunched beneath my stilettos—not the wisest choice of boots—as I walked down Fourth Street. Thankfully, the white stuff had stopped falling, but the fresh layer covering everything made the landscape look like one of those Norman Rockwell paintings. Disgustingly sweet.

I dug my hands deeper into the pockets of my bright-red leather jacket and blew out a visible breath. Yes, I realized my apparel choices made me appear like a lovesick fool crazy about the holiday, but my intentions were totally opposite. There was nothing cheery about my reason for being in Havenwood Falls, and I definitely wasn't a fan of Valentine's Day. I simply loved the color red, and it looked amazing against my sepia-brown skin. It hadn't eluded me that my attire was wrong for my profession either—supernatural mercenary slash dealer of lost treasures—calling attention to me like a beacon in the night. I just refused to resemble some demon-hunting warrior—even though I had killed a few demons during my lifetime—decked out in black leather and combat boots. So not my style.

People rushed past me and across the sidewalk trying to escape the freezing temperature. Had I mentioned my distaste for snow? It had little to do with the cold air, though. A little chill didn't bother empusai—a supernatural mingling of a vampire and a wendigo.

Personally, I preferred a much warmer clime. It made me happy while keeping the food supply sweet, and there lay the *real* problem with winter weather. I wasn't a fan of frozen meals.

Unfortunately, I wasn't in Havenwood Falls to eat. The iron-lined briefcase I carried had to be delivered, but while I waited for my next set of instructions, a stiff drink and maybe a little company would be nice.

I stepped inside a place called the Dirty Knuckle and surveyed the crowd. The saloon—a strange cross between an upscale joint and a dive—was packed with humans and supes. Their auras called out to me like fresh pastries. My mouth watered and my vision heightened, but indulging in even a small taste might get me in a heap of trouble. Besides, I'd promised my contact that I'd be on my best behavior.

Shrugging off my need, I steeled myself against the blaring music and pushed past the bodies on my way to the bar. As my vision returned to normal, I was hit with an anger-filled emotion. My back tingled, and suddenly I was on high alert. Whirling around, I glimpsed a handsome man—midnight-black hair, eyes like an ocean, scruff-covered face—glaring at me. First thought? He was beautiful. Second thought? Just the type of distraction I could use. My night seemed a lot more promising.

Lowering my sunglasses—a precaution, not a necessity—I gazed at the man. No. He wasn't your average human. This was a mage, a very talented mage. My interest was piqued.

"I'm Senora Graves," I announced as I bit my lip and twirled my long black hair around my finger. Touching him wasn't a wise move either. If he didn't know what I was by looking at me, it was best to keep it that way. Male supes had issues with empusai. They thought we were only about sex and eating—hey, I couldn't help the reputation, and I wasn't about to explain things to a meal.

"Not interested," he replied, annoyance coating his words.

I frowned. "Your loss."

How dare he reject me? It was probably for the best, though. Hooking up with someone so full of attitude—no matter how attractive—was a bad idea. He'd most likely give me indigestion. The girl who seemed to have his full focus—dressed as a gypsy, but even from here I felt the demon blood in her—could have the arrogant bastard.

I hit the exit just as my phone buzzed. Peering down at the screen, I saw the text summoning me. It was time to go to work. I'd find a meal later.

~

CLIMBING up the steps at the top of a mountain definitely fell under the category of despised work-related tasks. *Who the hell lives on top of a summit?* Sure, it made enemies reconsider an attack, but it also kept visitors from stopping by. Sadly, it wasn't my first trek up Mount Mae, but I was ready to make it my last. I'd been working discreetly for this person who'd dubbed himself the Collector for the last two months, acquiring trivial artifacts. Honestly, I thought the being was testing me —checking to see if I was as good as my reputation claimed. It was really unnecessary. All he—or she, I couldn't be sure—had to do was ask me. I never declared anything I couldn't stand behind. What the Collector couldn't do, though, was ask my clients or victims for a reference. Most wouldn't admit the association. The others? Well, digested food never talked back . . . much.

My contact—a dark, cloaked figure—waited for me at the top of the staircase, near a monolithic stone jutting out of the snow. From my previous trip here, I knew that stone held the magic of cloaking the Collector's estate. Instead of speaking—he never did—the figure led me through the enormous wooden front door. The howling wind slipped past us before the door closed. Another thing that had always bothered me about winter—the gusts of air reminded me of the hounds of Hell baying. Not a pleasant sound, to say the least.

Although the surroundings freaked the hell out of me, that seemed inconsequential to the eerie abode constructed of glass, stone, and metal. I had this thing about entering dark places—I just didn't do it. Shit happened in shady spots. And the Collector's residence was indeed gloomy.

Not an ounce of sunlight—or in this case, moonlight—touched the interior. It was dark and surprisingly warm, like a freshly killed body whose heartbeat had yet to fade. That thought alone resurrected my hunger. It took every ounce of restraint to push it back down. I didn't think my current client—could I assign that status to the Collector?—would appreciate me biting the hand that paid me.

I was led into a large dark room lit by the glow of a fire. Several seating areas graced the room, all the furniture antique. But the Collector, his face conveniently hidden beneath a cloak, sat in his usual spot—a high-backed chair near the fireplace. The dark garment didn't obscure the intense stare wafting off him. The unseen eyes dropped to the briefcase I carried. Inside it was another insignificant item from a foreign land. Although the magic it contained would only be helpful to a beginner witch, I kept it protected—it was my job. I set the bag down and took a seat across from the Collector.

"You succeeded," said the deep, raspy voice. The tone was oddly feminine and masculine at the same time. How was that possible?

As usual, the Collector rarely asked questions. He only delivered statements and expected me to provide answers.

"Yes. I always get the job done." I'd grown tired of this game. Not once had I failed to present a requested object. I'd always completed my assignments without any qualms. My virtual resume touted my accomplishments—over two thousand victories and zero failures.

Leather-clad fingers tapped the chair arm, but no words were spoken. The Collector simply stared in my direction.

The silence yawned on for several minutes, breaking my patience. I didn't need this type of aggravation in my life. I was hungry and horny —in that order—and a little tired. There were other people—human and otherwise—who'd gladly pay for my services. What the Collector offered was minuscule pay for dull assignments. Not worth it. Our relationship needed to end. Now. I opened my mouth, but the Collector lifted his hand, cutting me off.

"You want more of a challenge," he stated. "You also want more money. There is an item that would be useful to me."

Finally.

My only hope was it would be something worth my skills. Going after supernatural toys was a waste of time and effort. Moving to the edge of the chair and leaning forward, I asked, "Where is it?"

"In Havenwood Falls." The Collector's flat voice didn't match my enthusiasm. "Its protector is a member of the Fairchild family."

Fairchild. I'd heard that name since my arrival in Havenwood Falls. Something about a ghost . . . "Isn't that the family with its own ghost haunting their house?"

"You speak of Emeline." The Collector waved his hand in the air. "She is not your concern. Julianna is a student at Havenwood Falls High. Obtaining the object should be easy for you."

Great. Now I'd need to steal from a child. Taking things from kids went against my moral compass—yes, I had one. But if the price was right, I could make an exception. "How much?"

"Half your usual pay."

A fifty percent less payout? I knew that weed was legal in Colorado, but did the Collector smoke it? That had to be the only explanation for offering me such a bogus deal.

"I don't think so." We'd previously struck a bargain at a quarter of a million dollars. Half of that wasn't worth the risk of any job. "Information is the only thing that amount will get you."

"I don't need information." The sound of bones grating against each other filled the room as the Collector twisted his head to one side. "This assignment doesn't merit higher pay."

"Then give it to someone who works for crumbs," I said. "Unless you can afford to pay me, our relationship is over."

There. I said it, but my words didn't faze the being. He simply turned his head toward the fireplace and uttered, "If that is what you wish. However, there are more important jobs on the horizon. Higher paychecks come with them."

I salivated like a hungry fiend. When it came to money, I was like a hoarding dragon with a stash of gold bullion. The difference between me and the winged saurian, however, was I had a plan for my reserve. I had my sights set on an island paradise where I'd build a mansion and live out my days in isolated elegance—only seeking out humanity when the need arose. Far better than returning to my dreary life in New York City. But I wasn't about to stoop to collecting nickels from a shady character in order to fulfill my dream.

Pushing the briefcase across the floor with the toe of my boot, I stood and stared down at my former client. "Find somebody else. I'm out of here."

Emptiness settled in my bones as I sashayed across the floor, but I ignored it and continued toward the exit. My contact, not even looking in my direction, opened the front door. It slammed behind me as soon as I crossed the threshold. Before I descended the first step, my phone buzzed.

Don't leave town. Your business with the Collector is not over.

~

STICKING around Havenwood Falls was not my idea. I was supposed to drop off the briefcase, receive my pay, and head back home. Thankfully, the Collector deposited my fee into my offshore account—not like I needed it to remain in town.

It was good to know that he wouldn't squelch on our deal. I've only had a few clients try to whistle out of an arrangement. Needless to say, they could no longer count themselves among the living. Somehow, I didn't think the Collector would go away so easily. Besides, eating that creature would probably be like plowing through a bag of flour—a dusty, tasteless experience.

It was late, and I needed to find some place to lie low for a day or two. Because of some ridiculous Valentine's Day celebration at Whisper Falls Inn, I needed to find another spot. I couldn't stay there with all the couples hooking up. Not that I was jealous. It just reminded me of how the devastatingly handsome mage kicked my ass to the curb without even blinking.

Since I'd been here before, I had an idea of where I could go—NamaStays Inn. The bed-and-breakfast was located in a winery and offered yoga. Eva Blackstone, the manager, reluctantly gave me the key to the last available cabin.

I knew the reason for the hesitation. She was a witch hunter—someone who didn't care for empusai—but that was okay by me. I wasn't crazy about her kind either. The uptight yet classy female pursed her mouth before reminding me I couldn't go hunting in town for food.

It wasn't an issue. I could go a few days or even a week without food.

Unfortunately, my stay in Havenwood Falls stretched beyond Valentine's, and days turned into weeks. I hadn't heard from my new employer, so I couldn't leave. With a grumbling stomach, I had no choice but to check out the local fare. Personally, I would have loved to sink my fangs in a delectable morsel, but Eva reminded me—again—that tasting the locals wasn't allowed.

"Not a problem," I lied. "I wouldn't dream of it, but I do require a meal." I replied with just as much attitude as she gave me. The idea of settling for something akin to roadkill—a burger or a steak—didn't set well with me, but I had no choice.

Eva suggested Burger Bar—supposedly the best place in town for milkshakes and burgers. To my chagrin, the eatery—smelling of dead flesh and grease—was a hangout for the high school crowd. Sitting at one of the metal tables, I watched a group of teenagers gathered around a jukebox that seemed to be stuck in the sixties. A flash of lavender snagged my attention. The odd-colored hair belonged to a girl with deep violet eyes. I wouldn't have thought twice about her if someone hadn't called out the name Jules. It had been a few weeks since the Collector had mentioned the girl.

Could she be Julianna Fairchild?

She seemed to be a nice enough girl. Why would she be holding an artifact the Collector wanted? Perhaps I should find out more about her and this object before completely turning down the assignment.

CHAPTER 3

MICAH

I took in a deep breath, steadying my nerves as I released the frustration that always seemed to be building within me. But despite my effort, the sensation failed to ebb away. Instead my thoughts reminded me about what was at stake, and how close I'd come to losing the two people I'd vowed to protect with my life.

Fear wasn't something an angel readily admitted to feeling—despite the misconception that being Heaven-born miraculously made you immune to such human emotion.

I'd been raised in a garrison that drove that sentiment to the extreme. Fear was viewed as a weakness, one that no sane angel would ever admit to possessing. I grew up surrounded by such arrogance, that self-righteous attitude that elevated our kind above all others.

Had I not taken a stand and defied the orders of my superiors, I may have adopted such haughtiness. But I did defy orders. They saw a threat to be destroyed, yet once I held the small baby in my arms, there was no denying the truth I felt deep down to my core.

Holly.

She had a name.

She had a soul that demanded its chance to live and experience the world.

It wasn't by choice that she was born with such powerful and coveted gifts. From the second she'd gasped her first breath as a baby, she'd been hunted by every creature and being with even the slightest inkling of the marvelous and destructive powers that were just waiting to awaken within her.

It didn't matter that it would take many years before those gifts—her ability to manipulate time and see approaching portents—manifested. For some, it was all about the long game. They would patiently wait for their chance to swoop in and claim her. They could plan and prepare for their opportunity to corrupt and pervert a vessel for good.

Heaven had argued that allowing her to live was a risk too high to take, that the fate of the world hung in the balance each time she took a breath, each time her heart beat.

They failed to see *her*, a child who didn't see herself as either good or evil. She was too young to understand the labels. But I understood, and in an ultimate act of betrayal, I refused to kill Holly, instead beginning a life of secrets and constant hiding for the both of us.

I'd been successful in keeping one step ahead of those who followed.

I was vigilant.

All that mattered was her safety. When it came time for her to come into her powers, it would be her choice how she lived and used her gifts. It wouldn't be Heaven's choice, and it sure as hell wouldn't be Hell's.

Sometimes I wondered if there was even any distinction between the two. The lines were often too blurry to tell.

"Micah?" a soft voice came from behind. "Come inside. It's cold."

I closed my eyes and let out the breath I'd been holding, centering myself. Not that it helped. I was failing her. There was no hiding from the truth that rang louder than my feeble attempts to convince myself otherwise.

"You should be inside," I barked back, a little gruffer than I intended. It was more proof that I was losing control, something I couldn't allow. In a softer tone, I added, "It's late."

I didn't bother stating the obvious. Even with all the protective wards and magical safeguards, Havenwood Falls wasn't safe.

Austin's attack on Holly and Sedona had proven that. He had worked as a part-time employee at Shelf Indulgence—someone who had completely blindsided Sedona. Unbeknownst to her, the high school senior had been working for the Collector, and it had come to a violent end. The Collector, a new threat, had come so close to stealing away the two most important people in my life . . . my existence.

And then there'd been the second attack—this time with Sedona as the sole focus. I still wasn't quite sure why the Collector had come gunning for her again, other than to serve as a distraction.

One thing I did know with perfect clarity was it had driven home that brutal truth so hard that I couldn't fully relax until I found the answers I needed.

God, Sedona.

My chest clenched tightly thinking about the beautiful bookstore owner. I hadn't expected to find her—to fall so completely for her. Some angels felt it was beneath our kind to give our heart to a human, but to me, it made perfect sense. Once I quit fighting the chemistry between us, and surrendered to the way I felt when I was with her, it made that second act of betrayal easy to do.

I was a rebel angel on the run who was in love with an empath.

Did that make me weak?

No. It made me a formidable enemy should anyone dare threaten her safety.

Holly and Sedona.

They were my world, and I would burn everything to the ground if it meant they remained free to make their own choices.

"Micah?" Her voice was followed by the light touch of her hand on my arm. Holly sounded worried. Before turning to face her, I mentally pushed down my own frustration, so she wouldn't see it plastered across my face.

"Hmmm," I replied, wearing as sincere a smile as I could.

I should've known that while I had spent most of her life watching over her, Holly had been doing the exact same thing with me. She could see through my façade instantly.

"I haven't seen you this—" she paused as she searched for the right word—"distracted for a while. You and Sedona doing okay?" Holly studied me closely, a little too close for comfort.

I nudged her with my elbow before wrapping my arm around her shoulder and pulling her into my body. If only protecting her were as easy as this.

"What makes you ask that?" I answered, purposely pretending I didn't know her meaning. Gone were the days where I could keep her ignorant to most things. As a teenager, Holly was way more observant than I was ready for.

She shrugged, another favorite gesture of hers. "I know things were a little crazy there for a while. I know you try to hide stuff like that from me, but Micah, I'm not a kid anymore. You can trust me with the big stuff, you know."

It was hard not to agree with her. I wished there were a way to keep her young and innocent. I wanted to keep her untouched by the cruelty the world would show her, especially those who would take advantage.

Part of me knew that the time was fast approaching where she would need to be included in the big decisions, but even if it was just for tonight, I was determined to spare her from it.

"Sedona and I are okay, sweetheart. Don't you worry about us." I offered her another smile, this one not as tight-lipped as the first.

"Then what has you standing out here in the backyard at midnight, looking as though the weight of the world is pressing down on you?" She broke free from my embrace and stared up into my face, refusing to drop eye contact.

She jabbed at my chest with her finger. "Don't lie to me, Micah. Please."

I let out a heavy breath. Things with Sedona and me were good. That hadn't been a falsehood. Our relationship had taken a weird twist recently, but it wasn't something we couldn't overcome. All couples went through growing pains—some worse than others. No, it wasn't

Sedona that had me staring up at the blackened night sky, searching for answers in the stars.

"Holly," I began, my mind sifting through all the information I'd been gathering for some tidbit I could give her. She was right. Keeping her in the dark wouldn't be wise now that she was older. I hated it . . . hated that fact with a passion. "Do you remember why we don't settle down anywhere? The reason why I'm so strict about who we allow in our lives?"

She nodded instantly, the movement causing the lights from the back porch to shine on her dark hair. "You said some bad people wanted to hurt me, to control my powers, and make me do things I won't want to."

I returned her nod, and this time held her brave gaze. Sometimes it amazed me how courageous she was. "I can't ever let them close enough to harm you, Holly."

Understanding lit up her eyes. No other explanation was needed.

"Do we have to leave? I thought we were going to stay here for a while. You know, put down roots." There was a longing in her tone that broke my heart. Holly should have been worried about normal, run-of-the-mill teenager stuff. She needed the security of having a home, the chance to create friendships and memories with her peers. Instead, hers was a life of seclusion with an overly protective angel for a guardian.

This wasn't the life I would wish for her, and I hoped to God one day I could give her what her heart desired most.

"I don't know." And I didn't. Every cell in my body screamed to leave everything behind and disappear into the night with her. My heart, however, whispered that it was more complicated than that. I had opened it up to love, and now there was Sedona to consider.

She wasn't safe either.

She'd asked me to trust her . . . to trust the Court.

Trust. It was an expensive commodity when the only person you trusted was yourself.

I pulled her back in for another hug. "Go to sleep. Let me worry about where we live. For right now, Havenwood Falls is our home."

"But," she began to argue. I recognized the steely expression that now filled her features. She would stubbornly stand here all night if it meant she could wear me down. To prove her point, she planted her feet shoulder width apart, her hands on her hips. "Micah."

I placed a kiss on her forehead. "I know that's not what you want to hear, but that's all I've got for you right now. I swear—" I cradled her cheek in my hand—"when I have the answer, I'll tell you."

She held up her pinky finger, making me hook my own with hers. "Fine. Just so you know, if you break a pinky promise, you forfeit any right to complain about my choice in music and my book budget doubles."

When I went to correct her, she grinned. "Scratch that . . . it triples!" Lifting up on her toes, Holly kissed my cheek and hugged me one more time. "Don't give yourself an ulcer out here, okay?"

She was a good kid. She was growing into a remarkable woman.

I'd hoped Havenwood Falls would become our home—that it would become the home of her dreams.

Tomorrow would bring more answers.

Tomorrow I would go before the court again.

And this time, I wasn't going to leave until I was satisfied.

THE METAL DOOR slammed shut behind me.

I was furious—beyond furious.

For all the cajoling Sedona did in trying to convince me of the usefulness of the Court, they had failed me yet again. Abysmally so.

I wasn't sure what I had expected after demanding yet another audience with those in power. This damn town was governed by those who chose to keep everything close to the chest. You had to be one of the "chosen," from one of the founding families, before they would give you even a hint of truth. I was tired of talking in circles, of trying to convince the fools that I wasn't someone they could brush to the side. I had a hard time swallowing the party line that they were doing everything in their power to find out who was behind Austin's attack.

The boy had big dreams, but they didn't run on the diabolical side of things. He was no mastermind, and there was no denying his confession. He was working for someone—an unknown whose sights were set on Holly.

The Collector's moniker had been bandied about during the ten minute discussion, but they refused to listen, dismissing me as if my concerns were inconsequential. It didn't matter that I was there to warn them about this threat that had now attacked my family twice. For a governing body, they almost seemed blasé about it—turning me away because I didn't have enough evidence to prove that Havenwood Falls was in danger.

It was that last part that had rankled, adding fuel to the fire that was already burning inside me. I wasn't used to being refused. I also wouldn't wait until the only proof they'd accept would be me laying the dead bodies of Sedona and Holly down before them.

I wasn't one to beg, but I'd been ready to get down on my knees, desperation rearing its ugly head. Part of me had wanted to lower my own wardings and reveal what kind of being they were in the presence of. Witchcraft, magic—whatever claims they had on the supernatural —paled in comparison to the might and will of an angel.

But to do so, to drop the pretenses, would send out a beacon of pure light and divinity. It was bad enough the Court knew who—what —I was, without sending out a blinding signal to those searching for Holly and me.

I stopped before I hit the roadside curb, turning about so I could glare at the door I'd just exited through. Adrenaline still coursed through my veins as my temper remained stoked and ready to explode.

The Collector.

Who the hell was this person and how could I find him? I was done waiting for the next threat and attack. I was ready to hunt the bastard down and put an end to this once and for all.

The Court could sit and play amongst themselves, bickering back and forth, sitting on their dais all high and mighty. They had a certain order in how they did things. They were responsible for the entire town. Good for them.

I was responsible for two. They were my priority. I couldn't rely on Havenwood Falls to protect them. Once again, I was alone, and frankly, that suited me just fine.

"You were out of line in there."

I'd heard the door open and close, the soft click of heels on the sidewalk giving away her approach.

"I honestly don't care what you think, Ms. Stuart." Despite the mayor asking me to call her Barbie, I couldn't bring myself to do it. She was part of the problem, and as a Court member, she would always toe the company line. Whatever Millicent had told her about the attacks on her niece, Ms. Stuart would still place Havenwood Falls first, and foremost.

If she thought she could come out here and soften the blow that was dealt inside, she was mistaken. Sedona had once told me that she respected the mayor.

I was still reserving judgment.

She'd basically agreed with silencing me, ordering me to stop my own investigations into the threat against Holly, and instead sit back and wait for the Court to make their move.

"For the greater good" had been the line they all had tried feeding me. Like they understood anything beyond their own self-importance.

I was pissed and refused to see them as a helpful governing body.

Her features softened as she wet her lips. "I understand your frustrations, Micah. What happened to Sedona was horrible."

I raised my hand to stop her. I wasn't going to debate with her or be placated into sitting on my hands and doing nothing. The time had come and gone for that.

"Do you not see the danger that's right under your noses?" I countered. "Or has all that power gone to your head? Don't rock the boat and all that."

If Sedona had been here, she would've shushed me or elbowed me in the side. While she rebelled against her aunt and all the expectations that were stacked against her, she still had a fearful respect for the Court.

They hadn't earned mine yet.

"Don't forget whom you're addressing, Mr. Westbrook." There was that haughty attitude I'd come to recognize as her true expression. "I would hate for you to get on the wrong side of those who determine whether or not you're welcome in Havenwood Falls."

She stood there, a good foot shorter than me, but every inch ready to wield her authority. "Think of Sedona." Her lips curled into a half smile. "Or how about your young charge. You need us to help keep her hidden. How much longer do you think you would survive alone? Are you that eager to see?"

I clenched my teeth so hard that I was surprised they didn't shatter in my mouth. It was a bitter pill to swallow, knowing there was truth in her threats. I saw her words for what they were—play nice and do what you're told, or we'll withdraw our protection.

"Then give me something to do," I yelled, not caring who heard. The silence surrounding this new threat was deafening. "I've told you everything I know. I've been honest with you. Can you say the same?"

Barbie blinked, her gaze still guarded. "You've been given a task."

There was no holding back the snort of disgust. "Do you really think I'm going to sit idly by and do nothing?" I couldn't believe she thought I was so easily convinced.

"If you know what's good for you, you will." She said it so calmly and evenly that I wondered whether the woman had any kind of feeling. A cold shiver skated over my skin at the thought that this could've been Sedona's world had she not followed her own heart and desire.

"Is that a threat?" I cocked my brow at her. She was messing with fire.

"It is what it is. Don't push this. You will know more when the Court believes you can help. Not a moment earlier." She shifted the handbag on her shoulder, nodding slightly. "Good night, Mr. Westbrook."

Without waiting for my response, Barbie Stuart walked toward her car, pushing the toggle to deactivate the alarm.

I stared back at the building's door, debating whether or not to go back in and have it out with Saundra Beaumont and the others again. The Court's threat resurfaced, making the decision for me.

As long as they controlled whether or not Holly and I were welcome in town, I would stop pressing them so relentlessly.

I would go about my search for answers in secret.

I would find this Collector, and once I was done ensuring no more harm came to Holly or Sedona, I would then hand him or her over to the Court.

This changed nothing.

The hunt was on.

CHAPTER 4

HARPER

*L*ife was a conveyor belt of people with way too many problems and way too many dead ancestors. At least that's what Aunt Eloise—spiritual psychic extraordinaire and owner of Havenwood Falls' Into the Mystic new age shop—always said. The way my head pounded, my temple throbbing with whispered voices I couldn't quite comprehend as the late afternoon sun threw streaks of gold across the sidewalk, it wasn't hard to understand where Eloise's tidbit of wisdom came from. I was, after all, a Sinclair and my dead mother's daughter. Which meant two things: I was a spiritual psychic and a summoner. The former—a psychic who channels the dead through written words—was something I understood well enough because of my upbringing. The latter—someone who could conjure and control demonic spirits and lower caste fallen angels—was something I was working hard to get a handle on. Let's just say being a spiritual psychic with summoning abilities made reading and writing a bitch. In every sense of the word. It gave a whole new meaning to the old adage "the pen is mightier than the sword."

"*Harper Sinclair,*" a voice breathed, the melodious words sounding distant in my head, the echoing tone making my ears ring. I was becoming used to hearing my name whispered, even shouted in my head. Ever since I'd discovered I was more than just a spiritual writer, voices with no faces and shadows with no real bodies had become infrequent companions, the occasional shadow visits something I'd kept secret from those who knew me. The voices didn't come often enough for me to bother the Court about them.

A fountain splashed behind me in the town square, sweet summer laughter riding on the breeze as children ran around it, daring each other to climb into the large basin despite the trouble they could get into. July in Havenwood Falls was as beautiful and enchanting as winter was cold and brilliant, with warm temperatures that didn't feel too uncomfortable or completely unbearable compared to some places. It wasn't long until the Mathews River Paddlefest, an event held the last Saturday in July that was full of kayaking, rafting, and tubing up and down the river, and I could hear a group of teens down the street talking about who'd be brave enough to paddle the river after dark that night in the moonlight. I'd missed being able to do things like that at their age, because being around others had always been too big of a risk for me. The lighthearted banter and mischief of the kids free from the shackles of school, along with the sunny weather, clashed with my current apprehensive mood.

I stood on Main Street, just across from Coffee Haven and Shelf Indulgence. My heaven and hell. Today, I was skipping the hot chocolate I wanted desperately to order at the coffee shop and diving straight into the abyss, into a world of books and words. Seven months had passed since I'd discovered what I was capable of. I'd grown a lot in half a year, learning to read and write without being possessed by darkness. I could channel demonic spirits rather than be consumed by them.

Knowing this still didn't make entering the bookstore any easier. Only less intimidating. But if I didn't push myself, my powers and my control over them wouldn't grow.

My eyes drifted over the bookstore's showcase window, the space artfully decorated by Sedona Mathews, the owner of Shelf Indulgence, who also happened to be a witch and an empath. Beyond the display, cushy furniture and a hodgepodge of books invited passersby into the warm interior.

My cell phone dinged in my blue jeans pocket, and I lifted the hem of my oversized T-shirt to pull it free. A text flashed in the instant messenger app I'd downloaded, an angelic halo circling the contact name.

Elias: You don't have to push yourself so hard.

Even as comforting as his text was, I couldn't accept his words. Elias Jamison, a local fallen angel, had become my closest friend over the last few months, his support a constant reminder that I needed to take things slow. I'd lived my entire life sheltered and guarded, which meant I was more like a teenager or a child just learning how to use my powers than an adult who'd had them her entire life. His words from six months ago rang through my head, eerie and unforgiving: *You can channel darkness and attack people with their own nightmares.*

It didn't matter that my powers were scary. I had friends now—friends who depended on me—and my loyalty to them was stronger than my fears. Those friends came to me when they needed answers from the dark world beyond, and my desire to help outweighed my desire to run. Ever since Addie Beaumont arrived to help me with my powers on New Year's Day and ended up getting a message from the Infernum she hadn't expected, I'd been determined to get stronger. To become more powerful. Not because I was greedy for power, but because I was greedy to help those I loved. This was the reason I'd begun hearing the spirits even when I wasn't writing or reading. I chalked some of the voices up to guilt. I'd had trouble reaching the Petrans since January, following Addie's unexpected message, and it frustrated me that I couldn't find out more for her or for Michaela, Addie's best friend and the Petrans' daughter.

Taking a deep breath, I jogged across the crosswalk separating me from the other side of the street and stopped just short of the bookstore's door. Unease caused the hair on the back of my neck to rise, and I glanced over my shoulder, my gaze searching the street. The same familiar faces surrounded me. Willow Fairchild's lithe figure flashed against the window of Coffee Haven as she set up a display of pottery, no doubt created by Cressida Manos or her mother, both mountain nymphs renowned for their sculpting and art work. Rumor had it that the Manos family was having trouble with seventeen-year-old Cressida, that she'd recently been caught graffitiing buildings in Miller's Plaza and hanging out with Jack Peters, the hellhound shifter whose dad was the president of the local outlaw motorcycle club. But I knew there was much more to it than that.

My abilities—as scary as they could be—and my friendship with Elias were good for discovering things and information about our town most people, even some supernaturals, would be unaware of.

The voices in my head had been especially chatty lately, and I had notebooks upon notebooks full of odd, disjointed messages to prove it.

"Harper Sinclair!"

This voice wasn't in my head, the self-assured, feminine sound of it making me cringe. I wished it was a demon instead.

"Looking for a good read?" a blond-haired woman in her mid-twenties called out, her eyes sparkling as she sashayed down the sidewalk in denim shorts and a loose button-up blouse.

The hair on the back of my neck that had stood at attention before now threatened to jump right out of my skin. Shelly Martin was more than just your average human. She was Tase Roca's baby mama. Atanase "Tase" Roca was a moroi vampire with way too many issues, both family and personal. One of those issues—the love kind—included my friend, Addie Beaumont.

Shelly Martin was bad news. I didn't know how I knew this; I just sensed it. She'd run into me too frequently over the last few weeks, always finding an excuse to say hello or offer me a knowing grin. If I was the type to get paranoid—and I kind of was—I'd think she was following me.

"I was thinking about it," I answered carefully, keeping my gaze averted as she stopped before me. My hand slipped off the bookstore's door, falling to clench against my hip, the large folds of my shirt hiding my whitened knuckles.

Shelly grinned, flashing me white teeth. "Gotta watch what you read these days. Books just aren't what they used to be."

"That's true, I guess," I muttered, completely aware of the veiled threat beneath her words.

Maybe, anyway. *Was* she even threatening me? Or warning me? Did she even have a reason to?

I *really* was ultra-paranoid these days.

"Happy reading," Shelly added sweetly, continuing on her way before I had a chance to reply. My gaze followed her, my eyes narrowing. There was something distinctly not right about Shelly Martin, but I couldn't quite put my finger on it. Based on her barbed words, it was also obvious she knew more about me than she should.

Stop it, Harper, I chided, turning to push my way into Shelf Indulgence, Shelly's appearance enough to erase any trepidation I'd had about entering.

The overwhelming smell of books rushed me, the scent heady and addictive. I'd always loved the way books smelled. They had a distinct odor, the scent's type depending on the age and material of the tome. Titles yelled at me, the words printed carefully on the books' spines, and I glanced at them, the letters scrambling instantly out of order.

I blinked hard.

Voices rushed me.

"Harper."

It took everything I had to keep moving forward. I'd become used to words, to writing and reading once again. Enough so that Shelf Indulgence shouldn't bother me as much as it used to, but I knew this visit was different.

The shadows had wanted me to come today, had been insistent even. I'd written the name of the bookstore over and over on my bathroom mirror in lipstick the night before, all while sleeping.

It had been my pet shape-shifting weapon—an ancient wooden mace covered in bronze thorns that just happened to turn into a huge, talking, winged lion when needed—that had woken me, his voice petulant when he asked, "Want to explain the makeover you're giving your bathroom mirror at three o'clock in the morning? Because cleaning that is going to be a bitch."

The witching hour. My pale face and wild hair had stared back at me through loops of coral lipstick.

There were times when I really creeped myself out.

My head swam, my vision blurring. There was nothing more powerful to a spiritual psychic than words. And I was surrounded by them.

"Anything I can help you with?" a voice asked. Deep down in some distant part of me, I knew the voice belonged to Sedona, her ultra-sensitive senses no doubt detecting the multitude of emotions raging through me.

There was a reason the voices had wanted me to come here. There were enough words surrounding me to give a good portion of the spirits and beings in the Infernum a way to speak all at once. I felt like an orchestra conductor standing before a podium in front of a stage full of instrumentalists. Only, none of them knew what the hell they were doing. Most especially me.

"I'm fine," I answered mechanically, because I knew if I didn't say anything, Sedona might feel the need to contact the Court about my strange behavior. And that was the last thing I wanted. For now, I just wanted to know why the shadows were interrupting my sleep.

"Are you sure?" she asked, doubtful. It was pretty hard to lie to an empath.

"Just tired," I replied, moving past her, eyes on the floor. Tired was something I knew she'd feel from me. Anxiety, too, but everyone in Havenwood Falls knew I tended to fight that. Most just didn't know why.

A display of magazines rose up near the back of the store, and I paused before them, my eyes automatically homing in on the hobby catalogs, specifically those on photography. Taking pictures was how I made a living.

"*Harper.*"

My name was the only warning I got before I fell into a trance, my eyes swimming with written script. Spiritual writing was a straightforward form of communication. I could either channel the dead or spirits with a pen and paper, or they could speak to me the way they were now, through the typeface in the magazines.

Letters ran like busy ants across the display case, and then lined up at attention on an empty surface, looking oddly like scrapbooks pastings. *Chained people tied together. Items. Magic. Watcher watching. Waiting. United we stand against the one collecting power.*

I squinted, frustrated, my fingers idly and instinctively sketching words into the display case.

"Is this seriously what you brought me here for?" I hissed.

The letters danced, mocking me.

"This is ridiculous," I sneered. "It makes no sense."

It might be hard to understand most of the messages I received. I mean, the Infernum wasn't exactly a bubbly place full of grand conversationalists, but I usually at least got either sentences or fragmented words that clued me in to the spirits' intentions.

A human middle-aged woman with salon-fresh hair and a troubled brow threw me an odd look, clearing her throat as she brushed past me.

I stiffened, backing away.

Chained people tied together. Items. Magic. Watcher watching. Waiting. United we stand against the one collecting power.

What did that mean? And why did I feel the need to come to Shelf Indulgence just to see a message I could have gotten at home?

I was missing something.

Pulling my cell phone out, I glanced at the screen, at the unanswered text from Elias I hadn't replied to. Should I ask him about this? Should I get in touch with Addie?

And tell them what? That I'd gotten messages from spirits that made no sense, just so they could tell me it was probably my powers growing? I could hear their voices now: "This is a good thing, Harper. You're channeling. You can only get better at it from here. Stay strong."

My gut, however, told me I should worry, particularly about the words *chained people tied together.* My mind told me the spirits were probably talking about themselves, the dark shadows imprisoned and chained together in the Infernum. My heart told me they were talking about people outside the Infernum, people in Havenwood Falls. But how was I supposed to prove that?

Grabbing a photography magazine, so I wouldn't look like I'd come to the bookstore for nothing, I hurried to the store's checkout.

Maybe the message was about someone tied to Shelf Indulgence, and that's why I'd been led to come here?

Harper, stop, I berated myself.

If I kept this up, I was going to drive myself insane. Instead, I repeated in my head the same thing I knew my friends would tell me if they were here. *Your powers are going to grow, Harper. And the messages you receive and read are going to be full of weirdness while they do. Everything's fine. This is good. You're branching out. You've got this.*

Why did I feel like I was using my friends' pretend words to lie to myself? Why did I feel like the shadows I kept seeing peeking at me from the corners of my eyes were trying to tell me something crucially important?

CHAPTER 5

ADDIE

*S*omeone was burning leaves. The acrid fragrance drifted in through the open window on a breath of crisp morning mountain air. It smelled like fall.

The cool breeze caressed my cheeks, and I snuggled under the blankets, up against Tase, who still slept next to me. His arm tightened around me, pulling me even closer, the length of our bodies pressing together. Guess he wasn't sleeping anymore, as evidenced by his morning greeting growing against my thigh. His fingers moved to my hip bone, feathering slow circles over my skin. My hand slid over his ribs and slipped under his arm as I buried my face against his chest. We lay like that for several minutes. I could stay like this forever. It would never get old.

Life had finally settled down. Evened out. A crisis we'd been dealing with for years had finally been averted over the summer. We'd had two months since of near peace. Sure, I'd had to deal with some crazy shit happening around town, and Tase had a lot of work to catch up on with his businesses—the ski resort would be opening in less than two months—and his family. But the life I'd dreamt about since I was fourteen years old was possibly becoming a reality. I'd been trying not to raise my hopes too high, but damn it, we both deserved this. Us. A real life together.

"You know what would make this even more perfect?" Tase murmured, his chest rumbling against my ear. I expected him to say something sexual, but instead he answered himself with, "Coffee and bacon."

"Mmm," I moaned. That did sound good. "I can already smell it."

"Along with the burning leaves and snow."

"Snow?" I sniffed. "I don't smell snow."

"On the peaks. You can't smell it?"

"It must be a vampire thing."

"Bean," he said, shifting underneath me so that he could look into my eyes. "You're doing it again."

"Doing what?"

One brow arched. "Avoiding your other nature. Your hellhound side? Surely it can smell the snow."

He was right. I'd been avoiding half of my true nature for far too long. The process of breaking the curse on Tase and the Petrans had not only taught me to accept that I was half hellhound, but that it wasn't a bad thing. I'd still been struggling to truly embrace that part of me, though. I'd only learned about it barely more than a year ago. I'd always thought I was a witch, pure and simple, and when my biological father—who'd been living in this same small town all this time when I thought he was dead—dumped the news on me, I'd gone into complete denial mode. I wouldn't even admit it to myself. But everything that went down over the summer with Tase, the Petrans, and the Infernum required me to face the facts. Yet, since then, I'd done no more than have drinks with Savage, my father, one time several weeks ago. I'd still been reticent about actually *being* a hellhound.

With focused purpose, I closed my eyes and inhaled again, this time more deeply. And there it was. A scent I couldn't really give the right words to, but which immediately brought up memories of catching fat flakes on my tongue, building snowmen, and swishing down the slopes. I rolled over to look out the window. It was a sunny morning, not nearly cold enough for snow, but I could see the peak of Mount Sousa rising far above town, tipped in white.

"Winter is coming!" I said excitedly as I rolled back over, propping my forearm on Tase's chest and gazing into his greenish-gray eyes. The eyes of the moroi, a similar color to Michaela's. Not the bright green of the strigoi I'd seen hints of last summer. The strigoi were the immortal monsters moroi became if they killed too many times. Each life a moroi took also consumed a small piece of their own soul, until they had nothing left, transforming them into an unstoppable murderous nightmare. Tase had been on the brink of going down that path due to the curse. But now his eyes were clear, more gray than green, like they were supposed to be—a beautiful contrast against his olive skin and dark hair.

He smiled, dimples showing, as his hand slipped over the back of my neck, pulling me down for a kiss.

"*I* want to be coming," he murmured against my lips, before slipping his tongue in and delving deeper.

We'd just finished making love when my familiars started growing noisy, begging for their own attention. Chewie—Chewbarka for short —my wolf who could no longer fit in my hands but now could rest his chin on the bed, eyed us from the end, a half whine, half howl in his throat. Kylo, the tuxedo cat who'd also grown quite a bit over the summer, mewed from the hallway, while Skywalker, the raven, cawed from the kitchen. Only Princess Leia, the miniature dragon, remained quiet. Her gaze was just as intent as Chewie's, though, her eyes glowing from the darkness of her little makeshift cave in the corner of the bedroom.

"Guess it's breakfast time," I said as I swung my still rubbery legs over the edge of the bed.

"Coffee and bacon?" Tase asked, hope thick in his voice.

"Yes, that's my order. Thanks!" I gave him a smirk as my phone rang, causing me to jump out of bed and frantically search for something to put on. I had a weird thing about answering the phone while naked. Especially when I saw the name on the screen.

Tase saw the frown on my face. "Who is it?"

"It's my . . . uh . . . it's Savage?" It came out as a question, because my brain had already jumped ahead to thinking *WTF?*

"Are you going to answer it?" he asked.

I threw on my robe, then hit the Accept icon. "Uh . . . hello?"

Gah! Could he hear in my husky voice that I'd just had sex?

"Did I wake you?" His voice was even rougher, but it always was.

I cleared my throat. "Uh, yeah. I mean no. I mean, uh, what's going on?"

We hadn't talked since that one meeting for drinks about a month or so ago, which had been awkward as hell. We probably should have been trying harder, both of us, to form some kind of relationship, even if it never would be a father-daughter one, but life was busy. For both of us, I was sure. And we just weren't used to having the other in our lives.

"Can you meet me at the Dirty Knuckle later?" Savage was not a beat-around-the-bush kind of guy. In fact, he said as few words as necessary to get his point across. I supposed this was his way of saying he wanted to meet for drinks again. I guessed that meant he was trying, and I should meet him halfway.

"Yeah, I can do that," I said while locking gazes with Tase's curious one. I shrugged my shoulders, just as clueless about what prompted this as he was.

"I'll see you there at six." Savage ended the call. Well, it was a good thing I didn't have plans, since Tase had his own thing going on.

"Drinks again?" Tase asked, obviously having heard the full conversation with his vampire ears.

"He didn't really say, but I don't see him buying me dinner or anything, so yeah, I guess drinks again."

The beasts were making more commotion than ever, so I tied my robe and padded out to the kitchen, all but Skywalker following me. He was already on the edge of the pantry door, where I kept his seed, cawing and clicking.

"All right, all right," I muttered as I began to dish out everyone's breakfasts except for my own. Thankfully, Tase had come in and made me coffee.

"What time do you meet with Shelly?" I asked, after taking a sip of the delicious hot nectar.

Shelly Martin was Tase's baby mama. It'd been quite a shock to learn he had a kid about a year ago, shortly after Shelly had returned to Havenwood Falls after being gone for about five years. She'd been a fling of his during one of the "off" times of our on-again, off-again relationship, which had mostly been "off" up until now. Well, honestly, we'd never been more than fuck buddies and good friends—when we weren't breaking each other's hearts. Anyway, because of the memory wards protecting our town, she had no recollection of her time in our borders, including her baby daddy. Then Bent Brent, barkeep at the Haven Saloon, where she'd worked, apparently had called her to come back to town. She brought her kid with her, and when she returned, her memories flooded back. A little while later, Tase learned he had a son. Carter was his name. He was almost six now and had started kindergarten this year.

Tase couldn't really have anything to do with him, though. Not before, when he was cursed. He was too unpredictable, and we couldn't risk Carter's well-being. But now . . . now maybe things were different. That's why he was meeting with Shelly tonight—to see if maybe he could have some visitation privileges to get to know his son.

"She said to meet at six." He peered over at me. "You're still okay with this?"

I nodded as I leaned against the counter, watching him pull everything out to fry up some bacon. I didn't think he could get any hotter than he already was, but a half-naked Tase Roca cooking in my kitchen was sexy as fuck. He wore jeans and nothing else, giving me a full show of biceps and triceps and pecs and abs ending in a V that disappeared under his waistband. As the bacon began to cook, though, he covered up with an apron—spitting bacon didn't go well with bare skin.

"Of course. Any other plans today?" I asked.

"Not really." He gave me his signature sexy smirk as he pulled on the tie to my robe, bringing me over to him by the stove. "But I know what I want to do." He tucked me up against his side, and there was nowhere I'd rather have been. "You?"

I may not have *wanted* to be anywhere else, but life rarely gave me what I wanted. "Mmm . . . I'll have to check in with the Court, of course. I also thought about seeing what Harper's up to. She was . . . different at our last girls' night."

"Isn't she always different?" He pulled away to flip the bacon.

"Tase," I admonished.

"I don't mean that in a bad way. She's just a lot quieter than the rest of you."

My eyes narrowed. He did not just start bad-talking my girls.

He groaned. "I didn't mean that in a bad way, either. Except when you're all drunk. That can get bad. It wasn't a pretty sight when I stopped over at Callie's that one time." He gave me a devilish grin.

Now it was my turn to groan at the memory. I didn't want to talk about that night. I hadn't been able to stomach tequila for months afterward. Thank Goddess I was over that.

"Anyway," I said, getting back to the original point, "something seems to be up with Harper. I kept getting the feeling that she wanted to talk, but there hasn't been a good time to."

"Guess I'll see what Xan's up to then. If he hasn't keeled over from picking flowers and cake toppers."

I snorted. "Do you really think Michaela would even bother? She's had her shit picked out since we were ten. And trust me—she knows exactly which flowers. I'm just glad she hasn't called me yet."

I held my breath for a moment, sure I'd just jinxed myself and my phone would ring. Michaela may have decided on her perfect wedding years ago, but she was a woman and was exercising her every right to change her mind. Daily. Sometimes hourly. The actual wedding was going to be easy—they were getting married on the fucking ski slopes. That was my girl. It was perfect for the two of them. But the reception —she had all kinds of plans for how the ballroom at the inn would be decked out. Thank Goddess for Rhiannon Underwood at Fairy Tale Florists, who could grow anything, even for a December wedding. Christmas Eve, to be exact. Michaela had chosen the date in honor of her mother, who had been a romantic at heart and lived for the cheesy Hallmark Christmas movies. A Christmas Eve wedding likely had Irina Petran swooning in the Great Beyond.

My phone didn't ring, and I let out my breath.

Tase and I ended up spending most of the day together after all. I couldn't get a hold of Harper, and Xandru and Michaela turned out to be busy with inn work.

As the afternoon grew on, we both became fidgety, each of us on edge for different reasons. Finally, six o'clock approached, and we could leave.

Tase drove off in his Camaro after ensuring for the fifth time that I didn't want a ride. I'd always preferred walking around town rather than driving, and this evening's weather was too perfect. I crossed town square, turned right on Main Street, and then left on Fourth toward the Dirty Knuckle, enjoying the cooler air. The first day of fall—Mabon, which was also Founders Day—was last week, and now the square and businesses on Main were decked out in blue and silver for the homecoming game. Then everything would be covered in Halloween decorations, like much of the rest of the town already was. The holiday season kicked off early in our lovely little village.

At six in the evening, I was surprised to find the Knuckle's parking lot so empty. And even more shocked at two of the cars there—my mother's and my grandmother's—along with two motorcycles. When I walked in, the jukebox was off and the lights turned up. A group that included my mother, my grandmother, Savage, and Liam Peters, SIN's president, sat in silence. And there was nobody else here, as if the bar were closed. Not even Rhys, the owner, or his employee Casten were here.

"What's going on?" I asked, my steps slowing as I approached their tables in the middle of the room.

"We're wondering the same thing, but nobody here will talk," my mother said, her arms folded over her chest as she scowled. She looked like a middle-aged version of me—brown hair and brown eyes— although she was many decades older. We had great witch genes like that. Saundra, my grandmother, was born before the Old Families even founded the box canyon in 1854, but she didn't look a day over sixty-five.

"Melaina's on her way to explain," Savage growled, his arms crossed over his extremely broad chest.

I supposed, when it came to aging, I had good genes from both sides of the family. Savage was over three hundred fifty years old, but appeared to be in his early thirties. His hair reached below his shoulders and hung loosely around his face, which was in a perpetual scowl, sharply arched brows pulled together and eyes hidden behind the standard shades all hellhounds wore—except Melaina, my aunt, who had special contacts. Hellhounds' eyes could kill humans and even some supernaturals. Thank the Goddess my eyes weren't that powerful, but I continued wearing my glasses—now outfitted with special lenses—just in case. I didn't really need them anymore for my vision.

Next to Savage sat Liam, another hellhound, just as old as Savage while appearing just as young, with sandy-blond hair and a face that at times looked boyish and at others, sharp and terrifying.

"Actually, I'm here now," Melaina's voice called as the door opened. Talk about youthful appearances. The three-hundred-plus-year-old brunette strode in, wearing black skin-tight pants, a black fleece jacket, and black knee-high stiletto boots, looking to be not much older than me. With her were a blond woman and a familiar man—Shelly Martin and Tase.

What the hell?

I gave him an inquiring look, but he appeared just as bewildered as the rest of us.

"Go ahead and sit, Tase," Melaina said, her voice as gruff as Savage's, and her hazel eyes hard, a red tint glowing in them. "Shelly has something to share with us."

Tase took the seat next to me as Melaina turned to face Shelly, crossing her arms and jutting a hip.

"Well?" she demanded.

Licking her lips, Shelly took a few steps forward, glancing around at all of us. Dressed in a denim miniskirt and with her hands stuffed into the pocket of her soft pink hoodie, she looked like the girl next door. I'd never figured out what Tase saw in her, because sweet and innocent wasn't his thing, but maybe her working at the Haven Saloon, with Bent Brent, had taken some of her innocence. And maybe Tase had taken the rest. Or maybe she was completely different than I presumed, considering I didn't really know her. A Dorothy on the streets and Blanche in the sheets kind of girl? I shuddered at the thought and shoved it far, far away, never wanting to think it again.

Staring at her, I couldn't fathom what she had to tell us, nor why she appeared so nervous about it.

"So, um, I came to town six years ago as Shelly Martin, although I don't know if many of you really knew me then. Or now. But . . ." She paused, blowing out a breath, and all anxiety seemed to slip away as she stood up taller and her mouth twisted into a smirk. Right before us, her blond hair darkened a couple of shades, her nose softened, and her features became familiar—almost like I was looking in a mirror— even as her eyes took on a reddish hue. *Shapeshifter?* I wondered. "I think some of you might know me better as Rachelle Lyrica." She paused again, long enough for the three hellhounds to growl and my mother and grandmother to gasp, as though they all recognized the name. I didn't, although Lyrica sounded close to Lyra, my mother's name. Then she added, "last name Savage."

Savage's throat made some kind of rumbling noise. Tase stared at her in open-mouthed shock.

Shelly—Rachelle—walked up to me and held out her hand. "It's nice to truly meet you, sister."

My breath whooshed out of me. I stared at her, my mouth hanging open wider than Tase's. Others started rapid-firing questions at her. She lifted her hand to quiet them.

"I'm happy to explain." Her eyes looked triumphant, along with her smile, having received the reaction she'd apparently hoped for. What the fuck was up with her? She was a nutcase. She couldn't possibly be my sister—my twin—who'd run away from Montrose years ago. Could she? "I'm a witch just as much as I'm a hellhound. A powerful one at that, but you should already know this. That made it easy to disguise myself. *Mother,* you registered me yourself when I was a small child." She glared at my mom, while tapping a finger on her right hip. My Registry tattoo was in that same place on my own body, getting it one of my earliest memories. "So that made crossing the wards a non-issue, and since you all thought I was human, you completely ignored me. I was here for nearly a year—actually, two now —right under your noses, and none of you noticed. I don't know if that's a testament to my magic or to how self-absorbed all of you are."

More questions flew, but Tase's one-word statement caught her attention.

"Carter," he whispered.

She shifted her weight toward him, running a hand over his shoulder that made my body tense. "Carter is mine—and yours. I left when I found out I was pregnant. Hellhound pregnancies and births are difficult, and my disguise might have been blown. So I took off again, then forgot about this place. But then last year, I was called back and sent to return. Of course, I came back to all kinds of problems with you, Tase, so I had to bide my time and have full faith in my twin to resolve your little issue so we can move on to the important stuff."

"What important stuff?" he asked.

"Sent by whom?" my grandmother demanded, louder and more commanding.

Shelly tilted her head, her brows arching. "By order of the Collector. The big boss. And I'm here to collect."

"And just what do you think you'll be collecting?" Saundra challenged.

Shelly grinned at her unflinchingly. "Oh, dear grandmother, you know very well what's truly valuable in this town. And it's not just the *what* but the *who*. You'll see soon enough."

With that, she snapped her fingers and disappeared.

"What in the ever living *fuck?*" Melaina roared, making all of us flinch, even Tase. She swung around, knocking a chair over as she rounded on Savage. "Did you know this?"

He shook his head, almost imperceptibly, his eyes narrowed to slits.

Liam answered instead, his voice raspy, like Savage's and Melaina's. It was a hellhound thing, from having fire in your throat while in your other form, I supposed. "She disguised herself too well. I didn't even *smell* her. Did you?"

Melaina's head shook.

"Where did she go?" my grandmother demanded from behind us. "Do you know, Melaina? Savage?"

"I knew *nothing*," Melaina replied as Savage shook his head more noticeably this time, his long hair brushing over his shoulders. Though his eyes remained hidden, he still seemed to be glaring at the door, as though expecting his other daughter to saunter back in. "I've never even seen her around town before. She showed up at my club this morning and said she had something to tell all of us. So I made the calls. I don't even know where she lives."

"I do," Tase said through clenched teeth. He rattled off the address.

"Lyra, see if she's there," Saundra ordered. "I doubt it, but it's worth a try."

"I'm going, too," Savage growled as he stood.

"The hell you are," Saundra said, and they glared at each other, Savage in jeans and a leather cut, and Grandmother looking like she belonged on Wall Street. Liam stood, too, large and foreboding, but not quite as massive as Savage. Saundra still didn't back down. She knew who had the real power here. She, Mathilde Augustine, and Roman Bishop did, even over the rest of the Court. Though nobody ever said that out loud, we all knew the Luna Coven had the power, and the triad were our leaders. They *allowed* the MC to stay in town, and she could easily disallow it. "Rachelle had a message, and she delivered it. She's been here for over a year and didn't bother reaching out to any of you. Do you really think she'll see you now? She's not here for her daddy. She's here to fuck with our town."

The room fell silent for a long moment. I wasn't sure if anybody had ever heard Saundra Beaumont drop the f-bomb.

"She's right," Liam said, peering at Savage as he nodded his head toward the door. "Let's ride."

Saundra turned to my mother. "Lyra, take Tase. Rachelle might run if she sees you, too, but maybe not him. I need to call an emergency Court meeting. I don't know what she meant about the Collector, but Mr. Westbrook might have been right all along. We should have been giving this more attention. Adelaide, come with me."

Savage and Liam strode out of the bar while making plans of their own, and Melaina followed them out. Mom and Tase left in her Lexus. I slid into the passenger seat of my grandmother's black luxury sedan, already sending a text out to all the Court members.

They were all there by the time we drove the three blocks to City Hall.

Two hours later, after much outrage about how this could happen and arguing about next steps, we finally had a plan. And I had a new assignment.

"Adelaide, you're in charge of figuring out who this Collector is and how to eliminate him," Mayor Barbie said. "Form a task force to help you. Find out everything you can, including his weaknesses."

"Especially his weaknesses," Roman said, although I still couldn't help but wonder if he knew more than he was letting on. He'd definitely be on my list for questioning, with Elsmed present and in a magic-proof room so he couldn't block the fae's mind-reading abilities. I actually looked forward to seeing the tables reversed on Roman for once.

"This is now your number one priority, Adelaide," Saundra said. "But do *not* confront him. At least not until we know what we're dealing with."

I read over my notes as they wrapped up the meeting. I'd already started making a list of whom I'd be recruiting for this task force, starting with Micah Westbrook.

CHAPTER 6

MICAH

*B*elmont Park.

God, I hated this place in all its despair and starkness.

No matter how many times I came to the mental health facility, the smell of disinfectant and anguish always hit me like a freight train. There would be no getting used to it, which led me to my next thought: how the hell did everyone else walk around as though the oppressive atmosphere of sickness and madness didn't affect them?

I tried not to visit too often—not wanting to draw attention to the person I kept hidden away here. But when the doctor had called, telling me that she had begun screaming my name, I knew it was time. Dr. Collins was adamant that I held the answers to what had unsettled his patient. When he'd attempted to find out why she'd become extremely agitated, the only response he'd managed to get from her was a name—the Collector.

I'd come all the way to New York City immediately.

The flickering light above me did nothing to soothe my agitation as I patiently waited to be acknowledged by the woman sitting behind the plexiglass partition. She was absorbed in the crossword she was doing, her pencil twirling between her fingers as she slowly chewed on gum.

I couldn't fault her. The emotions and hopelessness that pressed down on me were enough to almost convince me to check myself in. As an angel, I'd witnessed many things across the span of time—wars, revolutions, discoveries, the advancement of humankind. They were a resilient group of beings. This, however—this felt almost too much to bear.

There was no way I would ever bring Sedona here, even if I desperately needed to involve her in this secret. Some things needed to be borne alone. Not just for safety, but because to share it meant allowing another to carry a heavy burden. Sedona would drown here. She would short-circuit her empathic abilities and descend into darkness. She deserved only the light—to be encapsulated by goodness.

No, this would continue to be my responsibility to shoulder.

I cleared my throat, the weight pressing against me all the encouragement I needed.

What did it say about this kind of place when an angel began feeling antsy?

The woman finally looked up, somewhat surprised to see me there. Based on the square plastic lanyard that was clipped to her crisp white scrubs, her name was Michelle Jefferson.

She pressed on the intercom button, and her voice came across the small speaker in front of me. "Can I help you?"

I cleared my throat again. "Yes, I'm here to see Jessica Potter." It was a fake name I'd given her, yet another measure in keeping my charge hidden from those who would not just hurt her, but destroy her.

"Does the doctor know you're coming?" She eyed me sharply. Doctor approval was required to visit the section of the hospital where Jessica was housed.

I nodded quickly. "It was Dr. Collins who called me himself."

She raised her hand in a signal to wait and used her pencil to punch in the extension number on the telephone. I watched as she spoke quietly into the mouthpiece, nodding as she listened to the person on the other end. Every few seconds she stared back at me, her gaze dropping as she assessed me. After a few moments, she ended the call.

"You're approved." Without waiting for my response, she slid me a visitor's badge through an opening in the partition. "You're to wear this at all times. Someone will take you to Ms. Potter and supervise your visit with her. Do not take it upon yourself to wander off. Before you enter, you're to remove the following items from your person: cell phone, keys, anything sharp that could be used as a weapon. If your shoes have laces, slip-on shoes will be provided. We reserve the right to end your visit at any time, should we deem it necessary. You will be searched before entering. Any questions?"

I shook my head. I'd visited places like this countless times, moving Jessica to different facilities in order to keep her existence secret.

"Then welcome to Belmont Park." Smirking, she pushed the buzzer. As I stepped through the door to the worker waiting for me, the lady had already returned to her crossword puzzle.

"Follow me," came the gruff command from the male orderly. He was already moving briskly down the hallway that led to another locked door. For a place that stated its mission was to provide a safe, nurturing environment where their clients could heal and thrive, there was no evidence to support it. It felt more like a prison than anything else.

If it wasn't for the fact it sheltered Jessica from those who would harm her, I'd have moved her.

As I did with each visit I made, I tested to see whether my magical wards and protections still held. I used the most powerful spells I knew —incantations that I'd gathered throughout the centuries for precisely this reason. I flicked my fingers—a small movement that would seem harmless to others—and sigils flared into sight. I'd spared no effort when I'd relocated Jessica here. The walls were covered with them, and to my satisfaction, they all remained pure and untampered with. I moved my fingers again, and they disappeared. From what I'd managed to ascertain, Belmont Park was run solely by humans. They couldn't see the magic I'd infused into the institution. Having said that, I wasn't about to take any risks either.

We stopped briefly by a room where the orderly stored my belongings and gave me a quick pat down. In a flat voice that revealed that he'd recited the speech more times than he could count, he instructed me with the dos and don'ts of the visit. I'd heard it all before —in all kinds of variations. It all boiled down to this: don't agitate the patient.

The hairs on the back of my neck rose. The air was filled with different sounds: moans, cries, the occasional scream for someone to stop. It was the last one that made me want to hurry.

Jessica.

I followed quietly as we passed through many secured doors, until finally, the orderly stopped us outside room 314. Jessica's room.

Nathan. I finally caught a glimpse of his name badge. "Just a word of warning. She's having another episode today. I don't know why the doctor approved this visit, and it's not my place to question him. Don't get too close. If you become afraid for your life, press the button by the door and I'll come get you. There are cameras in the room, so I'll be watching. Don't turn your back to her. You may think she looks normal, but don't underestimate the situation. Any questions?"

I had about a hundred but shook my head. I'd already made a mental note to start looking for a new place to hide Jessica, a new identity to give her. "I'll let you know when I'm done."

Nathan nodded once, opened the door, and gestured for me to enter. The second I crossed the threshold, I gasped. There was no holding my reaction back. It wasn't because of what I saw in the small cell-like room—the walls white, the bed neatly made. No, the involuntary sound erupted from the sheer desperation I felt emanating from the person huddled in the corner.

"Ms. Jessica, you have a visitor," Nathan said from behind me. He stood by the door, and catching my eye, pointed to the buttons on the wall. "Whenever you're ready."

I mouthed that I understood. Good God, this place was oppressive.

Left alone with Jessica, I wet my lips, momentarily forgetting why I'd come. I'd been in a rush when I'd checked her into the mental health facility. People had been getting too close, and I'd needed to get Holly to Havenwood Falls as quickly as I could. There hadn't been time to do a thorough evaluation, and in my haste, I hadn't stayed long enough to make sure she was in capable hands.

Staring down at the tiny form who was now rocking in the corner, I vowed I would do better by her.

Do better by Holly's mother.

"Jessica," I whispered in soft tones. When that didn't work, I stepped closer, crouched to the ground, and murmured, "Elizabeth."

She stopped rocking. She'd recognized her birth name.

I was tempted to move closer, to show her I meant no harm, to help her remember who I was. The mind could be a tricky thing. The last time I'd spoken with Elizabeth, the trauma she'd experienced at the hands of Holly's father had reduced her to an empty shell of her former self. Elizabeth used to be vibrant, full of life, a woman who smiled and laughed easily. It wasn't hard to see why Azareal had been drawn to her. She encompassed beauty and passion and hope—all traits that were coveted by beings who felt very little.

I tried again. "Elizabeth."

I kept my voice low and even, careful not to startle her.

I didn't move. I didn't say another word. I simply waited for Elizabeth to find her voice.

I don't know how long we sat there in relative silence. The noise from the others faded away. I did my best to ease Elizabeth's distress until finally, she spoke.

"She's in danger. You promised."

She was still in there, somewhere. Despite the trauma, she still recalled the promise I gave her to always keep her daughter safe until the time Holly could use her own powers to defend herself.

"I did," I answered, sitting on the floor near her. "And I've kept my vow."

Elizabeth's head whipped up, and we locked eyes. Her stare was penetrating. Bold. "The Collector is coming." There was a wildness in her gaze that churned up a wave of anxiety within my chest. I'd seen her expression before—when she'd seen something, her gifts surfacing. "No one will be safe."

I forgot about the rules as I scooted closer, now within arm's reach of her. "Who? What can you tell me?"

Elizabeth's whole demeanor changed. Gone was the façade of someone battling with their own sanity, and in its place, I could see that she was in full control of her faculties. There was a clarity that screamed that I needed to pay attention, that the words coming out of her mouth were not those of a mad woman, but of someone who understood the dire circumstances approaching.

"The Collector. Holly. She is in danger. She cannot be used as a weapon. She cannot be lost. Promise me!" And with that last demand coming out in a shriek, Elizabeth lashed out, gripping my arm with such force that she almost drew blood. I didn't flinch. "Keep. Her. Safe."

Gently, I touched her hand and felt her tight grasp soften. "You have my word. By my life, I will do everything within my power to protect her."

I let her search my gaze for the truth. I didn't blink as seconds passed. When she was satisfied with what she found, Elizabeth let out a long breath. "The Collector is searching, always searching. Power. Always for power, and they are close. So close."

One word instantly drew my attention.

"Who is close? Close as in how?" I cautiously pushed, careful not to trigger something within her. It was often like walking through a minefield where the wrong word, expression, or gesture could set off an explosion.

She swallowed hard and her brows furrowed. She began shaking her head as if she didn't agree with the voices or images in her head. "Keep her safe. The Collector. Havenwood Falls. So close." Elizabeth began rocking back and forth again. I was running out of time.

"What about Havenwood Falls?" The town's name on her lips frightened me, because I had never told her where I kept her daughter hidden.

Elizabeth banged her head back against the wall. Once. Twice. Three times. "No, no! I don't want to see! So much blood. So much magic." Then with one final burst of adrenaline and clarity, she threw herself at me, her small body pinning me to the ground with a strength I didn't think possible. "The Collector must be stopped! Find his weakness!"

Alarms started ringing, and the door to the room flew open. Nathan and another orderly came rushing in, pushing me to the side as they reached for Elizabeth.

"You need to leave. Now," Nathan ordered, using his head to point toward the door. As I slowly backed out of the room, my heart breaking over the sight of Elizabeth being restrained, I made another silent vow to find her a better place. No, it was stronger than that. I wouldn't rest until I made life safe enough for her to be free.

But not just for her.

For Holly.

For Sedona.

For us all.

~

MY VISIT to Belmont Park still weighed heavily on my mind as I watched Holly reading. While I didn't keep her in complete ignorance, I'd sheltered her from some of the harsher truths to protect her innocence.

I'd always said that once she reached a certain age, I would answer some of the questions she had. But there were emotions stirring within me, fatherly feelings, that whispered she would never be old enough to share the burdens I carried about her gifts. I dreaded the day she fully understood, because I knew it would also mean that child-like wonder she held about the world would crumble. She wouldn't be able to embrace the light so fully when she knew what darkness lurked in the shadows.

"Mr. Westbrook?" a voice jolted me from my thoughts, and reluctantly I dragged my gaze from Holly. I'd been standing outside

Shelf Indulgence and peering through the window at my young charge. Sedona was also inside, helping customers find the books they were wanting. It made me smile that in between that, she was bringing Holly other volumes that might interest her.

I'd fallen in love with Sedona, and I hadn't been alone. Holly was smitten by the young bookstore owner. There was no denying the two had established a bond that even I couldn't intrude on.

Turning about, I was surprised to find Addie Beaumont. I wasn't used to being approached on the street by other town members, and when I was the one doing the approaching, they usually quickened their pace to get away from me. In their defense, they were usually Court members.

It still rankled the way they kept brushing me off, not taking anything I said seriously. I'd been tempted to go and share with them what I'd learned at Belmont Park. They would have to take what Elizabeth said seriously because she was a seer. Yes, a crazy seer, but a seer nonetheless. They couldn't disregard her like they continually did to me.

I didn't, though, because I knew as surely as the Collector was here in Havenwood Falls, they would exclude me from the hunt. They would close ranks and give me some bullshit excuse that they had it under control.

I couldn't accept that. The Collector was a direct threat to Holly, and I refused to sit on the sidelines while others decided the fate of those I loved. While Havenwood Falls was my home for the moment, I owed no loyalties to the families and the Court. I owed loyalty to my Sedona. I would do everything within my power to protect her, but beyond that? It was better to ask forgiveness than permission. Not that I would ever ask them to forgive me.

I had one job, and one job only. If they got in my way, I would simply step around them.

Like now.

I moved to the side, hoping to find a reason to leave this conversation before it started. I didn't have time for pleasantries.

Whatever Addie Beaumont wanted, she would need to find someone else, because I wasn't interested. She must've realized my intentions because she stepped in the same direction, her gaze challenging.

"We need to talk, Micah." There was a seriousness in her expression that tugged at me.

"We do?" I replied, not sure what we could ever have in common. I cast a quick look over my shoulder at Holly. She was deep in an animated conversation with Sedona now. They were completely oblivious to the dangers that surrounded them.

Addie nodded and then spoke the two words I never expected out of her mouth, the two words that instantly captured my attention and humbled me. "The Collector."

"I'm in." My response came out so fast that it made her burst out into laughter.

"Just like that?" She tilted her head as she sized me up. "You don't even know what I'm going to say."

"I don't have to," I countered, holding her gaze. "He's a threat. The Court refuses to acknowledge it." And to prove that I meant business, I added the only piece of information I'd gleaned from my visit with Elizabeth. "And he's here in Havenwood Falls."

Her face went blank, lacking any emotions, as though she wasn't terribly surprised to hear that. I expected her to ask me questions, but instead she slowly nodded, looking about to see if anyone was close enough to overhear. "That's why I need you. We need you. The Court believes now the events with Sedona and Holly are related to other things going on."

"They acknowledged that the attacks were now connected?"

She nodded. "They believed before that different occurrences around town were simply random coincidence, but they no longer do."

"So they finally have the proof they need?"

"Enough. I'll tell you all about it if you'll help me."

"Like I said, I'm in."

Addie smiled and then her face went grim again. "Then welcome aboard." She stretched out her hand and I shook it. "This could get ugly."

Everything I loved was inside the building behind me.

"Then let's go."

CHAPTER 7

SENORA

*A*utumn and all its brilliance had arrived in Colorado. The crisp mountain air smelled like fall. A bearable time of year for me. The weather wasn't too cold, and the food supply was fresh. What wasn't acceptable was the atmosphere. It was like something was wrong. Every shop I ventured into had a residual, desperate energy—like someone was in a hurry to unearth hidden treasures or some other shit.

Get a grip, I told myself.

It was probably just my imagination getting the best of me—or my fear speaking up. If asked, I'd never admit to being scared. Empusai, as a whole, were valiant. We freaked the shit out of our victims—they could wrap their heads around fangs and having their blood drained, but being eaten afterward? That was the part they couldn't get with. Sadly, I understood it. The first time I'd witnessed a feasting—sounds much better than a killing—it sickened the shit out of me. But then I had my first meal. Eating the bones was like munching on chips or some other crunchy snack—not a big deal.

Back to the strangeness floating in the air . . .

A premonition or a warning from the spirit world were better explanations. Something was brewing in town. It was ancient and malicious and I suspected its source, but I didn't want to admit it. Not yet. Unfortunately, it didn't matter if I acknowledged it or not. Returning to Havenwood Falls was a dangerous and stupid endeavor even for someone like me.

The first reason should have been obvious. My bestie, Izzie Itzae, was in town, which meant I could run into her. She was fleeing from a pussy-hungry, very human mafia boss—Kazimir Chekhov—but it wasn't a romp in bed he was after. Not anymore. Losing three million dollars will quash lust faster than ice water poured on a nut sack. Well, in all honesty, he didn't lose it. Chekhov knew exactly where—or I should say who—had his money. Yeah, my super bright friend stole the money from the Russian. Why? She wanted out of her agreement —the one she inadvertently activated by fucking the bastard. Chekhov had a lame-ass policy that made females dumb enough to sleep with him exclusive property. You know, sex slaves. The only way out was to give him three million dollars—what he thought any woman he owned was worth. Izzie stole from the company and held the funds as ransom. She claimed she'd release the money once Chekhov tore up the contract.

I wasn't saying that Izzie was stupid—*yeah, right.* It was more like she was desperately horny. Delayed transformation did that to naguals. They resorted to doing dumb shit, like fucking Chekhov, trying to scratch the proverbial itch. Her actions made me glad to be an empusa. There was no such thing as late bloomers with us. You got your fangs, your stomach growled, and you quickly learned how to soothe the hunger. End of story.

Anyway . . . After Chekhov announced that she belonged to him, Izzie looked for a way out. What I didn't understand was that she knew I had money—I'd told her I had this mega trust fund that I tapped into from time to time. All she had to do was ask me, and I would have gladly helped. I could have bought out her agreement *and* put Chekhov out of his misery. She'd been free of the arrogant bastard, and I would have been belching vodka. Everybody happy.

Of course, the immature nagual didn't choose the easier option. The female never listened to common sense. So I did what any friend would do. I told her to run—get her ass so far away from New York

City that it wasn't even a memory. I even gave her the key to my cabin here in Colorado, but the girl couldn't read a fucking map to save her life. Izzie got sort of lucky—the verdict is still out on that—when a resident found her and escorted her to the town hidden in a box canyon. The last I heard from my friend, she had planned to stay put in Havenwood Falls. I suspected her remaining in the town had more to do with meeting a hot nagual shifter than hiding from Chekhov. For her sake, I hoped his men, all members of Bratva, didn't find their way to Havenwood Falls. It was my sincere wish that Izzie's potential mate could handle whatever shit came her way.

The second, more insidious reason I didn't want to be in town had to do with the being called the Collector—the real threat facing Havenwood Falls. We had unfinished business from my last visit, so I was fairly certain it was why I'd been summoned. Frankly, I had no problem with the request—outside of the aforementioned reasons. We needed to reach an understanding about the incomplete assignment and move on.

There was something strange about that last text message, though. Normally, when one came across my phone, my contact's signature—a distinct and dark essence—came with it. Not this time. The impression was wrong somehow—a strong sensation of cloaking and secrets, which begged the question—was it really my normal contact sending the message or someone else? The question churned my insides and intensified my already wary nature.

Trying to decipher a supernatural puzzle wasn't worth the time and effort. If I wanted an answer, I had to go to the source. In this case, it meant pushing aside my apprehension and porting back to Havenwood Falls. Porting in and out was an ability from my great-aunt Hecate, the queen of witchcraft. That ancestry didn't make me a witch, but it granted me a small assortment of powers. One was the ability to transport wherever I needed to go—much better than a commercial flight.

What I couldn't do was transport up the side of this frigging mountain. Besides the fact that I didn't like heights, this peak was protected by barrier spells. So I tamed my fear and made the treacherous climb—something I swore I wouldn't do again. Unfortunately, I only had more questions by the time I reached the summit.

Like where was my contact? The shadowy figure draped in a cloak usually waited at the top and ushered me into the Collector's estate. This time the only thing waiting was the howling wind. I really didn't need the contact to enter. All I had to do was press the monolithic stone with my palm. It took a moment before the estate appeared. I ignored my quivering gut and continued to the door. It stood open, with nobody to greet me. For the first time, I crossed the threshold alone. An overwhelming cold hit me. I rubbed my hands over my arms, but the feeling of ice water drenching me wouldn't go away.

Something was . . . off in the structure. Was it an oddity or a harbinger of horrors to come?

Run, said the little voice in my head.

Now, my gut added its opinion.

The possibility of fattening my bank account, however, won, and I edged forward.

Thankfully, I warmed up, but the heat didn't come from a usual source—no fireplaces in the hall outside the main room. My gaze bounced around the narrow space, but I saw nothing out of place. I sensed a foreboding presence, and it disturbed my delicate balance. The predator within was on alert. My heightened eyesight kicked in, and I searched the shadows for hidden threats, but there was nothing. Common sense told me not to take that barrenness for granted. Lives got snuffed out when you let your guard down. Instead, I stopped and scanned the area, seeking the masked soul in the darkness. When I inhaled, the faint smell of brimstone hit me. Dragon? I closed my eyes and listened. It was hard to hear it at first. Then it grew stronger. The heartbeat was too small for a beast, but it belonged to an animal. Dog? Wolf? Shit—hellhound! My pulse quickened as my eyes flew open.

"Afraid?" The disembodied feminine voice approached me. "You should be."

I prepared myself—ready to transport out of danger if needed. Heels clicked across the stone floor and stopped in front of me. My eyes swept over a skinny female with dark blond hair and slightly reddish eyes. She didn't look like a hellhound, but she gave off that vibe along with something else—a damned witch. "Who are you?"

"An ally, nothing more and nothing less." She laughed briefly and then continued, "Relax. We're on the same side. The Collector wanted me to contact you. Keep my number handy."

I like how she sidestepped my question, but I wasn't here to hang out with a supernatural Barbie. "Where is he?"

The female pointed toward the main room's door and faded into the darkness. Good riddance.

As usual, the space was overheated and dimly lit. The Collector was in his usual spot. As I took my seat, I asked, "Why am I here?"

My client studied me for a long, uncomfortable moment. "You left town before we concluded our business."

As far as I was concerned, we were technically finished. I'd decided I wasn't stealing shit from a kid, no matter how tempting the offer. I'd told him this months ago. "I do have a life outside this town."

"Have you acquired my asset?"

Another unimportant relic. Frankly, I was tired of gathering trinkets—my job until I went after what the Collector really wanted. I hadn't acted on it, because we'd never finished our negotiations.

Was he deaf? Or maybe he really smoked a joint or two? I sniffed the air, trying to detect the herbal blend, but found none. Just what was this creature's problem? "No. We never agreed to any terms."

The Collector steepled his glove-clad hands, leaned forward, and exhaled loudly. The stench of his breath stretched across the space between us. The funk slapped my face. I gagged and swallowed hard.

"You're difficult," he uttered in that familiar, raspy voice. "New terms. I'll pay twice your standard fare provided you also acquire another artifact."

Now that was more like it. I crossed my leather-clad legs and swung my foot lazily. "You do know my standard is half a mill?"

He nodded.

Part of me was doing the happy dance—butt naked in a stack of

Benjamins. The other half—my more sensible part—pumped the brakes and warned me not to count the cash so fast.

"Before I agree, what's this other item?" My inner voice smiled at my levelheadedness.

"It's a piece of a whole—the Elan Chain. The links have been scattered."

Was he kidding? I was supposed to find something that could have been scattered all over the world. I hoped he had a map.

My boss continued, "I've already been disappointed once by a failed attempt."

"What happened?"

I swore I heard a slight chuckle from him. "Let's just say that I don't take disappointment well. Death comes to those who fail me."

Death? Oh, hell no!

"So how am I to find the piece?" The longer I was in the Collector's presence, the more I grew certain that the creature was batshit crazy.

"Work with Rachelle. She—"

I jumped to my feet and shouted, "You want me to partner up with the Barbie doll? A hellhound? I don't think so." I'd never met one that I liked.

Despite not seeing the face of the Collector, I felt his intense glare. It hollowed out my bones and sent a soul-numbing chill down my spine. A palpable warning—interrupting my customer was ill-advised. Pressure landed on my shoulders. Slowly, I sank back down, lowering my eyes as I shifted on the chair. This was the Collector's doing, not mine. I tried lifting my head but couldn't. Clearly, I was no longer in charge of this conversation—if I ever had been.

"As I was saying . . ." His fingers strummed the chair's arm, and he continued as if nothing had happened. "Rachelle is excellent at obtaining information. She'll let you know of any tips she receives. Your job will be to follow up and bring me what you find."

With a little justified hesitation, I ask, "That's *if* I take the assignment."

"You *will* take the assignment," he replied with confidence.

He shouldn't be so sure of himself. Yes, the Collector could force me to my knees and make me appear remorseful for my sassy tongue, but he couldn't make me take the job. First, there was the issue of getting that damn lantern from a kid. It didn't matter that she was no longer in school. Second, I have always worked alone. It was easier and not as messy that way—nobody got hurt and nobody blabbed to the authorities. I learned in the beginning that partners eventually became meals. After devouring my first ten associates and getting a bad reputation because of it, I operated alone. Third, there was that whole dying thing.

As if reading my thoughts, the Collector dangled a bigger carrot. "Three times your usual allotment."

I licked my lips. With that kind of payout, I'd be able to fulfill my dream in no time. Still, I didn't want to seem too eager. Much like sex, it was better to draw out the negotiation and get a more satisfying reward. Pushing to my feet, I stared down at my employer—yeah, taking the assignment would change my status and not in my favor. It was the other reason for my saying, "I'll think on it. I need to head back home, take care of some things, and then I'll be in touch."

"Stay in Havenwood Falls. I'll deposit half of your pay to your account. Call it an act of good faith."

So tempting. *Maybe* I could lie low and avoid Izzie.

"Leave," added the Collector, "and the deposit, along with a seventy-five percent penalty, will disappear from the account. That penalty comes from your total account. Call it a restocking fee."

Fuck!

WELL OVER 2.6 million dollars of my hard-earned money. That's a hell of a lot to lose just for turning the Collector down. I probably could survive the loss. Honestly, it wouldn't break my bank account, but it had the potential to leave a lasting impression—one that I didn't like at all. As I paced the floor of the NamaStays cottage, I considered the pros and cons of the situation.

The biggest plus was that I stood to gain a lot of money. With what the Collector offered, I could easily pay for my island retreat. Hell, maybe I'd buy my own mountain hideaway. The other positive was I could finally give up the mercenary life. Who knows, I might even find the time for a regular fuck buddy or two?

Doubt it, said that little voice.

Unfortunately, I agreed. Empusai normally didn't find love. It was too difficult to find a partner who didn't fear us or consider eating us.

Being alone wasn't a great fear, but the cons of taking the job worried the hell out of me. What if I ran into Izzie? I'd have to explain why I was in a town most people didn't know existed. The girl was too smart for her own good, though. She'd question my appearance and slowly put two and two together. She didn't know me as a hired gun, and it needed to stay that way. I was still digesting the last roommate who stumbled upon the truth.

Besides Izzie and the money issue, there was the simple fact that I didn't like what the Collector was doing. No, I didn't know what his plans were, but I sensed he was scheming and it wouldn't be good for anyone involved with him. That fact troubled me enough to seriously think about taking the risk and refusing the Collector's generous offer.

The more I thought about it, the clearer the choice became. It was time to be proactive—remember my heritage as a niece of Hecate— and act accordingly. Besides transporting, I could leave behind a believable apparition of myself or someone else. It wasn't something I shared with anyone. If I had, I was sure the Collector would have used it to his advantage. Handy for what I needed to do.

It was still daytime when I appeared outside the bank located on a tiny island in the Philippines. Waving my hand, I manipulated time, and every person within a hundred-mile radius froze. I entered the building and headed to the first available associate poised in front of a computer. I wiggled my fingers, and the woman became a convenient puppet. She was obedient and located my account. The deposit the

Collector promised was there. Now to make sure it remained in its resting place. First, I used my helper to block access to the account the Collector used to deposit my funds. Next, she destroyed any paper trail to all of my other accounts. Finally, in case the being or that dreaded Barbie doll investigated, my sycophant created a fake trail that would inevitably lead back to the Collector. If he tried to take funds from me, twice the amount would magically disappear from his account and show up in one of my other accounts around the world. By the time he figured out what happened, it would be too late. Once put into motion, this account, along with any traces to it, would disappear, and the funds would be distributed amongst the others.

Nobody took advantage of me.

Protecting my finances was done, but I had no desire to return to Havenwood Falls right away. Instead, I waved my hand and faded to Chekhov's location. I just needed to make sure Izzie would be safe.

As my image dissipated, activity returned to the bank—nobody the wiser that I had ever been there.

CHAPTER 8

HARPER

*A*utumn in Havenwood Falls was a patchwork quilt of colors, the changing and falling leaves a plethora of beauty that called to the photographer in me. My mind took mental snapshots, my cold hands warming against a mug of hot cocoa cradled in my palms, my body warmed by a pair of worn skinny jeans and an old sweatshirt that hung to my knees. Fingers of fragile light leaking through the canopy of trees surrounding my small mountain home stroked the wooden porch where I stood, stopping just short of touching me. As if it was afraid of me.

I didn't blame it. I was afraid of me.

"You have a perfectly warm cabin to ruminate in, and you choose to stand outside in this?" Desi complained, the mace bouncing in a wooden rocking chair beside me, causing the chair to sway in the stillness.

Creak, creak.

The sound should have comforted me, the chair's movement merging with the symphony of early morning nature to crescendo with the whistling birds and rustling breeze. Instead, it grated on my nerves.

A nightmare had woken me before the sun had crested the mountains, and it still lingered in the corners of my brain, chasing away the beauty of the day.

. . .

"Hello?"

My voice echoed down an empty, dim hallway full of unopened doors, my only reply the questioning 'hello'. Below me, the floor was rough, a hewn, unfinished wood that left splinters in my skin. A corridor, the walls of equally rough stone, closed in on me, and my heart raced, anxious sweat beading on my brow.

Standing on shaky legs, I glanced down to find myself cloaked in an old-fashioned white gown with ruffled sleeves that ended at my elbows and a pink-ribbon-adorned hem that came just below my knees, leaving the rest of my legs and feet bare. The wood below dug at the bottom of my feet, sharp and unforgiving, driving tears I refused to shed into the corners of my eyes.

Fog came out of nowhere, filtering down the hall and swirling against me, the chilly wetness rubbing me like a cat looking for attention.

"Hello?" I called again, because not *speaking felt scarier somehow.*

A lucid dream.

I wasn't a stranger to dreams or visions like these, the kind where I woke up inside a whole new world aware that I was dreaming. They happened too often, but I'd never woken up in a place like this. The worst place—until now—that I'd found myself in was a pitch-black darkness faced off against a demon named Levi.

The fog around me thickened and darkened, like white clouds turning gray just before a storm. Streaks of odd lightning shot up, highlighting the wood-and-stone hallway to showcase doorways that looked nothing alike. There were big doors and small doors, arched doors and rectangular doors, decorated doors and plain doors.

"Harper." The fog spoke to me, the sound disembodied and deep, before growing and growing, becoming an army of shadow people with no faces. Walking silhouettes.

One of these shadow people glided to a door painted bright red. Like blood.

"Come," it beckoned.

There was no way in hell I was listening.

"What's in there?" I asked.

The shadow person grew, quivering, and I wondered if I'd angered it, if this was what my demons looked like when they were unhappy with me.

"Come," it beckoned again.

The wood beneath my feet grew sharper, the splinters eating at my skin, causing me to bleed. The tears I'd wanted so badly not to shed slid down my cheeks, but I didn't cry out. If the hallway was this bad, whatever was beyond the door would be worse. Somehow, I knew that it would be better to bleed to death.

"I won't," I whispered firmly.

I wasn't a loud person. To most, I came off as meek and quiet. Not cowardly, but certainly not brave. To them, anyway. But people didn't always need to be loud to be brave or badass to be fierce. Strength came in many forms.

The shadow person grew so large, it left me surrounded by pitch darkness, the only light the lightning streaks, leaving me in a storm that was sucking the very life out of me.

"What's beyond the door?" I gasped, falling to my knees, the rough wood skinning me, staining the hem of the white gown with drops of blood.

"You," the shadow person screamed. Its shriek pierced my ears, and my hands flew up to cover them, my palms instantly wet with blood.

I was going to die here.

"Me?" I whimpered.

"Everything you could be."

The walls and the floor suddenly changed, going from rough and cold to soft, wet, and pliable. Lightning highlighted the space, and I found myself fighting the urge to vomit. I was kneeling inside a human brain. I didn't have to be a doctor to know what an internal organ looked like.

"Oh, God," I breathed.

Pitch darkness came again, and with it, any bravery I'd been feeling.

I kneeled, blood seeping from my feet and knees into a freaking human brain.

The scream, when it came, was desperate.

. . .

"Want to talk about it?" Desi asked, shaking me out of my thoughts.

I shook my head and sipped my hot cocoa, the now cool liquid sliding down my throat as I peered over the rim of the cup into the mountains beyond my porch.

I'd been trapped inside my own brain in the dream, and it had been an unforgiving place. The doors had been entrances to places within myself I'd never explored before. All of them dark places, because I'd been born of darkness. Darkness I could no longer ignore.

"You aren't exactly an easy person to find these days, Harper Sinclair," a voice I knew all too well said gently. It was late afternoon, and I'd left my disquieting morning behind to sit at a table at Coffee Haven sipping hot cocoa and eating a grilled cheese sandwich, my go-to stress relief.

Until now.

Addie's boot-covered feet stared up at me, and I let my gaze wander up over a slim frame to land on brown inquiring eyes behind black-framed glasses.

Addie Beaumont. The granddaughter of Court member Saundra Beaumont. Witch extraordinaire. Half hellhound. Amazing tattoo artist. And, most importantly, my friend.

Shoes thudded over hardwood floors as customers crowded in front of a long marble counter, most of them deep in conversation. A harried Willow Fairchild scrambled to meet their needs, along with Davis, the manager. Light spilled in through a large picture window, highlighting indoor plants, crystals, and local art. Coffee Haven brought in crowds all year round, but during the fall and winter, when chilly breezes and falling temperatures drove people toward hot drinks and food, the shop bustled with business.

A tall man with brown hair and blue eyes I wasn't acquainted with stood just behind Addie, towering over her, his face stern.

"Your aunt told me we'd find you here," Addie continued.

I stood, nodding respectfully, because I wasn't sure if Addie was here for business or friendship. Had the Court realized I'd been seeing the shadows more frequently recently? Had they figured out that I'd been discovering new ways to communicate with the darkness? It wasn't that I was trying to hide it from them; I just didn't know enough about what was going on with me to come forward with the information.

As for the man with Addie, I got an oddly familiar feeling from him.

"You're an—" My words trailed off, my gaze sweeping the crowded coffee shop to land on Irene Beckett and Biddie Half-Moon, two of the town's most notorious gossips. "I'm guessing this isn't a good place to talk?"

"You're a bright one after a few cups of hot chocolate," Addie teased, lightening the mood, although her eyes told an entirely different story. She was worried about something.

Leaving behind the half-eaten grilled cheese sandwich I'd been nibbling on, I followed them quietly onto the sidewalk outside—away from prying eyes—before letting them lead me next door into Shelf Indulgence, through rows of books, and into a storage room at the back of the store. Shelves lined with organized tomes greeted us, heightening my power and making me shiver.

As soon as the door clicked shut, Addie faced me, and I picked up where I'd left off in Coffee Haven, my gaze on the man instead of her. "Are you an angel?"

His brows rose, sudden wary interest flaring in his gaze. "You're perceptive."

It didn't sound like a compliment. Angels were extremely powerful, so much so that their powers were beyond the Court, and it didn't sit well with them when people were able to see beyond their human disguise.

"She's got experience with angels," Addie revealed, light humor lacing her words.

I was never going to live down my affair with Lucas Fox, a fallen

Seraph who'd literally swept in and out of my life like a shooting star, dazzling and brilliant.

"This is Micah Westbrook," Addie introduced. Being at Shelf Indulgence made sense now. I'd heard Micah's name around town, but this was my first time interacting with him.

I offered him my hand. "It's nice to meet you."

Micah shoved his hands into his blue jeans pockets, his eyes narrowed. He was a kind man—I could see it in his gaze—but he was also suspicious. He had ancient eyes, the kind that had seen too much. The kind that didn't trust too often.

And considering the kind of powers I called on, I wasn't exactly the kind of person he'd want to make friends with.

Addie pulled a notebook and pencil out of a messenger bag she had slung over her shoulder, the movement breaking the tension, before holding it out to me. "We need you, Harper, and not just for information. I'm rallying a team to figure out something the Court desperately needs to know."

I had a weakness for the word *need*.

"You need *me*?" I asked, because it bore repeating.

Addie bumped the notebook against my hand. "Yes, you. Can you channel spirits for information about someone called the Collector?"

The name triggered me, sending whispered words rushing through my head, words I'd read on the shelves of Shelf Indulgence only months before. *Chained people tied together. Items. Magic. Watcher watching. Waiting. United we stand against the one collecting power.*

The Collector? Was that what a collection of power had meant?

A collection of power. Had the spirits been trying to tell me about this moment?

United we stand. Had they known Addie would come to me?

I accepted the notebook, flipped the cover over, and let myself fall cross-legged to the floor. I didn't need to sit to do this, but I wasn't about to go all weird and possibly faint in front of an angel I'd just met. It was safer to do this sitting.

Addie sat opposite me, her gaze focused on my face.

"What is she going to do?" Micah asked, still standing, his voice gruff.

"I'm a spiritual psychic and a summoner," I replied for Addie, without looking up. "I channel the dead and spirits. Through words."

Well, not just through words anymore, but I wasn't willing to share that yet.

Setting the notebook on the floor before me, I let the pencil dangle from my fingers, my eyes falling closed. "Tell me about the Collector," I murmured.

Addie and Micah hadn't told me a thing other than a name, but spiritual psychics were well versed in working for clients on little information. Sometimes nothing at all except maybe a coarse command of, "You're the psychic—you tell me what I came for."

Words whispered in my head, a cold numbness settling over my body. Dark, heavy, and suffocating. This feeling wasn't new to me, but it had become stronger over the last few months—so strong, I'd become afraid of my own head. Which was a terrible thing, since I'd just started to become comfortable with it to begin with.

"The Collector," I repeated.

The dark power that held me was strong and painful, and my fingers clenched around the pencil. Micah stiffened, his body primed for a fight. "There's darkness here."

"That's what she channels," Addie told him, her gaze remaining on the notebook.

The pencil in my grip flew across the page.

Scratch. Scratch. Scratch.

In truth, I didn't need the notebook. The shadows yelled at me inside my brain, fighting to get free, to use me as a host rather than the pencil and paper. I had become more powerful than words.

I struggled to hide it, to tamp down the shadows where they fought within me, angry and pooling in my gut, so that Addie wouldn't see the conflict within me. My body was a civil war ground.

But I was losing this war. Deep down, I knew that.

Power, sharp and uninviting, shot out of me, springing forth a horde of dark shadows that circled the storage room.

"Fuck!" Addie cursed. "What the hell, Harper?" She'd seen the shadows before, but these shadows were darker. Bigger. More malevolent.

It was too late for me, my body a channeling vessel of terrible things. Words spilled out onto the paper, the script messy and uneven.

Chained people tied together. Items. Magic. Watcher watching. Waiting. United we stand against the one collecting power. The red door, Harper. You should have opened the red door.

Vaguely, from a distance, I heard Addie ask, "What red door?" before my body fell over, the convulsions taking me—and them—by surprise.

"Power," I gritted through chattering teeth. "Whoever this Collector is, he has a lot of power."

My pencil had spilled words onto the paper before I lost to the darkness, and I knew when Addie gasped that my secret was out. At least in this room. I'd become stronger, and I'd been hiding it from everyone.

"Harper, you've been holding out on me," Addie accused, giving voice to my thoughts.

Micah spoke, the words something I'd never heard before, but they chased back the shadows, sending them reeling.

The red door.

Something told me if I'd just been brave enough to enter, I'd have answers to more of Addie's questions.

Right before I blacked out and completely embarrassed myself, I found myself thinking about another angel. The only one I truly trusted. Elias Jamison.

CHAPTER 9

ADDIE

I sat in the ritual circle near the waterfall, eyes closed, breathing deeply, trying to meditate with my familiars surrounding me in their appropriate positions on the circle. Trying not to think about the chill creeping into my ass from the boulder I sat on. The smell of burning wood wafted in the air, along with the fragrance of the falls and the muskiness of the dying forest floor. While today wasn't terribly chilly, last night had brought yet another hard frost. We'd had flurries a few nights before, and our first true snowfall could come any time.

I normally didn't trek here to one of the many Luna Coven circles scattered about the forests surrounding town. I normally didn't have need for what we used for larger rituals to protect the town and its people. Things were different now, though, and this one had the most power, being so close to the great falls and the magical aether in the water. It was also not too close to my home and on the opposite side of town from Tase's house. I needed to be as far away from him as possible at the moment. I couldn't even go to my own altar room in my house these days, because his energy was constantly intruding.

Tase was pissed.

I couldn't blame him. A year ago, some one-night stand showed up out of the blue with a five-year-old, claiming the kid was his—which had been confirmed by a supernatural doctor as well as three trusted mediums—but because of his personal situation, he hadn't been allowed to do anything but give her money. Money she likely didn't need if she'd been working for the Collector all this time. And now that Tase could finally have something to do with his own kid, she took him away. Nobody had been able to find Shelly—Rachelle—nor Carter since she'd dropped her bomb on us over a week ago. Tase was livid and on a rampage. He was impossible to be around.

I admittedly had mixed feelings being around him anyway. I was pissed, too. We'd never had any kind of commitment to each other until recently, and I still wasn't even sure what we had right now. Happiness. That's what we'd had. For a brief moment in time, anyway. But as much as I tried to be supportive and understanding that the only man I'd ever loved had a kid with someone else, on the inside, part of me had been in agony. And then to find out the baby mama was the twin sister I never knew I had? And she'd known all along? Sometimes, it was all just too much to think about. And I thought learning I was half hellhound was a difficult truth to accept.

So I could barely handle my own feelings, let alone piling Tase's on top of them.

At least we could do something about his problems, though. Maybe. If we could find anything about Shelly and this Collector person. If the bitch hadn't basically threatened my hometown, I'd admittedly be fine with never finding her again. Except, not really. Because I didn't know if Carter was safe with her. And while he might be the child of my boyfriend's lover, he was also the son of the man I loved. Possibly my future stepson. Oh, and definitely my nephew.

What a fucking mess. Somewhere along the way, my simple life had become one that belonged on a trashy daytime TV show.

I inhaled deeply, silently counting as I did, then exhaled slowly, letting go of those thoughts as though they were balloons and the breeze could carry them away. Inhale. Exhale. Draw in the clean air and magical energy. Release the stress and worry. Ground deeply into the earth. Pull in the Goddess's power, letting it flow through my body.

My mother's approaching energy tingled down my spine long before I heard or smelled her. I tried to ignore her, but I could sense the agitation in her aura, and so could my familiars. The beasts started to grow restless. So much for the deep meditation I so desperately needed.

"Can I come in?" She paused at the edge of the circle.

I released what little serenity I had achieved and pushed myself to my feet, rubbing my hands over my ass to warm it up as I turned to face her. "How'd you know where to find me?"

She pulled her knee-length black cardigan around her, crossing her arms over her stomach. "I felt you pass by my place on your way here."

I hadn't realized she'd been home when I'd hiked here through the Beaumont estate in Havenwood Heights. Although there was plenty of room in Grandmother Saundra's mansion—the main house—Mom lived in one of the extra homes on our family's property that butted up against the falls. The Bishop and the Augustine estates also bordered the falls, giving us all direct access to their magic.

"I needed a quiet place to meditate." If she understood that meant I wanted to be alone, she pretended not to.

"I wanted to let you know that I researched that energy blip we all felt the other night."

I lifted my chin, my interest piqued.

When the town's protective wards were tripped, everyone in the Luna Coven felt the energy shift. We usually paid no attention to it, especially if it was a familiar energy, as it was most often just residents coming and going. If it was an unfamiliar energy, which meant they weren't registered, we made a mental note in case we needed to come back to it later, if there was trouble. Mom and a few others, however, kept detailed notes, giving us long-term written records. Just in case. The energy blip the other night had felt vaguely familiar—like I'd felt it before—yet strange at the same time. Not like any other supernatural we had in town. Unfortunately, we knew it wasn't Rachelle, but I'd hoped . . .

"Please tell me you found the Collector."

"I wouldn't exactly know if that's who it was, being unregistered and all, but according to my record book, we felt the same type of energy signature last winter. On Valentine's Day, to be more specific. Whoever that was hadn't stayed in town long enough at the time for us to track them down and register them."

"But they're back?"

"They were. Or someone like them. We've lost them again, though."

I growled as I kicked a rock. "That's not helpful, then. It could just be a tourist. Someone obviously not staying long enough to cause problems."

"Unless it *is* the Collector."

I tapped my finger against my lips. Harper had said the other day that the Collector was here, in Havenwood Falls, but nobody sensed any unexpected or unusual energy. At least, nothing we'd been able to track down yet. We'd guessed that he must have been a null or a void —someone immune to magic—or somehow able to cloak himself from our wards.

"So let's say it's the Collector. If he can hide and unhide himself like that, then he wouldn't be a null or a void," I said.

"Unless he's using some kind of artifact, like Alex Newton has."

"The Elan Chain?"

Mom nodded. "Has anyone talked to Savannah Bast yet?"

"Yeah. She didn't know anything. Hadn't felt anything. So maybe it's more of a cloak. But why play with us like that, blipping in and out?"

"Isn't that what the Collector does?" Mom asked with a tilt of her head and a raise of her brow. "Play with us all?"

I scowled. "Yeah, I guess it is. And I hate being a plaything."

"On the other hand, the signature could be one of his minions coming in and out of town."

My scowl deepened. "Or being cloaked once they get to town. By the Collector, of course, so we can't track what they're doing. Which means he has more than just Shelly working for him."

My head dropped back, and I exhaled sharply as I stared at the naked tree branches against the blue sky. We'd known the Collector had others working for him before, but we thought maybe we'd taken care of them all. All except the shapeshifter, anyway. We still weren't sure where that thing was. And we didn't think this blip had come from it—the shapeshifter tended to take the forms and auras of people who were registered so we'd pay them no attention. So the Collector possibly had multiple minions, coming in and out of town, and we had no way to track them. Just how many did he have?

"Fuck!" I finally groaned, stomping my foot.

Mom sighed. "Yeah, I agree."

Calling my familiars to follow—Skywalker and Princess Leia in the air and Chewie and Kylo on my heels—I stomped my way home, more frustrated than when I'd left.

My fingers drummed on the wooden table as I sat in the SIN conference room, waiting for Liam Peters, Savage, and a guy who went by Axle, but I knew his real name as Monte, who were pow-wowing in private. My chin rested in my other hand, my elbow on the table, and one leg bouncing on the other knee as I glanced around the room. I had a feeling this was where the members voted on what murders and other crimes they'd commit next. They called themselves a club and publicly denied any lawbreaking, but I worked for the Court. I knew better. As long as SIN kept their lawbreaking outside of town, the Court allowed them to stay. Also as long as when the Court itself needed laws broken, SIN would be at their beck and call.

The place smelled like leather, sweat, sex, booze, and pot. Lots and lots of booze and pot, especially out in the main room that was obviously the party room, decked out with pool tables, a bar, cocktail tables, couches, and a jukebox. A shudder ran down my spine as I thought about what a black light would expose in this building.

I forced my thoughts somewhere else—to the meeting I'd had with Gwen Facharro earlier today. A Seelie fae who owned Tragic Ink, she did most of the tattoos around town that I hadn't done. Hers could come with a different kind of magic than mine, though. Rather than working with the town's wards, like mine did, hers were infused with fae magic that made them come to life. Exactly as it sounded—they could actually peel off the skin and become what they depicted. Like weapons. I'd really, *really* hoped she'd join the task force and help us when it came time to take this fucker down.

She'd actually let me into the studio that was on the second floor, above Howe's Herbal Shoppe, which had been a surprise in itself, considering she was closed. Gwen had always been more of a loner, although after what happened last Valentine's Day, she'd come out of her shell a bit. She'd never been girl-next-door friendly, though. A hard nut to crack, as Eloise Sinclair, Harper's aunt, would say. So I'd thought the fact that she'd even let me in the door had been promising. But when I told her my purpose for being there, she'd immediately backed off.

"I don't know," she'd said, running a hand through her short blond hair. "I don't think I should be involved."

"Really? But our whole town could be in danger," I insisted. She'd been the first one to so easily turn down my request for help.

She squared her shoulders as she turned to look out the front window at town square below. "I have my reasons."

My mouth fell slightly open. "That's it? Our town could be under attack, and you refuse to help? You have an endless supply of weapons at your disposal."

She brought her green gaze back to me, narrowing her eyes. "I don't *like* doing what I did. That's not me."

Then I understood. She didn't want to have to fight. "Okay, I get it. I just thought . . ."

I shook my head, not finishing. I just thought everyone would be willing to do what I was to protect our town. But knowing what little I did about Gwen and the way she'd always been treated, I could understand how she'd have a different perspective.

"Look," she said, "I also don't like giving others the power that my ink provides. Too many want to abuse that power. So I only do those kinds of tattoos on people I know I can trust. And, well, if I can trust you, I can give you, maybe a couple others, useful tattoos. Only ones on my own body replenish, so you'll only be able to use each one once, but I can help in that way."

I bit my lip, nodding. I didn't know if we'd take her up on the offer, but at least it was something. I'd rather have her fighting alongside us, but I couldn't and wouldn't force anyone.

Heavy thuds of motorcycle boots and the clanking of chains hanging out of their jeans pockets brought my mind back to the present as Liam and Savage filed into the room with Monte behind them. All three of them were way over six feet tall, but Monte's build was slight compared to the other two, and Savage was built like a fucking brick wall. Of the three of them, Monte's were the only eyes I could see, the others' hidden by sunglasses. Monte wasn't a hellhound, although we'd learned that the hellhounds' gazes couldn't harm me, being one of them and all. It must have been habit for them to keep their shades on.

"We haven't been able to find anything," Savage said as he and Monte sat across from me while Liam took the chair at the head of the table.

Liam tilted his head toward Monte. "Axle's been researching and monitoring the dark web. He hasn't found anything helpful."

I looked over at Monte, slightly surprised. A mechanic at Havenwood Falls Garage & Tow Service, he came across as nothing more than a grease monkey and outlaw biker. Definitely not a computer geek.

"There are many on the dark web who collect things—stolen art, cars, jewelry, data, you name it. Even magical artifacts, especially of the dark kind," he said. "If they think there's money in it, they'll gladly claim to be our guy or know him. But every lead ends in a dead end. If the Collector's even using the dark web, he knows how to cover his tracks."

"Or he has minions who do," I muttered before turning back to Liam. "And you've checked with your other chapters?"

He nodded. "We have. Everyone's keeping their ears to the ground, but nothing so far."

"Shit." I rubbed circles into my temples. I'd hoped with all the connections they had, SIN would have been able to find some kind of clue about our Collector and his whereabouts. With the kind of pressure they knew how to apply, you'd think someone would have squealed by now. "You'll stay on it?"

"Of course." Liam leaned forward. "But as I already told Saundra and the rest of the Court, if we find this guy outside of town, we take care of him *our* way."

The implication didn't need further explanation.

"He threatened our own," Savage growled anyway, sending a chill across my skin.

"As long as this town and her people are safe, I don't give a fuck how it's done," I said, standing, and one corner of Savage's mouth curled upward as though he was proud of me. Shit. I didn't want to make him proud. I didn't want to be like him at all.

But the hell if someone was going to come in and threaten *my* own and get away with it.

~

THE NEXT DAY, I paced the Court's meeting room as Micah's imposing figure leaned against my desk.

"We've done everything I can think of," I said as I made a turn, Chewie's eyes following me as he lay under the table. "We have the Luna Coven at work, including Roman Bishop, although I'm not sure if he'd even tell us anything he found. SIN is all over it in ways we don't want to know. Elsmed's taken it to the Seelie Court and all over the fae realm. Elias is in contact with the fallen and the damned. Harper's even channeled the dark side. We've picked up tiny clues, but nothing has led to anywhere yet." I stopped in front of him and dropped my hands to my hips. "You have to do it."

The thick muscles of his arms tightened across his chest. "Absolutely not."

"Why the hell not?"

He stood up to his full height, towering over me. My inner hellhound began to rise at the threat.

"I said no. It's not an option, so forget about it." He began to stride toward the door.

I followed after him. "Then why the fuck did you agree to help if you're not really going to help? You're the only one who can access the divine. You could find out in a heartbeat what nobody else could possibly know!"

He turned on me so fast, I stumbled backward a few steps. Anger filled his dark eyes with a kind of danger I didn't want to know. "I will do anything but that, Addie. I can't risk it! You have no idea what you're asking."

I refused to back down. "I know that you could be our town's only hope, and you're being a stubborn asshole."

His nostrils flared. "I cut those ties. What you're asking—it could bring a bigger wrath on this town than the Collector."

Crossing my arms over my chest, I cocked my head to the side. "And how would you know? How do you know the Collector isn't doing their bidding if you won't even check in to find out? How do you know he's not after Holly himself?"

Micah glared at me for a long moment before turning on his heel and throwing open the wooden door. He strode out of it without another word.

Without his help, we could be running in circles for months. But with it . . .

Maybe he was right. He knew better than I did. Maybe the Collector wasn't the worst thing we could face. As far as we knew right now, he wasn't really all that dangerous, considering we'd been able to thwart every attempt his minions had made so far. Since we hadn't heard a peep from Shelly in weeks, maybe she was just full of shit.

But something told me that wasn't right. Something told me deep in my bones that the Collector had only been testing us so far. If Micah wouldn't tap into the one resource that could tell us everything we needed to know, then we'd have to figure out another way.

I was just at a loss for what that could possibly be.

CHAPTER 10

MICAH

I walked away from that discussion knowing two things for sure.

One, despite the "no-brainer" attitude Addie used when laying out her plan and expecting me to agree to her crazy suicide mission, there had to be some other alternative. Taking the risk of being detected by tapping into the angels' collective consciousness couldn't be the only option on the table.

Two, calling me a stubborn asshole wasn't the way to motivate me.

Unfortunately for me, her use of Holly to remind me there was more at stake than my pride was.

I just couldn't bring myself to commit. After all these years of being on the run, and narrowly escaping surprise attacks, it left a bitter taste in my mouth. Even with the constant thrumming of truth that this was for the greater good, I still couldn't shake the feeling that while the Collector was dangerous to the town as a whole, there was always the slight chance that a miracle could happen. A way could open so Holly and I could slip out of Havenwood Falls and disappear again.

As long as that hope still burned within my chest, my answer had to be no to Addie. We would just have to keep searching and researching whatever leads surfaced.

We had to exercise faith—even if it was only in ourselves.

Our conversation lingered in my mind all night and hadn't budged most of the morning. I'd successfully kept my concern from both my young charge and Sedona—a feat that wasn't always possible the closer Sedona and I became. Energetic boundaries blurred the second we consciously crossed the line within our relationship. It forced me to be especially careful around my empathic girlfriend.

While I'd opened up to her, there were still secrets I'd sworn to keep.

The more she knew and understood, the harder it would be to walk away if the time ever came.

Unable to sleep, I'd gone for a late-night walk, hoping to clear my head enough so I could think straight. It was in the act of moving that I did my best problem-solving. With nothing but the stars twinkling above and the soft crunch of leaves beneath my feet, the knot in my gut slowly began to unravel.

There had to be an answer. That thought was the driving force behind everything. I just needed to see around the obstacle—the fact that Addie had been right.

There had been a sinking feeling that wouldn't go away. Sooner or later, I was going to have to connect with the divine collective that linked all angels together. It was simply a matter of when.

That's when I'd bumped into someone who jogged a forgotten memory.

Not everyone socialized in Havenwood Falls, so I hadn't considered visiting the dark and formidable mansion up in Havenwood Heights. The home belonged to Marcus St. James, the town's hermit who rarely left his lodgings. He had a manservant, however, who did. A Mr. Phineas Knox.

I'd made a point to study the town's members and evaluate who the movers and shakers were. I'd needed to know who may become a threat to Holly, and who I could turn to in a case of an emergency.

St. James had been hard to investigate because he kept to himself —preferring to safeguard his privacy. From what I'd managed to glean, he was a blood drinker in search of the cure. Gypsies had cursed him, and seeking vengeance had brought him to the town.

It was Knox I'd bumped into running errands late at night.

It was him I was now going to meet, at his home up in the Heights. To say that I was optimistic may have been a stretch, but knocking on the door, and waiting for something to answer, I prayed that this would save me from performing the reunification ritual.

Footsteps approached from the other side of the thick mahogany door. I remembered this house from the tour around the neighborhood I'd done when first canvassing the town and getting the lay of the land, so to speak. It did me no good protecting Holly if I wasn't familiar with the town.

Holly would die if she knew where I was standing right now. Everything about the reclusive St. James intrigued her.

If it hadn't been for Addie and this business with the Collector, I wouldn't be bothering the man. I understood the need for privacy and respect of others. If he didn't want to be involved in all the festivities and events Havenwood Falls had throughout the year, then it was his prerogative.

We all had our secrets to hide.

"Mr. Westbrook, welcome." Knox swung the door open, and with an air of civility, bowed his head in greeting. "Please, come inside."

As I passed by him and over the threshold, the young man leaned forward and looked to the right and left.

I had the distinct impression that nothing escaped this man's gaze. He held himself with the same vigilance I'd seen time and time again. This was someone who preferred to fly beneath the radar.

In my experience, these were the people who had the real information about a town. You had those who manufactured and maintained a certain façade, and then there were those who operated from the shadows. They saw everything.

The hope that had been quietly flickering inside me flared, growing brighter. This was a really good sign.

"I appreciate your willingness to meet with me." I stuck out my hand for him to shake. "Will your employer be joining us?" I glanced

about the spacious foyer. It was clear that no expense had been spared
—from the twinkling lights in the crystal chandelier to the
Renaissance artwork that graced the walls. Even the granite tile had
flecks of gold in them. It was hard to stand there and not gawk.

Beauty was something that always drew my eye and dazzled me.

"I must admit that I'm curious about what I could possibly help
you with." With gentlemanly manners that spoke of yesteryear, Knox
gestured for me to enter the open French doors to the right. I could
hear the crackling of a fire coming from the room, and sure enough,
one was blazing in the bricked hearth. "Although I regret to inform
you that Mr. St. James has declined your invitation to talk." There was
no further mention of him, or why he'd refused to meet with me.
True, I was a stranger to him, but we'd also never had any kind of
negative interaction with each other.

There was being a hermit, and then there was being antisocial in a
town that thrived on knowing everyone else's business.

"Surely I could coax him to come out and say hello." I didn't want
to sound as desperate as I felt. If the employee knew things that might
prove valuable, I could only imagine the wealth of information the
boss would have. Records had shown their arrival at the town's
boundaries before the 1880s. Roman Bishop had been the one to
welcome them and officially accept their living here.

They had to know something.

Knox didn't blink or skip a beat. With a calm and level tone, he
shook his head. "That won't be possible. Now," he once again gestured
for me to take a seat. I looked about the large room, wondering how
much of this was just for show to appease me. This was more formal
than I'd expected. "How can I help you?"

He held my gaze. There was no shiftiness about him, and I sensed
no ulterior motive.

"Can I be frank?" I'd considered how I'd approach this request,
and from the relief that filled his eyes, my new acquaintance
appreciated the offer.

"That's all I ask. What is honesty, if not the courage to speak
boldly the things in your heart and mind?" He sat forward, pointing to

the tea set that was on the coffee table between us. "Can I tempt you with something hot to drink? I have tea here, but if that's not to your liking, then I can always brew up a pot of coffee."

I shook my head. I was ready to get to the point of our meeting. "I understand that you've called Havenwood Falls your home for over a century."

Knox slowly nodded as he looked over the teacup he was sipping from. "That is correct. Have you come for a history lesson?" His lips curled at the edges. There was no fear in Knox's features. He was every bit as comfortable in this room as if he was the lord and master of the house.

I let out a short laugh. "I wish." It was my turn to scoot forward. There'd be no relaxing into the comfortable couch and pillows. "Actually, I'm looking for information that isn't quite so easy to find."

That caught his interest. Placing the cup and saucer back on the table, Knox tilted his head. "And you assume I might know something about this information you're seeking."

He was evaluating me. He didn't hold any kind of threat or powers that concerned me. I'd learned that he was an alchemist-in-training when St. James had brought him into his home. Details were sketchy at best, but Knox was more a chemist or scientist than creature. One who'd obviously learned how to stop the aging process, considering his age and youthful appearance.

"I'm hoping you might." I glanced back over at the closed doors we'd come through. "That's why it would be great if Mr. St. James could join us."

This made him laugh and completely break character. Gone was the stuffy, formal man who resembled the butler on the TV show Sedona liked watching. In his place, a lively man sat with a softer, more approachable appearance.

"I would give the tiny fortune I keep hidden under my mattress to have you convince Marcus to come out here and chitchat. Hell, I'd be happy if he let you get close enough to his private rooms to speak to him. Many have attempted and failed."

I furrowed my brow at his last comments. "Not much of a people person, huh?"

That earned me an even louder round of laughter from Knox. "You have no idea." Shaking his head, he slowly regained his composure. He was back to being serious again. "Thank you for the amusement, Mr. Westbrook."

"Micah. Please."

He relented. "Micah, then." He took a smaller sip of his tea this time. "I don't think I can help you, but is there anything specific that you have in mind? A century is a long time, and I won't ever say or do anything that might incriminate him."

I took a deep breath and went for it. "What do you know about the Collector?" I didn't add anything else to it. My hope was that he would answer freely, and possibly fill in the blanks.

Knox went stone cold. Nothing. He didn't even blink at the name.

"He's the one responsible for an attack on my girlfriend in her store."

Understanding made his eyes widen. "Ah, you're here on behalf of Sedona Mathews. I heard that her employee had shot her when she'd foiled his plans. It was your charge, I believe, that was the true target."

So, he'd done his research on me, too. "Yes. His name has been linked to other incidents around town. Something enigmatic and dangerous is here, and I hope you can understand why it's important that I find where he is."

Knox threw me a sympathetic smile. "I've also heard those same rumblings. Power is a great influencer and corrupter. There will always be someone behind the scenes—making puppets out of fools while they claim more power for themselves. It's one thing that hasn't changed over time. If you follow the clues, it will always lead you to someone who wants to hold the ultimate control over others." When I didn't say anything, Knox brushed his blond hair back from over his eyes, tucking a few strands behind his ear. "I'm not a stranger to such games."

"That's the thing. This isn't a game for some. People are going to get hurt. Lives are in the balance. This Collector holds all the cards right now, and I refuse to sit idly by while he threatens the ones I love."

I couldn't get a read on him yet. "It is an admirable quality to have, Micah. I still don't understand how this involves me or Marcus, however. As you've mentioned, we don't associate with anyone here in town, and we're unlikely to be heroes in this new adventure of yours."

I didn't like the way this conversation was going, or the sense of condescension that crept into his voice. I didn't need to know the horrors he'd seen or what living with a vampire was like. His business was his business. I just needed to keep my family safe.

"I'm not asking you to take up the sword and join the fight. You don't have to participate or get your hands dirty."

"Oh, but you are. If I were to share the things I know, how can you guarantee my involvement won't get back to this Collector person, making me a new target? Let me be brutally honest with you now." Gone was his friendly tone and hospitable demeanor. "I have one task, and one task alone. It doesn't involve getting caught up in small-town drama. I serve one master, and you are not him. I'm sorry that I've wasted your time, but I can't help you."

"Can't or won't?" I countered, not willing to throw in the towel yet. The alternative was to accept the inevitable . . . the ritual.

"Won't." Knox rose to his feet abruptly, and I took his meaning immediately. It was time to go. Sharing time was over. Or so I thought. "I'm sorry."

We walked back through the foyer in silence. There had to be something that I could convince him with. Anything. I wasn't choosy.

"Knox," I started, turning about, and refusing to move. "Anything, no matter how small, can help. I'm not asking you to betray a trust or go against your conscience. I'm asking you as a fellow protector . . . help me keep my girls safe. Help me remove this threat."

He let out a lengthy sigh. With his hand now at the top of the open door, Knox drummed his fingers against the hardwood. "I know nothing about this person, but—" Once again, he studied the street as if expecting to find people hiding. "There is someone who might be able to help. He has lived up in the mountains since before the founding families came here. He knows truths that others have spent a lifetime trying to uncover. Go see him, and perhaps you'll find the answers you seek."

A small, torn piece of paper appeared in the center of his palm. Written in clear and concise letters was an address.

"Visit the shaman." As I turned to walk away, my mind already three steps ahead of me, Knox called out, "Don't come here again, Mr. Westbrook. Not for these purposes. The next time you bring possible drama to these doors, I won't be responsible for my master's response."

It was a clear threat.

I nodded that I heard him.

"Thanks again." With a wave of the paper still in my hand, I didn't wait for him to close the door. Our conversation was over.

I just hoped that it had borne good fruit.

I'D WAITED until nightfall before venturing out to where the shaman lived. It was my goal to send Addie a text tomorrow morning that I had good news.

I needed to prove that she hadn't been right.

I didn't like being wrong.

A light shone from around the bend as I quietly drove down a long and windy driveway. I'd assumed that the glow in the sky was from his home, and it didn't disappoint me as I came to a halt.

My intention had been to arrive in the car I'd borrowed from Sedona—the noise from the engine and tires announcing my approach. But that all changed when I spotted a second car.

The shaman wasn't alone.

He had another visitor.

Indecision warred inside my head. This could be something harmless—someone from town visiting the healer for any of a variety of reasons. Sedona had been trying to get me to admit that not every shadow held an enemy, that I sometimes let my paranoia get the best of me.

It didn't pay to be lax, I'd countered. It wasn't paranoia if it was true.

I'd seen enough through the ages to trust my gut. Right now, that instinct was telling me to exercise caution and not rush in. Slipping the car into park, I sat there in the dark and silence, watching the humble-looking house. There was nothing spectacular about the lodgings. It was definitely a far cry from the wealth and opulence I'd witnessed up in Havenwood Heights earlier.

Just when I thought I'd either need to go inside or come back another time, the door opened, and the last person I expected to see stepped out.

Roman Bishop.

What was one of the most powerful warlocks in town doing here with a shaman?

The feeling I'd gotten from Knox was that this shaman operated on the seedier side of things. That in itself didn't make Roman's appearance surprising—the Bishops didn't exactly have a squeaky clean reputation. But why was he here? What business would he have with this shaman?

That was the million-dollar question, and one I couldn't wait to hear answered.

Once I was sure Roman wouldn't be returning, I approached the house and banged on the door. Fresh hope burst to life in my chest as the sound of footsteps came closer.

"May I help you?"

The voice came from behind me. Somehow, the shaman had surprised me by not being where I'd expected him to be. To others, he may have dazzled them with his unexpected appearance, but I'd seen enough parlor tricks to know he wanted to keep me off balance.

I jumped right to the point. "I couldn't help but notice Mr. Bishop just left." I glanced over my shoulder to the road he'd driven away on. "Seems late to be receiving visitors."

The shaman's gaze narrowed. "Yet you stand on my doorstep wanting an audience with me." His glare was meant to intimidate.

I answered with a chuckle. "Touché, sir. Touché." I stuck out my hand to officially introduce myself. "My name is Micah Westbrook."

The shaman, who hadn't moved from where he was standing, peered down at my extended hand. "I know who you are, and even why you are here. Unfortunately, you've made the trip in vain. I made a promise long ago not to involve myself in troubles that don't include me. I have honored that oath successfully."

I was tired of continually coming up against brick walls. Every lead I followed or hunch I investigated resulted in dead ends. All the while, I could still hear Addie chiding me in my mind, telling me that I was wasting my time because the answers we sought could only be found by my reconnecting with the divine.

"What if I told you that it does affect you? What happens to the town will bleed out into the surrounding areas. How long do you think you could stay here if . . . *when* it's destroyed?" I wasn't too proud to beg.

The shaman waved his hand dismissively, actually tsking at me. "It matters not to me."

I could feel the magic that ran through my veins heat and sizzle. Peering down at my hands, I could see a slight golden glow. I was fed up with being dismissed.

"Before you waste more of my evening, why not ask what you truly want to know? Perhaps I will humor you with a response." The shaman walked around me and stopped right before entering his home. "Time is of the essence, however."

Questions flooded my mind, each demanding that I give it utterance. Something told me that even if I did ask, this strange man who lived in the mountains might not answer honestly.

"Why was Roman Bishop just here?" The question blurted out, but I saw the wisdom in it. It was time to evaluate everything—big or small —for a possible connection. If it didn't seem to fit, it was questioned.

The shaman's lips curled into an eerie smile. "Ah, young Roman. His father and uncle used to visit me when they first arrived in Havenwood Falls. They would often seek my counsel on matters, and it developed into a long-lasting friendship. Roman has upheld that tradition."

"So he was here asking for advice?" I asked, surprised that the arrogant warlock would actually admit that there was something he didn't know.

The man shook his head. "That is not for me to disclose. Only that he occasionally visits to honor his father and uncle."

The lackluster revelation caused my brow to wrinkle. Another dead end.

But was it?

I'd sensed something dark about the shaman and his magic. And it was no secret Roman's father and uncle had been accused of using dark magic—it'd been at the root of Emeline Fairchild's death a century ago. Plus, from what I'd learned, it was the reason for their banishment from the town.

Did this mean Roman was carrying on with their ways, but outside of the wards and too far for the Blackstone witch hunters to detect? And why was there no information about this shaman, someone who'd apparently been living so close for so long?

I'd come hoping to find answers, but instead, I had more questions. Roman Bishop had always left me feeling somewhat suspicious. There was something about him I couldn't quite put my finger on. Nobody said much about him except that he was a member of the Court. And a Bishop at that.

A new thought rose to the top of the whirlwind currently sweeping through my mind.

Could the shaman be the Collector? Or working for him?

Maybe.

I was more certain of the possibility that Roman Bishop had answers, and I needed to uncover them. Secrets had a way of festering in the darkness, and it was time to shine some light on his relationship with the shaman.

I needed something to bring to Addie—information that would eliminate any need to tap into the angel collective.

And maybe, just maybe, I'd discover his connections to the Collector.

CHAPTER 11

SENORA

*O*f course, shit can't be easy. I figured I could relax while I waited for the perfect moment to confront Kazimir—the notorious son of a mafia boss. Frankly, I was looking forward to getting rid of him. He'd threatened plenty of females, not just Izzie. But as soon as I sat down on the hillside—all prepared to keep an eye on Kazimir's private jet—he jumped into a dark sedan and sped off into the night. According to the human who serviced the rental car, Kazimir's driver asked for directions to Grand Junction. He and his team had been in Colorado Springs for a few hours. Thankfully, I would be able to locate him with a tracker spell, but in the meantime . . .

It wasn't a good situation for my friend.

I whipped out my cell phone and sent Izzie a message. But after five minutes there wasn't a reply. So I sent a second and then a third message, all the while my heart thumping loudly against my chest. Being patient wasn't my strong suit. Yes, empusai were rumored to be overly tolerant. It was a necessary evil—one never knew how long it could be between meals—but I wasn't a typical empusa. Waiting made me anxious. Anxiety made me hungry. And hunger . . . Well, that made me dangerous. Instead of waiting, I called and got Izzie's voice mail.

"Why the fuck aren't you answering your phone? You need to get the hell out of there," I shouted into the speaker. "Kazimir's jet landed in Colorado Springs a few hours ago. My sources say he's on his way to Grand Junction. Go south. Now. Give me a location, and I'll meet you. You can't handle him alone."

I disconnected the call and slid the device into my rear pocket. What the hell was I supposed to do? I'd never forgive myself if something happened to Izzie. No. It wasn't my fault that she got tied up with Kazimir, but I should have watched out for her better. After living a few centuries, I'd learned to spot an asshole from a mile away. My immature nagual friend was just a kid. She deserved my full attention.

My ass tickled thanks to my phone buzzing. I pulled it out, hoping it was Izzie, and peered down at the screen—it was the hellhound-witch Rachelle. The Collector wanted me to give a report on his most recent assignment and my success—or failure.

I quickly typed Rachelle a reply—something that amounted to a written "kiss my ass."

SG: I'm busy and can't be bothered now.

HellWitch: If you're busy, does that mean you're working on acquiring the asset?

SG: Can't talk now.

With that last text, I was tempted to turn off my phone and put it away, but I needed it a bit longer. The last time I spoke to Izzie, she gave me a phone number with the explicit direction to only use it in case of emergency. I would think her impending doom was dire enough.

SG: Have you seen Izzie?

In a matter of seconds, a response came across.

Contact: No. Not for a few hours. Who is this?

There was no easy way of delivering the news.

SG: My name is Senora Graves. I'm Izzie's friend. I've been texting her all night, but haven't heard from her.

Sending messages back and forth was a pointless endeavor. I called the digits stored in my phone. After a few seconds of listening to a ringer, I started to disconnect.

"Hello?" The voice was gruff, agitated, and very male.

"This is Senora." The level of frustration in my voice matched his, not a good way to start, so I toned it down and practically purred into the speaker. "What's going on with Izzie?"

"I'm not sure. Do you know Kazimir Chekhov?"

I guessed I was speaking to Izzie's mate. The girl wasn't too trusting. I seriously doubted she would have told her tale to anyone without a vested interest in her survival.

"Bad news in a handsome package," I stayed. "He's after Izzie."

"Then you know about the money?"

"Hell, yeah." I exhaled loudly. "Izzie stole three million from him. She would have returned it after he set her free."

"Set her free?"

Naturally, my best friend left out some details, so I shared some. I had checked into the situation, and long story short, Kazimir bought Izzie. I hated telling that news to Izzie's mate. I could only imagine how hurt the shifter might be. Shit, I wasn't her mate, and not being told the truth fucking stung. I thought Izzie and I were closer than that.

Her mate's anger filtered across the phone. "According to my sources, Kazimir has her."

If I could talk to the shifter's sources, I could have easily found Izzie. Something told me that wouldn't happen easily, so I opted for the logical choice.

"Where are you? I can be there in a few minutes."

The call went silent. *Did I scare him off?*

When the male didn't speak, I added, "I'm an empusa. All I need is a mental image, and I can be there."

Izzie's mate rattled off a location, and I transported with the phone still in my hand.

THIRTY MINUTES LATER, I stood about a half mile past the border of Havenwood Falls' notorious town wards. They provided protection for its residents, making sure no unwanted creatures crossed the proverbial line. If anyone was stupid enough to try, they'd be met by the town's sheriff.

Three figures on motorcycles slowly approached—one exceedingly tall, one slightly shorter, and the last one made like a damn bull. I walked over to the trio with my hips gently swaying. If these males weren't my welcome team, I planned on having a good time and a healthy-sized snack afterward.

The large one barked, "Are you the empusa?"

The faint smell of sulfur crossed my nose. Either a fire demon or a hellhound was close by. Then I noticed the dark glasses on the one who just spoke.

Hellhound.

Damn. There'd be no fun with him on the team.

"I am," I drawled in a captivating voice. My gaze darted from the speaker over to the exceedingly tall shifter and then landed on the one who must be Izzie's mate. Her scent wafted off his skin. "I'm guessing you're Izzie's mate."

He removed his helmet. "I am. So tell us how to find Chekhov."

"Here's the thing." I sauntered over to the shifter and dragged a finger down his leather sleeve. "I don't believe Kazimir has her."

The third member of the team decided to finally join the conversation. "Why do you say that? I got a message saying otherwise."

"May I see it?" I held out my hand for the device while keeping my gaze locked on Izzie's mate. Once I gripped the phone, I peered down at the screen. There was a strong signal coming from it, but it wasn't magic. No. This was human intervention—a fake message. "Whoever claimed to see Kazimir with Izzie lied. This message isn't genuine."

The mate's nose wrinkled as he shook his head. "Sorry. I don't believe you can tell that from a text."

Man, I hated it when creatures wanted to argue with me. For some unknown reason, everybody just assumed that I didn't know what I was talking about. Humans used the excuse that I was a mere female and couldn't be that smart. When it came to supes, however, they stuck to mythology. One of these days they'll realize that not every empusa only wanted a fuck and a snack. Well . . . almost every empusa.

But I digress.

There were things I needed to share with them, especially Izzie's mate, but not out in the open. "Is there someplace we can talk?" I glanced over my shoulder. "The forest has ears."

The mate jerked his thumb toward his bike seat.

Perfect.

Testosterone, snatch, alcohol, and stale cigarettes hit my nose as soon as the door to the clubhouse yawned open. No rank amateurs in that room. Every eye narrowed in my direction as they scanned me like groceries on a conveyor belt. Instead of a happy beep, the machine was screaming, *put it back!*

Thankfully, my escorts ushered me past the scorching glares and into a sizable room near the back of the building. Sadly, the closed door didn't block the noxious smells.

I perched on the edge of the table and looked at the males before filling them in on all I knew about Kazimir and Izzie. "Of course, I can help you find her for a price."

The one called Hunter asked, "How much?"

So good to know he paid attention. There was nothing worse than trying to make a deal with someone who thought I worked for free. I tilted my head to the side and considered how much I should charge and what I'd actually ask for.

"Keeping this town secret is very important to all of you." I pointed to Hunter. He was another easy male. Whatever Izzie wanted, I was certain he'd break his neck trying to accomplish it. "Plus, you'd do anything for Izzie. Since Kazimir is sending me a nice chunk of change, I'll do it for . . ." I tapped my chin for a long moment, watching the males sweat. "One million."

The one with Axle emblazoned on his cut swallowed hard. "Dollars?"

"I'll pay it," Hunter quickly volunteered. "I need a few hours to transfer funds."

"Pleasure doing business with you," I said, before strolling to the door. "I'm sure we'll see each other again."

CONTRARY TO POPULAR BELIEF, I found no joy in stalking my prey. It was never an easy venture. The quickest method involved scaring the shit out of people. Of course, there were other ways of getting the job done—seduction, weaponry, and even knock-out drops to name a few. Tonight, I'd use a combination to get to Kazimir.

For a long moment I stood in the shadows watching the black sedan. His driver exited the vehicle and walked toward the convenience store.

Witnesses.

Never a good thing. And having my cell go off again pissed me off.

Reaching into my pocket, I pulled out the phone and peered at the screen and saw a text message.

HellWitch: The Collector needs to see you.

I had no time for this nonsense. Quickly, I sent my reply.

SG: I'm in the middle of something. Unless you want to become my next snack, do not call again. I will be in touch.

With no time to waste, I jogged over to Kazimir's sedan. Before rapping on the window, I waved my hand and cast a privacy spell. Anyone looking at the vehicle wouldn't see a thing.

Now to go to work.

Kazimir's eyes widened as the window lowered. "Do you have what I need?"

"Not exactly." I yanked open the door and slid onto the seat beside him.

"What does that mean?"

In my line of work, fear was the quickest way to a man's heart . . . stomach . . . and all the yummy other parts. Kazimir's worst fear wasn't being gunned down on the streets. It wasn't even about being snuffed out in his sleep. No. His nightmare involved a stint in prison where he'd be passed around from cellmate to cellmate like a Thanksgiving turkey. It was no secret that the man was the biggest homophobe in existence, but he had no problem sticking his dick in a woman's . . . You get the picture.

And so did Kazimir. Sadly, the fool had a heart attack before the fun began. Unable to enjoy my meal, I gobbled down the bits and pieces, licking my lips as I swallowed a toe.

I twisted my head to one side as the part caught in my throat. A bubble lodged in my windpipe before a loud belch escaped my lips. Uggghhh . . . I was going to be belching vodka all night.

My eyes darted around the interior of the sedan. No signs of a struggle and not even a hair follicle left behind. I popped open the back door just as the driver exited the store. Time to go to the Collector's estate.

BY THE TIME I reached the mansion, the mob boss had finally been digested, and I no longer tasted the Grey Goose he'd recently imbibed. Rachelle waited for me at the door when I reached the top of the stairs.

"What kept you?"

I held up my palm and sucked my teeth loudly. "You don't want to mess with me. I ate my last meal quickly, but I wasn't satisfied." Leaning toward the hybrid hellhound-witch, I said, "I have room for more. Hellhounds are quite spicy."

Rachelle narrowed her eyes and stepped to the side. "The Master is in the drawing room."

"No shit."

As I stepped into the room, I felt his cold glare. He followed me until I took my seat. That's when I noticed the strumming fingers. I'd pissed off the Collector—dumb move.

"You've kept me waiting, and I don't appreciate it."

"Understood. I needed to feed," I lied. "You didn't want me to bring my food with me, did you?"

His stare intensified. "Have you completed the job?"

"First," I started, crossing my legs. "We didn't agree to any terms. You suggested what you wanted me to have. Second, I don't work while I eat."

The Collector exhaled loudly, and the stench was worse than rotting flesh. "Enough! This is your last chance. Deny me and you shall regret it."

"Fine. I'll take the—"

"Forget the asset. I have something else for you. A task worthy of your skills."

Oh, this should be good. "What is that?"

"This next . . . artifact . . . is a person, but not just any person." Bones cracked as the Collector twisted his body toward the roaring fire. "I'm in need of a Scottish fae with dark magic."

"That's it?" I asked, surprised. "Anyone in particular?"

"No. Your choice. The result will be the same."

Something told me that this was a test. Scottish fae meant I had two choices—Seelie or Unseelie. One would be a cinch to catch, and the other would require a little maneuvering. But only one was dark. "The price?"

The Collector shook his head. "Everything is about money for you."

Duh! Why else would I do what I do?

"Very well. Bring back a Seelie, and I'll pay your standard price." The creature leaned forward. "But capture an Unseelie, and I'll double it."

Hallelujah! I wanted to dance for joy, but knew I had to play it cool. Letting the Collector think he had the upper hand wasn't going to happen. Despite my calm demeanor, I sensed a change in the Collector. If he had a face, I swore he smiled.

"We have a deal?"

Pushing to my feet, I said, "Of course we do. Give me a couple of hours."

I practically skipped out of the room and down the mountain steps. All I had to do was prowl the streets of Havenwood Falls and find out where fae liked to hang out.

~

It didn't take long for my *artifact* to make an appearance. As I neared Miller's Plaza, I saw a figure leaving one of the shops. Her glamour shimmered when she noticed me. She snarled and attempted to move past me.

"Not so fast, fae. There's somebody who wants to see you."

"Who?"

"An old friend."

Just when I thought the creature would let her curiosity spark, she vanished. My eyes darted around the parking lot. I picked up her scent near an SUV. Her eyes glowed as she stared back at me.

Two could play that game, I said to myself.

I held out my hand, flicked my wrist, and cast a protection spell. The Unseelie shot her own magic in my direction, but mine held tight.

When she held up her hand to try again, I twisted my fingers. The fae's palm snapped and folded in on itself. She dropped to the asphalt screaming in pain. Thankfully, my spell muffled the noise. Before she could realize what I was doing, I moved closer and placed my hand on her shoulder.

In a matter of seconds, we stood in the Collector's drawing room. My employer was just where I'd left him.

"That was incredibly fast," said the familiar voice.

Damn, I didn't notice Rachelle.

"You have proven your worth to me," said the Collector. "You'll need to remove the block on your account or give me access to another if you want to be paid."

The fae writhed and moaned at my feet. "Do you want me to heal her?"

"No need," the Collector said. "You're free to do with her as you wish. Rachelle said you rushed through your last meal. Take your time with this one."

The being pushed to his feet, and a cloud of mist rose with him. He floated out of the room, leaving me behind with my meal.

I'd never been one to turn down a freebie. Yes, the Unseelie was a dark, malevolent being, but once her soul exited, none of that mattered.

I knelt beside the fae and looked into her pain-filled eyes. The Infernum was her greatest fear. No surprise there. I reflected the confines of that supernatural prison into her mind. The fae's weakness was intolerance. She despised those who had no tolerance for her kind. Her flaw wrapped around her like a chain. Snapping her neck was easy.

While her heart slowed, I nibbled on a finger. The flesh was sweet and juicy—just the way I liked it. In minutes, I'd torn apart the body. Crunched on bones and lappedup entrails. My eyes rolled back as her liver squished between my teeth. The darkness trapped inside the fae affected her flavors, making every bite a delicacy. By the time I swallowed the last eyeball, I was satiated.

"Content?" Rachelle asked.

I wiped the juices from my lips. "Care to find out?"

The hybrid pivoted on her heel and stalked out of the room.

CHAPTER 12

HARPER

*M*y skin itched, the irritating sensation leaving crawling trails of frustration from my face to my legs. I refused to scratch, because in truth, I wasn't suffering from a skin infection. I was suffering from something much deeper, something I was beginning to think I'd never learn how to deal with.

Ever since I'd channeled the darkness for Addie and Micah, I'd been suffering from an ever invasive deluge of shadows, dark dreams, and dancing letters spelling out words I didn't want to read. Dark figures popped up out of the corners of my eyes, eerie silhouettes that vanished when I tried to look at them.

My house had become a haunted mess of sights, sounds, and unidentified guests, the kind that would make any sane person pack up and move out immediately. But it wasn't the house that was haunted. It was me.

Which was why I found myself marching determinedly down Eleventh Street, a large specially rigged backpack thrown over my back, a struggling, mumbling Desi nestled within it, his iron barbs digging into me even with the padding inside the bag. I rarely brought my talking mace to town. It was too risky. Desi—short for Destroyer —wasn't exactly the best behaved sentient weapon in the world. After centuries living it up as a hero of legendary battles, he didn't quite understand why it was important *not* to alert the humans to the supernatural aspects of Havenwood Falls.

In other words, he wanted to be appreciated and constantly hailed a hero. Which was why, when I told him about my meeting with Addie and Micah, minus my embarrassing fainting episode, he was ecstatic. There was nothing more alluring to him than a potential battle he could be the victor of. My mace was narcissistic.

Elbowing my backpack, I hissed, "If you don't be still in there . . ."

Desi cackled when my words trailed off. "It's more effective if you finish the threat."

Havenwood Falls was in that transition period between holidays. Most of the shops and houses had taken down their Halloween decorations and replaced them with Thanksgiving décor. Others—the ones in love with Halloween—were stubbornly and proudly displaying skeletons and scary décor a week after the holiday had passed. Yet others—the yuletide lovers—were all decked out for Christmas, ready with lights, trees, and wreaths way before Thanksgiving had even come to pass.

I had mixed feelings about the holidays. The season reminded me of my loneliness growing up, but it also reminded me of two kinds of love: the love I had for my Aunt Eloise, and my first taste of romance. In truth, I'd learned a lot of things from the holidays. Not only loneliness and love, but fear, desperation, and triumph. I'd faced a demon during the holidays and won.

Desi bumped me, and I grunted, elbowing the backpack as I approached my aunt's shop, Into the Mystic New Age Books and Gifts. Aunt Eloise was one of those people unwilling to give up Halloween. The door to her shop was covered in fake spider webs, with eyes peering out at me between the thick strands. Fog curled out the door and circled my ankles when I entered, and I groaned.

"You could at least put the fog machine up," I called out.

The store welcomed me, the mist from the machine moving over purple walls, brightly painted bookshelves, random, colorful display cases, and scarf-covered, candle-laden tables. From the back of the store, beads clinked together, turquoise flashing as Aunt Eloise exited her 'reading' room. Like me, she was a spiritual psychic. Unlike me, she didn't channel darkness, and she certainly wasn't bound to it.

"You missed it." Eloise paused and picked up a handful of crystals splayed haphazardly on a table, no doubt the victim of a curious child left unsupervised. "I just channeled the great-great-grandfather of this family visiting from out of town. Funny thing is, he appeared along with both his deceased wife and his deceased mistress. You should have seen the paper I was writing on. Apparently he had an open marriage with the women, and there was this thing with their children . . ."

Her words trailed off, her perceptive brown eyes flicking to my backpack before finding my face. Wisps of auburn hair tinged with gray kissed her flushed cheeks, the green and orange striped leggings and ghoulish green tunic she was wearing clashing with her skin and hair.

"She stops just when the story was getting interesting," Desi mumbled from the backpack.

"Why do you have that hellish baseball bat with you?" Eloise asked, ignoring Desi. "Something bothering you?"

Aunt Eloise knew me too well. The bag wiggled, Desi's annoyance obvious.

"He's reassuring," I answered. Irritating, narcissistic, and sarcastic, but definitely reassuring.

"And you need reassurance because?"

Desi answered before I could. "We're going to be heroes," he said, struggling. "Can you open this thing now?"

Eloise frowned. "Heroes?"

I cleared my throat. "He has delusions of grandeur. Just ignore him." Taking the backpack off of my shoulders, I placed it on the floor, unzipped it, and watched as the dangerous-looking mace hopped out. "I've been asked to help Addie Beaumont with something for the Court. We're trying to find someone ca—"

"They asked for *you*?" Eloise asked, interrupting me, her face softening.

For the Court to approach me for help about anything always put a smile on her face. After living a life pretty much shut away from the citizens of Havenwood Falls and under constant surveillance from the Court, it felt inclusive and relieving to be one of them suddenly. A help rather than a hindrance.

"Don't get too exc—" I began.

"Wait, it's not dangerous, is it?" she asked, interrupting me again.

I gave her a pointed stare.

She threw her hands up. "Okay, okay, I'm sorry. I'll let you finish. I just get excited."

My lips twitched, because seeing her excited always got me excited. Even when it was something that wasn't particularly exciting. Boy, that was a lot of *exciting*s and *excited*s rolling around in my brain, the word in big bold print and italicized. Spiritual writers tended to think in written words.

"Have you heard of anyone called the Collector?" I asked. "Addie's been tasked with finding out some information about him."

Eloise stared, her mouth frozen in a half smile, half frown, her brows creased. "Sounds familiar. I've heard tidbits and things from the spirits about a Collector. Just the name. Nothing concrete. I've never given it much thought. You know as well as I do that we sometimes channel words that make little sense. There was nothing about a Collector that seemed bad enough to go to the Court."

I frowned. "Maybe not. But whatever he is and whatever he's doing, the Court is interested. Which means it's not nothing. We may need your help when or if the time comes. For information, that is. We may share psychic gifts, but you're much better at reading the spirits than I am."

"That's because you hold yourself back," Eloise scolded.

"That's exactly what I told her," Desi whined, the mace almost hidden completely by the fog wafting along the floor.

"You have unlimited potential," Aunt Eloise added.

My hand flew up, my fingers touching my lips. "Shh."

Whenever my aunt said things like this, it meant a two-hour discussion about what I was capable of and the missed opportunities I would never get back if I didn't try harder.

"The Collector?" I reminded her.

Eloise sauntered to an old record player before setting a record on the turntable. "It's old."

"*It?*" I asked.

She placed the needle on the vinyl. "I've never been able to tell what it is. Male or female. Spirit or person. It's too hard to tell from a reading. Every time I've channeled anything about it, the information has been vague. But whatever it is, it's been around a long time. I talked to a spirit once who seemed to know someone called the Collector personally, and this spirit was hundreds of years old."

"And you didn't say anything to the Court?"

Eloise threw me a look. "When did being hundreds of years old in Havenwood Falls become a strange thing?"

She had a point.

Silence fell, the only sound the record whirring on the record player, a Van Morrison song rising slowly over the room. Eloise had an obsession with Van Morrison music.

"Help us," I said suddenly, my gaze finding hers.

Eloise froze. "I'm getting a bad feeling about today. About you showing up here. About that baseball bat—"

"Mace!" Desi interrupted.

"That *baseball bat,*" Eloise continued, "being with you. About the Court and your involvement. I'm getting the same vibes I did last year when you faced off against that demon."

"You're just worried about me," I said, waving off her words.

"Yes, I am," she replied without hesitation. "Which is why I'll help if you need it."

"See?" Desi asked. "What did I tell you?" He bumped my leg, and I winced when the iron thorns on the end poked me in the calf. "I told you your crazy aunt would help."

Eloise cried out, stepping toward us. "Now, see here—"

I moved between them. "He turns into a giant winged lion, Aunt Eloise."

"And?" she asked.

I laughed. "Never mind."

Aunt Eloise's face grew bright, a smile overtaking her features, my laugh changing the mood. "You want tea?" she asked, rushing away to grab two mugs. "There's nothing better than a fresh herbal brew to clear your mind."

Desi groaned.

I scratched at my skin, the hairs rising on the back of my neck. Something was coming. I didn't know what, but it reeked of death.

~

TWILIGHT WAS DESCENDING on Havenwood Falls, the shadows outside growing longer, the temperatures dropping dramatically. Somehow, after leaving my aunt's shop, I found myself walking the streets, completely consumed by the dark thoughts in my head and the phantom itch in my skin.

Desi remained still in my backpack, his mood matching mine. I'm not sure when he realized something was wrong with me—maybe during tea with Eloise—but he'd gotten mysteriously quiet and uncharacteristically obedient when I pulled the backpack out.

"It's cold," I whispered, my breath fanning like smoke from my lips, the thick coat and fur-lined boots on my feet doing nothing to get me warm. And not just because of the temperatures.

I had no idea where I was going. For some reason, I just felt compelled to walk. Pedestrians passed me by, but no one spoke to me.

I didn't stop until I was standing in front of a green house on Thirteenth Street, my gaze landing on the dark windows.

Eyes stared back at me. Phantom eyes that glowed violet in the dimming light.

Desi struggled in my backpack. "Let me out!"

"Shush!" I warned. "Be quiet before someone hears you."

My voice didn't sound like my voice. It sounded distant, distracted. In front of me, the house seemed to breathe, the walls billowing out, and I knew I was imagining it. There was no way a house could breathe.

Was there?

"*Harper.*" My name came to me on the breeze in a hundred voices. Male and female. Young and old.

The phantom itch in my skin grew worse, and I realized whatever was behind the violet eyes was causing the itch, its power so potent it was making my skin prickle.

"What are you?" I whispered.

Desi struggled harder. "Let me out, Harper!"

"*The Indrori,*" the hundreds of voices yelled at me.

Nausea doubled me over.

"Harper!" Desi cried.

My skin didn't just itch anymore. It hurt. The power coming from the house was strong, so strong it connected with the darkness on a different level from me.

"I can't breathe," I gasped.

In the distance, a truck rumbled around the corner, slowing as it approached the house. Vaguely, I heard a truck door open and slam shut. Big, warm hands cupped my arms.

"Harper." Elias Jamison's familiar deep voice invaded my ears, calming me and chasing away the darkness, his broad shoulders protecting me from the cold. A beard covered his strong face, his gaze sharp and ready for anything.

The pain in my skin disappeared.

"You smell like death," Elias breathed against my ear, causing me to shiver.

"What—"

"I heard the Destroyer's call." Elias answered my unfinished question. He was an angel, a divine fallen, and since Desi was a gift to me from another angel, it made sense they could communicate.

"I'm not cold anymore," I said, surprised, inching closer to Elias. "And my skin doesn't hurt."

Elias glanced up at the green house. "What's in there, Harper? You reek of power."

I gulped. "I don't know. Can you take me to the Court? They need to know about this."

My exhausted gaze found his, and his grip on me tightened.

"Why didn't you tell me you were getting this strong?" he asked me. "Why didn't you tell me you were having a hard time controlling this?"

I didn't say what both of us knew. I didn't tell him because we weren't in that kind of relationship. We were friends.

This wasn't the kind of thing you burdened a friend with.

Elias sighed. "Come on, I'll take you to the Court."

Things were going afoul in Havenwood Falls. Not only was there a Collector we knew little about loose among us, but there was a dark spirit in the house on Thirteenth Street. And it was deadly.

The Indrori.

CHAPTER 13

ADDIE

I dropped my elbows on my desk and rubbed circles on my temples, my hair falling forward to curtain my face and allowing me a moment to feel like I was somewhere else—a moment of reprieve from the craziness. The Court members sat at the table on the dais, firing questions at each other, Harper, Liam, and a couple of local demons about the Indrori. Harper had come to me last week with the news that some kind of conglomerate of dark spirits had escaped the Infernum and reached out to her. The Court had immediately gone into action, because the last thing our town needed was another threat of attack. Our leaders didn't seem to know what to do about it, though. They'd asked Liam and Savage to enter the green house on Thirteenth Street and try to escort the souls back to the Infernum—that was a hellhound's purpose, after all—but something had prevented them from even being able to cross the threshold.

"We have another possible solution we're pursuing." Saundra's voice broke through the din from the front of the room.

"The Lizard Man is a myth," Lawrence Mills growled.

"And so are frost dragons," Saundra snapped uncharacteristically, making me look up again. All of this was getting to her, too. Old Man Mills only narrowed his eyes, knowing she had a point. Not even half the people in this town believed his kind existed. "We've found another possible Lizard Man, or woman, in this case. Tasha Young. We're not sure that she is the same kind of being, but if so, she could be the one to take care of this Indrori."

"Roman brought up the Lizard Man idea," Mayor Barbie said, "but where is he tonight? He seemed so interested in this situation last week, but he couldn't even show up for this meeting?"

Nobody seemed to know, but Elsmed muttered, "Roman is Roman, and he'll be wherever he damn well wants to be. We're not his keepers."

"Anyway," my grandmother continued, "we will find out more about this Tasha Young and see if she'll be willing to help us. If so, we'll have to be careful about it. We'll want to make sure she can do what the Lizard Man could do, and if so, then we'll need to put all the preparations in place. We'll need the hellhounds on standby to help." She gave a pointed look to Liam, who nodded. "We will not put this woman's life at risk. That's the last thing we need."

"Do we have a timeline of when this will be resolved?" Michaela asked.

"Next week is Thanksgiving. Let's hope before Christmas Eve," Saundra replied with a small smile to Michaela. Then her chin dropped as she turned her attention to Harper. "You'll let us know if you sense this Indrori gaining in strength." She didn't make it a question, giving Harper no choice but to nod. "Very well. The house has been secured with our own wards to keep people from venturing too close, since we don't know what this thing is capable of."

"And the public seems to remain completely unaware of the Collector, as well," Mathilde Augustine added.

Saundra nodded. "The only other piece of business is the ring that was brought to Adelaide on Samhain. Savannah Bast confirmed that it's a link of the Elan Chain."

She referred to a relic two teens had found in Peacock Lake—an enchanted lake whose magical waters were more sinister than those of the great falls. They'd caught me on my way to a Halloween party to turn it over, and thank the Goddess they had. It definitely contained a darkness that didn't belong in anyone's hands, especially a couple of teenagers.

"It has been secured?" Old Man Mills asked, his eyes gleaming with interest. "My vault is available."

"Roman has locked it away with the other artifacts in his charge," Grandmother answered.

I personally didn't know how good of an idea that was—entrusting Roman Bishop with such valuable and powerful relics when Bishop Enterprises was in the business of trading such things—but I wasn't on the Court yet, and such decisions were not within my pay scale. When I brought it up to Saundra while at her home for dinner last week, though, my grandmother assured me once again that Roman could be trusted. She also assured me that in no way would he or anyone else have all of the links of the Elan Chain in one place. Nobody needed that kind of power.

The Court adjourned, and everyone filtered out, only Michaela trailing behind, as usual.

"Nina said my outfits will be ready for a fitting on Saturday," she said excitedly as we made our way down the hall, toward the stairs. Outfits—plural—because she needed one for the slopes and one for the reception. "You can come with me, right?"

I tried to think about any plans I had Saturday—and about normal life, in general. The idea of going on with a wedding and even everyday life sometimes seemed so preposterous, with everything happening. But that was the whole basis of our town and our primary directive, so to speak—protect the secret. And that meant protecting our town and her people without letting on that anything was out of the ordinary, even when it was completely opposite of ordinary. The good news was, though, that we'd yet to be attacked.

Maybe Shelly was full of shit?

Yeah, I doubted that.

"Earth to Addie," Michaela called.

I hadn't even realized we'd already climbed the steps and passed through the metal door to the outside world. Our breaths plumed out, and a few snowflakes drifted lazily from a partly cloudy night sky.

"Uh, yeah, I'll be there," I said absentmindedly.

"Good. We need to finalize what you and Aurelia will be wearing, too."

"Just let me know what time, and I'll meet you at Dress Perfect." That was Nina's shop for her custom-designed clothing.

Michaela and I parted ways at Eleventh Street as she headed south and I turned north toward home. I'd only gone half a block by myself when I sensed someone following me. I spun, surprised to find Micah striding down the sidewalk toward me.

"Hey, you're out late," I noted as he caught up with me.

"Did you know an Unseelie fae has gone missing?" he asked, bypassing any kind of cordial greeting. He stood in front of me with his fists stuffed in his pockets and his shoulders hunched near his ears, as though he were cold. Did angels get cold? I didn't think they did.

I murmured a muffling spell to ensure no prying ears heard. He shouldn't be spouting such things in public. "Yeah, we heard mention."

"And you're not looking into it? Your police? Anyone?"

"Sheriff Kasun said he found no trail. Fae leave all the time. She probably went back to Unseelie in Faerie, and good riddance for us."

His dark eyes narrowed. "What if it's the Collector's doing?"

"We can't blame everything on the Collector, Micah. Seriously, this isn't really that unusual, and if we're rid of another dark soul, so much the better. You, of all people, should agree with that."

He lifted his chin. "And what about Roman? Do you know what he was up to tonight?"

I tilted my head, and now my own eyes narrowed. "Why?"

"He wasn't at your meeting."

"How did you even know there was a meeting?" While this one had been open to more than just Court members, we hadn't exactly made it public knowledge. We rarely did.

Micah ignored the question. "I was watching him. I've been following him."

My brows shot up, and my eyes scanned the area. I grabbed Micah's coat and jerked him closer.

"Keep your voice down," I hissed. "Meet me at my place in ten."

I didn't care if I had our conversation muffled or that I could cloak us to prevent anyone from seeing us even talking. For one, it was too late for that—if anyone was around, they'd see us suddenly disappear, and that in itself would raise questions. And secondly, there were those powerful enough to break through my spells. Specifically, Roman himself. We didn't need to be on his bad side. At least, not any more than we usually were. Micah needed to respect Roman's power a bit more. Maybe he was impervious to it—I didn't know—but I didn't want to find out if I was.

Tase and my beasts greeted me at the door five minutes later. I gave him a quick kiss before getting to work spelling my place for privacy.

"Micah will be here any minute," I told him. He'd apparently been doing his own research on the computer, still searching for Shelly and Carter, but coming up with a whole lot of nothing.

He turned his full attention on me. "You two sure are spending a lot of time together."

I rolled my eyes. "We're on a mission. The same one you are, remember? You can't seriously be jealous. Besides, trust me when I say he only has eyes for Sedona. Everything he does is about her and Holly."

He rose to his feet and strode over to me, pushing the full length of his body up against mine. Almost like he was marking me—or at least scenting me. *Men.*

"Okay," he breathed against my ear before sucking on the lobe. "Then why is he coming over at midnight?"

I had to move away because he was doing things to my body that I didn't need at the moment. Too distracting.

After testing my spells to ensure my house was warded, I went over to the front door. "The idiot's been following Roman."

I opened the door then, knowing Micah was about to knock.

"I'm not an idiot," he growled. "I know how to make myself unseen."

I motioned him inside and quickly shut the door. "And he knows how to detect those who are trying to hide. He's powerful, and he's ruthless."

"And I'm more powerful," Micah said easily. He didn't sit down. He stood just inside the door, a massive mountain of muscles and bone.

"So why are you following him?"

Micah glanced at Tase and back to me.

"I'm on this task force, too," Tase reminded the angel.

Micah sighed, then told us what he'd learned about the Bishops and a shaman in the mountains.

"So just because his father and uncle—who, by the way, haven't been in this town in over a century—knew some shaman in the mountains, you thought . . . what?" I asked when he was done.

"According to Knox, the Bishops and that shaman were probably up to no good. The older Bishops were known to dabble in the dark arts."

I nodded. "Yes, that's well known. And that's why they were banished. I know I taunt Roman about practicing dark magic, but I also know he'd be banished if he actually did. The Blackstone witch hunters would know."

"If he did it in town," Tase clarified, and I couldn't argue with that.

"He's been leaving town a lot," Micah said, dropping his hands to his hips. "He went out of town tonight, in fact."

Tase mimicked his pose. "That's probably just business, though. I've done business with him before. It's not unusual, especially since Ronan's been staying close to home these days."

"Except it is," I said, thinking about the djinn I'd registered last February—the djinn kept in hiding at the Bishop estate. "Because Roman also has reasons for staying close to home. So wouldn't he be calling you, Tase, to handle something if he and his brothers couldn't?"

Tase shrugged. "Maybe. Depends on what it is."

"I doubt he'd call Tase to handle anything with the Collector," Micah said, making an excellent point.

That conversation, combined with the fact that we had nothing else to go on, led to Micah and me hiding out in a coffee shop in Provo, Utah, three days later, spying on Roman Bishop. Although I'd enchanted us to change our appearances, my stomach was tied in all kinds of nervous knots. Roman Bishop was not one to double-cross.

I trusted him about as much as Micah did—which was why I'd even agreed to do this—but my grandmother and the rest of the Court truly did trust him. She and my mother and even Savage and Liam all agreed Roman was an arrogant, narcissistic asshole, but that he also did care about the town. If anything, because he needed it for his own purposes. They had over a century of experience with him, compared to my twenty-five years and Micah's less than one.

But if he was so trustworthy, why was he meeting this Unseelie fae in a coffee shop so far away from home? Why did the whole thing reek of suspicion, even for Roman Bishop? He used a muffling spell of his own, so it was impossible for even an angel and a hellhound to eavesdrop on their conversation. When Roman and the fae stood, Micah and I both hid behind our menus, watching them over the tops.

"Fancy seeing you here, Adelaide." Roman's voice whispered in my ear, making me jump. My head whipped around, as I expected to find him right behind me, but he was already striding out the door—twenty yards away.

"Fuck," I muttered. "I told you he could break our spells."

Micah didn't care, though. He was already up, headed for the door, looking like a middle-aged dumpy guy who probably still lived in his mom's basement. Appearing as though I *was* his mom, I hurried after him, ignoring the raised eyebrows at the senior citizen nearly sprinting out the door.

"I got Roman. You go after the fae," Micah murmured over his shoulder once we were outside and saw that our targets had split up.

Turning left, I followed the Unseelie, wishing I could drop my disguise. I could see in the reflection of the windows I passed how ridiculous—and attention-grabbing—I looked. But I couldn't lose this guy. Finally, he turned left into an alleyway. About halfway down, we turned left again, and I ran straight into Micah.

"What the fuck?" I barked as I bounced off him. "Where'd he go?"

Before Micah could answer, my body suddenly flew through the air and slammed against the brick wall, taking my breath away. Micah went flying, too, but he instantly blocked the spell, stopping his trajectory before he hit the wall.

"You disappoint me, Adelaide," Roman said as he stepped out of a shadowed doorway. "Following me? I thought you were better than that."

"I thought you were better than doing business with an Unseelie," I retorted lamely. I wasn't normally one to be so judgmental, and I didn't like it.

"I do business with whomever the fuck I want," Roman growled.

"Including the Collector?" Micah just flat out asked, like Roman would actually answer honestly.

The warlock turned angry, stormy ocean eyes on Micah. "I told you before to stop following me, angel. This is your last warning."

"*Are* you doing business with the Collector?" I asked, trying to distract Roman more than anything so Micah could do his thing—whatever it was. Some angel thing to get us out of here. "Is that who that Unseelie is?"

Roman laughed before he suddenly appeared right in front of me, his lip curled and his nostrils flared. "Like I said, I do business with whomever I want. But are you sure that was an Unseelie you saw? Where is he now?"

He studied my face as my brows scrunched, questioning myself and what I thought I'd seen—what did happen to the Unseelie when I turned into this alley?—while Micah silently rose up behind him. Just as Micah was about to attack, Roman thrust his hand out. Micah's body jolted and then collapsed to the ground. He sprang up in a heartbeat, but Roman was already gone. Right before my eyes.

Rocking my head from side to side as I shook off the ache from hitting the wall, I threw my arms in the air. "Well, that was fucking productive."

"That was actually really fucking stupid," said a female voice from the far end of the alley.

Micah and I both whipped around to see Shelly—Rachelle—sauntering toward us. She looked more like me now than I cared to admit, especially as she was dressed in a miniskirt with holey thigh-high tights held up with garters that reached down below her exceedingly short hemline. It was not my kind of look except maybe on one day of the year, and Halloween had already come and gone. My twin's stilettos clicked on the cement as she sauntered toward us.

"What are you doing here?" I demanded. There was nothing suspicious at all about this. Yeah, right. "Were you posing as an Unseelie now?"

"And working with Roman?" She laughed as she stopped in front of us. "Please. I wouldn't trust that asshole to hold my coffee, let alone anything important." She lifted one shoulder as her torso twisted from side to side. "Now, my boss, on the other hand . . . who knows? The Collector's powerful enough to easily keep Roman Bishop under control." She eyed Micah as he leaned over her. "And you, angel. Trust me—you're really no match."

"What are you doing here then?" I asked. "And what have you done with Carter?"

She rolled her eyes. "Carter is perfectly safe. I'm his mother before anything else, and I will keep him safe. You can tell that to Tase. And I'm here to deliver a message—*another* message."

I lifted a brow, but said nothing, waiting for her to continue.

"I'm not working with Roman, but he's doing something important. So *back off*." She growled those last two words, her eyes glowing an orangish red to drive her point home. "And be careful, twinnie. The Collector's game has leveled up. You might want to watch your people. You, Addie, are wanted very badly—you and I make a matched set, you know, and collectors like their matched sets. But there will be others first—we have our eyes on quite a few who would serve us well." She looked over at Micah again, her gaze traveling from his head to his feet and back up again. "Havenwood Falls is populated with some very valuable beings, isn't it, angel?"

With that, she disappeared, just like she had from the Dirty Knuckle. Like Roman had just a few minutes ago.

"Holly," Micah rasped, and then he vanished, too, leaving me alone in an alley in Provo, Utah.

I made a portal for myself and appeared behind my desk in the Court meeting room in Havenwood Falls. After I contacted Saundra and shared Shelly's threat, our town went into lockdown. Of course, none of the residents knew anything had changed, but the Court, the sheriff's department, the hellhounds, and others began combing the streets and the forests surrounding the town. Everyone except the one Unseelie fae seemed to be accounted for, and she had disappeared weeks before Shelly delivered her message.

The Court ordered routine sweeps, though, three times a day. Elsmed was now involved in questioning every newcomer, poking into their minds to ensure they told the truth about anything they might know about the Collector. We tracked every coming and going of supernaturals—and Roman seemed to be staying put now, which only made him more suspicious in my mind.

I got my wish to sit in on Elsmed's interrogation of Roman, but it wasn't as fun as I'd hoped it would be. He either managed to keep the fae from his most incriminating thoughts, or he really was on the up and up. I laughed and laughed at the latter thought. No, he'd definitely found a way to keep Elsmed from his darkest secrets. If I knew anything at all, it was that Roman Bishop had many dark secrets. I could only hope the Collector was not one of them.

Thanksgiving weekend—and the opening of the ski resort—quickly approached. Our busy season was about to start. More than a week had passed since Shelly's threat, and everybody was, for the most part, fine. Much of the Court was again starting to doubt Rachelle, her connections, and her seemingly empty threats.

But I didn't. Neither did Micah, so I'd keep pushing him until he broke.

"You have to do it, Micah," I said the afternoon before Thanksgiving, as we stood outside the home he shared with Holly—and sometimes Sedona, if I wasn't mistaken. "You can't stay by Holly's side twenty-four seven."

"I will if I have to. And I have wards. I can protect her."

I nodded. I'd had to face those wards myself when I'd driven up. Micah had had to come out to free me.

"But you know there's more you can do," I persisted. "When are you going to admit that to yourself?"

Turning and stomping back toward the house, he growled over his shoulder something that sounded a lot like "Fuck off, Addie."

CHAPTER 14

HARPER

I was sneaking through the woods, quietly tracking a red-tailed hawk with my camera ready, the first time Tasha Young contacted me.

The voices in my head, the strong presence of spirits, and the irritating itchy skin had gotten worse over the last few weeks, my run-in with the Indrori on Thirteenth Street a catalyst to something bigger. Something terrifying. I'd gone to Addie Beaumont with my concerns, followed by a meeting with the Court, about an evil presence made up of hundreds of spirits residing in the green house. Elias waited on me outside while I met with them, which was a relief, because I was honestly afraid to admit what I'd felt in that house.

My powers were growing, and I wasn't sure I wanted anyone, other than a select few, to know. I'd been monitored by the Court, the things I could do limited while growing up because of my untrained, unpredictable abilities, and I didn't want that to happen again.

I felt like a supercharged conduit for the dead and the darkness with no idea how to control it, but I wanted the freedom to figure it out at my own pace.

Which was why when Tasha contacted me, the federal agent's soul having been sucked into the spirit realm, her desperate voice had taken me to my knees, so loud and insistent, it felt like she was standing next to me rather than being miles and miles away.

My hands trembling, I reached for my camera bag, sliding my unsteady fingers into the pocket where I kept extra pencils and notebooks when I wasn't at home. The way Tasha sounded in my head, the way my pencil flew over the page as soon as I opened the cover of the notebook, felt different somehow than any channeling I'd ever done. I usually channeled spirits by talking to them and then recording their response through words, but with Tasha, I was having to write down *my* words in order to communicate with her. Everything felt wrong. Everything about my powers had felt off lately.

My heart raced.

Dread consumed me when I realized she was inside the green house on Thirteenth Street, trapped by the spirit I'd felt within. The Indrori was no joke. It wasn't like anything I'd ever felt before. It was stronger than any shadow or demon I'd ever faced.

Tasha needed me. What she was up against wasn't something she could take on alone.

It was with this thought, and because of her cry for help, that I went to her, my fear a palpable thing that I struggled to hide.

The green house on Thirteenth Street mocked me when I arrived, the door an evil mouth waiting to swallow me whole. But there was a woman on the other side of that door, trapped and desperate. Fear be damned. I wasn't the kind of person who deserted someone in need.

There was no time to lose.

When I was finally inside the house facing Tasha, I could see her. Not in the typical sense. She was a shadow, just like all of the other shadows I'd seen, but she was more colorful somehow.

Probably because she was alive. Trapped, but alive.

It was obvious from the uncertainty I felt wafting off her that Tasha felt my fear. My fear was too big a thing to hide from her. From anyone really. But my resolve was much bigger than the fear, the determination masquerading as bravery.

She gave me quick instructions, ordering me to go find a trap upstairs and shoot the Indrori with it.

It was then I noted my surroundings. The inside of the house was strangely normal and clean. Large bay windows filled the space with light, bouncing off stainless steel appliances and designer-selected decorations.

The only odd things were the dark, foreboding feeling crushing me from all sides and a wooden doll sitting on a mantle. I'm not sure what made me look at the doll, but something about it drew my attention. It was a vintage female toy, the girl wearing an ancient green dress yellowed and faded by age, the paint on her nose and neck chipped. She wore an apron and bonnet, which should have made her look quaint and humble. Except she had black eyes. Completely black eyes, the orbs colorless and cold.

Even with the desperation hanging in the air, I hesitated when I saw the doll, shaking off my unease to run up the stairs. My heart pounded so hard, it felt like it was fighting its way outside of my body, one *thunk-thunk* at a time.

On a bed inside an upstairs room, two bodies lay sprawled, one a man, the other a beautiful woman with long black hair. It looked like a messed up scene from Snow White. As if the woman was a fairytale princess sleeping next to a corpse. *This* was Tasha. Who the man was, I had no idea.

Tasha talked inside of my head, telling me what I needed to do before suddenly pausing. She was beginning to doubt me.

"*You know what?*" Tasha said. "*I've changed my mind. This is too dangerous. You need to get out of here before it comes back.*"

I hated when people doubted me. I defended myself, using the brave words I threw at Tasha to pep talk myself as much as her, but all of my bravado disappeared when I *felt* the Indrori. The feeling hit me before the spirit revealed itself, a huge violet aura that literally drank my fear and courage, feeding off of it. My skin suddenly felt swollen, the itch in it so bad, I almost whimpered as I fought not to scratch.

It was then I learned how much I still needed to grow as a summoner and a spiritual psychic. It was then I learned that, despite being able to control the darkness, I knew little about it.

The Indrori used my powers against me, throwing me backwards and defeating me so easily that I was ashamed of myself, ashamed of how little I knew about what I was.

As a last-ditch effort, I summoned the shadows and urged them to fight with me, only for the Indrori to swallow them whole, using the darkness to strengthen itself and leaving Tasha in a worse predicament than she'd been before. Apparently, I wasn't the only one out there who drew strength from darkness.

So, I did the only thing I knew to do. I ran.

Leaving the house to go after Desi and the help I needed to assist Tasha, I promised the spirit agent that I would return to help save her.

Only, nothing went as planned. Nothing.

I heard Tasha's screams in my head before I'd even accomplished what I'd left to do, and I reached out to her.

It was then that all hell broke loose.

After a phone call with Roman Bishop, which resulted in an amazing revelation, I showed up at the house with Desi ready to fight.

"Leave her alone," I screamed. Desi shifted, becoming the massive lion with wings he became when things were dire.

But I never had a chance to do anything.

It was too late when I realized why *this* fight and *this* house bothered me so much. It wasn't just the Indrori or how powerful it was. The Indrori wanted Tasha, not me. Her fight with it was her story. Not mine. They were the bait used to attract me. I knew this the moment my gaze landed on the creepy doll on the mantle.

The doll wanted me.

Tasha screamed out a warning just as I saw the doll on the mantle look at me. Actually *look* at me, its head turning, its black eyes meeting mine.

"Hello, Harper. I've been waiting for you."

It was like a scene from a horror movie, the doll jumping off the mantle, her green dress swishing against her legs, the bonnet on her head casting a shadow over her face. It hooded her already black eyes, which was somehow scarier than seeing the eyes themselves.

"Play with me," the doll said sweetly.

It was the most terrifying thing I'd ever seen, and I'd seen a lot of terrifying things. But the reason people feared dolls so much was because no child's toy should ever become something evil. It twisted something innocent into something ugly and wretched.

"Play with me," the doll repeated, her singsong voice rising in the blinding whiteness to a screech that hurt my ears. Her head lifted, the black orbs where her eyes had once been now a glowing vomit green. Her carefully carved red rosebud lips suddenly smiled at me, revealing razor sharp teeth. "Hello, Harper."

My world disappeared. With a blinding white light and two words from a doll apparently no one else could see moving, I vanished.

And here I thought the strangest thing I'd ever seen in Havenwood Falls was the family of tiny tree gnomes I'd once spotted near the roots of an ancient tree in the mountains. They'd reminded me eerily of the Smurfs from the movies and the cartoon, only less blue and less cheerful. The evil doll that kidnapped me was on a whole new level of strange.

The world went from blinding white to pitch black, my last thoughts of Eloise, Elias, and Desi, the two people and one pet I cared most about.

My body was heavy, but I never passed out, my eyes wide. Why is it that people open their eyes wide during a blackout? As if opening them wider would somehow make it magically possible for us to see. When all it did was add an eerie dimension to an already black world.

Out of nowhere, glowing green eyes stared at me.

I couldn't help it. I screamed. The doll was with me. I couldn't make out its body, but it remained with me, its eyes watching. Not being able to see its body, what it was doing, or how far away it was from me finally threw me over the edge of reason.

My scream echoed back at me, loud and deafening.

A faint, pulsating glow began to fill the space, revealing a long hallway full of doors, all of them different. All of them flanked by sharp stone walls and rough wooden floors.

I was inside my nightmare; the one I'd had with all of the doors, the one where I'd bled and refused to go through the red door.

From the end of the hallway, her rosebud mouth twisted and her head cocked, the doll stared at me. "Welcome to my home," she said invitingly.

Above me, flickering white fluorescent bulbs appeared, the lights throwing sporadic sparks onto the floor, the sparks bouncing off of the wood rather than setting it on fire.

"The inside of your head is fascinating," the doll said.

She walked toward me, one slow step at a time, her voice changing from its singsong childlike pitch to something strange. Not quite female and yet not quite male either.

Ancient and all-knowing.

"Who are you?" I stammered.

The doll laughed. "I'm disappointed that you don't know. I assumed after all of the time I've spent inside your mind, you'd at least recognize me, Harper."

Tendrils of fear snaked through me, like smoke rising from flames. Although I'd never met him before, the psychic in me knew on a gut level I couldn't ignore who and what this was.

"The Collector," I whispered.

The doll sat on the floor a few inches away from me, relaxed.

Freaked out, I stepped back. "Are you the doll or are you just using the doll?" The doll's lips twitched, and I waved my arms at it. "Don't smile! Please don't smile." I couldn't handle its razor-sharp teeth at the moment.

The doll didn't smile. "This toy is an artifact. I'm just using it as a vessel."

My mind whirred, a million thoughts running at each other. Confusion ate away at me. But most of all . . .

"Is Tasha okay?" I'd been taken before I could help her. This bothered me more than dying. More than anything else.

"She's fine," the doll answered. "Help came. Although she's capable enough on her own. Trust me, I've got my eye on her. What an interesting woman Tasha Young is." Reaching up, the doll rubbed her chin, her wooden hand clicking against her wooden face.

"Why are you doing this?" I asked.

The Collector watched me, and I wondered if it was the doll's green eyes staring at me or if they were actually his. "I'm helping you."

"Bullshit!"

The doll sighed, a deep sigh that tugged at me, pulling my body toward her.

I dug my boot-covered heels into the floor.

The Collector laughed, and like the sigh, it tugged at me, too. "Oh, Harper. Do you even know what you are capable of? Do you even understand yourself at all? I've been watching you for a long, long time."

Jumping up, the doll danced in place, as if being a doll gave the Collector the right to dance a little jig in the middle of a creepy-ass hallway. "You are a gem!" the Collector informed me. "An absolute gem. Rough and uncut. Untrained but loyal to a fault. And so, so much stronger than you realize. Do you know how valuable this makes you to me? How valuable this will make you to the people you care about?"

The Collector's speech was emotionally moving in a peculiar way, the words messing with the complex feelings swirling in my heart.

Was the Collector attempting to hypnotize me?

"Don't!" I cried, covering my ears. "I won't listen to you."

The doll frowned. "The only fault you have is an inability to trust based on instinct." She stepped toward me. "You're going to learn a few things while you're with me, Harper Sinclair. Whether you wish to or not."

The doll started to vanish, and even though I wanted it gone, I panicked. "Where am I?"

Laughter floated on the air. "Inside a dollhouse you can't escape from. Go through the arched blue door. There's a bed there. Rest, Harper. You're going to need it for what I have planned."

Inside a dollhouse? Then why was the doll still smaller than me?

"Because what you fear and what you see are the same things," the doll replied. The Collector could read my thoughts, and he was right. For some reason, I was more terrified of him as a talking child's toy than I would be if he was the same size as me. Growing up, I'd always been afraid of dolls the way some people were afraid of clowns. He was playing on my childhood fears.

"Why are you doing this to me? Why are you doing this to Havenwood Falls?"

The doll was almost gone now, but her glowing green eyes stared back at me, as clear and green as they'd been before she started to fade.

"You should have gone through the red door, Harper."

My brows creased. "The red door?"

"In your dream, the door the shadows were trying to get you to walk through." The eyes vanished and then reappeared, as if the Collector had blinked. "This dollhouse and the doll are interesting artifacts. They make you face your own demons. They make you face the inside of your mind in ways you've never faced it before. You should have walked through the red door, Harper. The shadows were helping you. If you had, you would have discovered I was coming for you."

With that, the green eyes vanished, leaving me inside an eerie hallway with flickering lights and nowhere to go.

"Harper!" Familiar voices shouted, echoing around me. Tasha. Addie. I turned, desperate, my gaze searching, but my friends were nowhere to be found. It was a relief and a disappointment. A relief because they weren't trapped with me, but a disappointment because I was afraid of being alone.

"Harper!" they called again.

Where were they? Were they still at the green house? Was the doll still sitting on the mantle? Could that be why I heard them?

"Tasha!" I yelled. "Addie!"

If they could hear me, they didn't respond. My body sagged, exhaustion a disease that overtook my limbs.

The arched blue door led to a bedroom, right?

"I don't know what to do," I whispered.

"*Sleep*," a voice called, tendrils of darkness leaking into the hallway. The shadows. I wasn't scared of the shadows as much as I was the doll. The shadows I was used to.

Had they really been trying to help me in my dream?

"*Sleep, Harper.*" The shadows' voices were insistent, the darkness beginning to wrap around me. I was used to me controlling them, not the other way around. Maybe it was weakness from fighting the Indrori, but I was helpless to fight them off.

They lifted me, carrying me, shivering and scared, to the blue door. The way it creaked when the door opened was the last thing I remembered.

Darkness took me away.

CHAPTER 15

MICAH

*A*ddie's demand wouldn't stop tumbling about inside my mind, making it hard to concentrate on anything else. Which was a real shame, because my current view was breathtaking.

Leaning against one of the tall trees in the town square, I didn't need to squint my eyes to get a clear look at the woman who owned my heart.

Owned my heart. It still felt completely foreign to think like that— let alone feel the emotions that accompanied it. Angels weren't meant to indulge in such weakness, the elite often looking down their noses at humans.

I'd personally avoided developing any kind of attachment for a simpler reason.

I couldn't afford to. One wrong slip, or even the slightest distraction, could be the opening Holly's enemies needed to snatch her from my protection. From the moment I'd taken charge of her— rebelling against my superiors with my refusal to destroy the baby girl —I'd accepted that everything else would be sacrificed to keep her safe.

A small part of me had wanted to believe that Havenwood Falls could be a safe haven for the young oracle. I'd lowered my guard and let love in.

I'd let Sedona in.

And now, there was the very real possibility that this being had Harper Sinclair.

It was that last part that terrified me, because it was the one thing that made me actually consider doing the unthinkable.

It was a strong enough reason to risk everything I'd done to keep Holly safe, and tap back into the angelic divine.

He could find us.

Havenwood Falls would be leveled to the ground by a mere command from him.

He made this Collector being look pitiful in comparison.

But.

There's always a damn but, I cursed under my breath. Another quick glance toward Shelf Indulgence showed me Sedona hadn't moved from her spot at the front counter. The last customer had left about ten minutes ago, and I could almost guess what my beautiful girlfriend was thinking.

She was contemplating locking up and calling it a day. Even though she was adamant about doing okay, there was no disguising the fact the year had been a tough one for her. Attacks had rattled her world and the belief that she was safe within the confines of the store.

That was my problem.

If I tapped into the angel consciousness and listened in, I would be helping protect Holly and Sedona. Not just that, but also the town both of them loved deeply.

I could see whether or not the Collector had Harper.

If I tapped in, however, and they detected me? The outcome could be catastrophic for everyone.

"So, what's the greater threat?" I murmured out loud. A headache was developing, and the pounding of my temple matched the beating thoughts in my head.

"Does it matter?"

I closed my eyes briefly and softly smiled. I should've known there'd be no getting rid of Addie. I'd gone toe to toe with countless people through the ages, so I was a good judge of character. One look at the brunette, and I knew she'd be stubborn. There'd been a glint in her eye that screamed that she wouldn't take crap from anyone.

I guessed it also meant that she would hound a person until they finally caved and did whatever she wanted.

"It always matters," I countered, not turning around. A few seconds later, Addie Beaumont came up beside me, her own gaze directed toward Shelf Indulgence as well.

"See, that's where I beg to differ." She stepped around me and blocked my view of the store. She wore a determined look on her face, eyebrows cocked as though she was itching for me to disagree. "Life isn't always about right and wrong. Good and bad. Sometimes you've got to choose between completely fucked up things." Addie sounded so matter-of-fact that I felt a touch of sadness. She was too young for such bitterness.

I couldn't argue with her logic, either. "I don't think you understand what you're asking me to do." I shook my head, rubbing my mouth with my fingers. "The pain alone is excruciating, but it pales in comparison."

"To what?" she fired back, still unimpressed. "I hate to break it to you, but I'm not afraid of whatever bogeyman you're hiding from. This is my home, and screw whoever thinks they can threaten it."

"Darkness," I spat, with the same sense of urgency that continually stirred in my gut. Holding her gaze, I didn't blink while she searched my face for something. Then with a voice that was calm and level, I continued. "Death. Destruction. The end of all things."

Each word rang out, its weight pressing firmly down on my shoulders.

Addie scoffed in return. "It's all in how you look at the situation, Micah. It also depends on whose shoes you're standing in. To me, darkness is darkness. If it's coming here, I'm going to stand up to it and tell it to fuck off." She leaned in closer. "That includes the big bad you keep looking over your shoulder for. They're all the enemy."

That made me pause and look at her with a different set of eyes. "So you're telling me that whatever threat arrives in Havenwood Falls, you'd be there to help protect and defend? Even if it has nothing to do with you." I just wanted to be clear.

"I swear it. I don't know what your situation is, and frankly, I've got my own shit to worry about, but I have your back. The question is —" Addie stepped forward. "Do you have mine?"

That was the question.

I looked beyond Addie to Sedona again, who was now laughing at something Holly had just shown her. They were completely oblivious to the danger that was always lurking around the corner.

"Look. I'm only going to ask one more time, and before you answer me, consider this. Whether it is the Collector, your threat, or freaking Darth Vader himself, Havenwood Falls is at risk. Doesn't matter what the evil looks like . . . are you ready to do whatever it takes to keep her safe?" Addie nodded her head toward the bookstore.

Flashes of the torturous ritual I'd performed when I severed ties with Heaven caused a ripple of tremors to spread through me.

Pain.

Agony.

Fire.

Screaming.

Was I truly ready to relive that?

Slowly, I looked away from the building. My spine straightened and the muscles in my jaw tightened. The warrior mindset that I'd allowed to soften since meeting Sedona returned with a vengeance.

"Yes."

Addie smiled.

"I'm ready."

THE AIR WAS OPPRESSIVE, making it hard to breathe.

Worse were the tendrils of darkness and fear that whipped about my senses.

"How are you doing?" Addie peered at me from where she placed the last candle.

"Just peachy," I replied quickly as a bead of sweat fell down the side of my face. I gritted my teeth. "How much longer?"

We were currently inside the mausoleum that also served as a portal to the Infernum. It was almost impossible to think standing this close to such power and energy. Addie and I had been banking on that when we decided that this would be where we worked the magic needed.

"You can't rush this, Micah. Sorry." She reached out and adjusted one of the candles that stood at each point of the pentacle. "Everything has to be just right. It's the difference between a simple love spell and summoning a demon from Hell." She threw me a grin that I think was meant to make me laugh. The corners of my mouth turned up, but my own smile didn't stay long.

There was nothing amusing about this ritual. I had openly defied Heaven when I refused to destroy Holly at the order of my leaders. They'd seen her as a threat that needed to be eliminated for the greater good, but I'd believed differently. Not everything was set in stone—absolute and unchangeable. The young baby needed to be given the opportunity to choose, the chance to grow into her powers and align herself with the angels. Yes, there'd been the very real possibility that she could be corrupted, but to kill a newborn? It was monstrous and without honor. I'd accepted the task and then run with Holly.

I'd severed my link to the network of information accessible to me as a warrior and being of light. I'd magicked specific runes and spells to hide my own powers, having collected different enchantments from around the world. I'd spared no expense or effort in ensuring that I wasn't a beacon of energy, and buried the sword gifted me as my angelic birthright. I'd only kept with me my wings, but even those had been diminished underneath the weight of a heavy magical warding.

I'd had to adjust to being at half strength, but the sacrifice had been worth it so far.

And now I was looking at reversing all my hard work, at risking exposure again after painstakingly erasing any evidence of my existence.

I couldn't remember the last person to purposely repeat the ritual so they could join again.

And there wasn't a single account of that same individual working the magic a third time.

"I hope you understand the cost here," I repeated as I let out another calming breath. "When I finally reconnect, there can be no interruptions or sounds. Under no circumstance can there be anything to distract me. I have precisely two minutes to go in undetected and get out. I'll listen for any information about the Collector, then I need you to stab me with the blade." I pointed to the special sword I kept hidden. In a confrontation, it would be the only weapon I'd need to smite my enemy. "No chickening out."

Addie snorted. "I don't chicken out. You need me to stab. Gotcha." She stood up again and dusted her hands off. "Everything's ready. Where do you want me?"

There must've been over twenty white candles of different shapes and sizes scattered around the pentagram, the black ones already flickering and creating dancing shadows against the walls.

I pointed to the spot beside the sword. "Whatever you do . . . no matter what I say . . . do not break the circle of holy oil." I'd spared nothing in preparing for the ritual, taking every precaution.

"You sure you want me to light it? Won't it bind you within its power field?" She scrunched her brow.

"Trust me," I answered, tugging my T-shirt off over my head. I rubbed my chest, where the scars that I'd inflicted over a decade ago were now faded. "If this backfires, it'll protect you from what may show up. They'll be trapped with me, and under no circumstances should you extinguish it and break the circle. You do everything you can to keep Sedona and Holly safe." I demanded she hold my gaze. "Swear on it. I won't continue until I have your word."

Addie nodded, a solemn expression cast over her features. "You have it."

"Then you'd better hope that the Luna Coven's protection spell doesn't falter. That, along with the energy emanating from the Infernum, is just enough of a distraction to camouflage this."

Before she could ask what I meant, I stepped into the center of the pentagram and bent over to pick up the athame at my feet. "Start praying or whatever the hell you do."

And with a hard swing, I plunged the knife's blade deep into my chest, twisting it over and over until I'd made a hole. I ignored the pain that set my veins on fire and the way the blood gushed between my fingers, leaving a trail of blistering, molten heat down my abdomen. Tossing the athame to the ground, I dug into the gory mess of flesh, and with an angelic breath, whispered a few words in Enochian.

"What the *fuck*?" Addie exclaimed, and after all the warnings I gave her, she took a step toward me. Thankfully she caught herself, but it didn't stop her eyes from going as wide as saucers. "Micah."

"Runes," I grunted from exertion, my body wracked in tremors. "Must. Remove. The. Runes." Magic pulsed through me and a white glow began building within my center. It was working. Over and over, I repeated the Enochian phrase that would undo my spell work. With each utterance, dread and apprehension followed. Then, from somewhere in the midst of that glow, a spark flashed out and there was a tinkling ping that echoed in my ears.

My own personal wards were gone.

I was vulnerable.

"Now!" I screamed. "When an angel is stabbed with that blade, they briefly return to the source of their divinity. You need to send me home." Fear unlike anything I'd ever felt exploded, and I almost broke the barrier myself in my need to make sure Addie understood the next part. "Two minutes. Two minutes, then you stab me a second time . . . this time with the blade coated in my grace. It will blast me with enough healing magic that I can escape."

We locked gazes.

Addie nodded, and pulled back her arm before thrusting the sword forward.

Directly up into my chest.

It was as if the fiery pits of the Devil suddenly opened up their malignant maws and swallowed me whole. I could hear myself screaming as wave after wave of volcanic pain crashed against me. My senses immediately reached out—hoping against hope that I was still alone and not surrounded by enemies and beings determined to use me as a portal into Havenwood Falls.

Nothing.

Darkness and emptiness engulfed me as I began spiraling upward. I was returning home. I was about to see the one place I'd vowed never to go. Seconds passed painstakingly slowly. All the while, I reached out with my grace, waiting for the precise moment I could feel them.

I wasn't prepared for the way it struck my heart when that familiar energy emerged.

I'd once been happy here—fulfilled.

Respected.

Two minutes, I mentally scolded myself. Nothing has changed.

I sent out tendrils of my energy, seeking amongst the collective for any hint of news. I was instantly bombarded by the thoughts of every angel, the sensation like wading through thick sludge. Every being—regardless of the spirit. It was hard not to drown in how overwhelming it was after a decade of silence.

Shaking my head hard, I forced myself to stop and breathe. I ignored the pull to focus in every direction. Then in the eye of the storm, came the whisper . . .

The Collector.

Power.

The angels were scared. This being was perceived as a threat.

Flashes of faces swam before my eyes.

Shelly.

Harper.

And the next one made me forget all else as Holly's sweet face came to a halt before me. So it was true. This person was coming for her as well.

I kept searching.

What do you want with them? I silently asked.

The angels were angry that their own research into the identity and motivation for the Collector hadn't borne the anticipated fruit. They were just as much in the dark as we were, except for one small piece of information—the Collector was a deity from another realm.

Other images came flying at me. A woman with . . . something. A flash of jewelry. But before I could register their meanings, I felt a sharp tug and then that familiar burn as Addie plunged the sword back through my chest. Frantically I tried to prolong my return to the last possible second, hoping to understand the ancient symbols that filled my view.

There was no holding back my screams as I fell to the ground in the mausoleum. I was covered in a slick coating of sweat, and my heart pounded loudly in my ears.

"Tell me you got something, Micah!" Addie cried. She wore a mixed look of fear and horror. Her hands were covered with my blood. "Tell me you found something." There was a slight tremor to her fingers as she raised her arm to rub the back of her neck. "Holy shit."

I tried to answer her, but I still hadn't caught my breath.

She began pacing back and forth—no doubt because of the residual energy that still filled the air. It sizzled across my skin, and with a sudden surge of adrenaline, I barked one more order at her.

I slowly pulled myself up and staggered forward a few steps before I corrected my balance. When she didn't budge, I waved her away.

"The Collector has the angels in a panic." Her brow furrowed with confusion until I bent over to pick up the athame. "And I caught glimpses of someone else . . . a victim or an accomplice, though, I don't know."

"Micah?" Addie's eyes kept darting from my face to the bloodied mess I now was.

"Go. I can't remain vulnerable like this. I need to replace the runes I erased. We'll talk more later." I pressed the tip of the blade against my already cut skin. I wouldn't die from what remained of the two mortal wounds. The grace that had coated the sword had already began repairing the damage.

Bracing myself, I heard her quietly leave. I was alone again.

"You will not win," I exclaimed as I began recurving and weaving the protective magic.

The Collector would never win.

CHAPTER 16

SENORA

*P*ersonally, I was not a fan of the holidays and the tedious, endless celebrations. Who cared about exchanging gifts and inducing sugar comas? It was all a huge farce, anyway. As soon as the clock struck midnight for the new year, humans returned to their trifling ways and quickly forgot about those they claimed to love just minutes ago.

Staying in Havenwood Falls wasn't on my agenda either—not at first. But after saving Izzie and finishing that last so-called job for The Collector, I had no choice but to hang around. His insistence, not mine.

To keep my bestie from getting too nosy, I told her that I missed her terribly and wanted to stick around. As luck would have it, I convinced that tall drink of handsomeness—I think his name was Monte—to vouch for me with the town's supernatural court. Instead of getting an easy pass, though, they gave me a provisional permit until they could check out my credentials. Apparently, my reputation proceeded me, and they had doubts that I wouldn't try eating the residents.

Someone might be looking for that dark fae I ate. It didn't help that Kazimir's driver put out a missing person alert.

Damn that creature I worked for. The Collector put me in a bad position. I didn't know that while I'd been snacking on the fae, Rachelle was recording the incident—proof easily delivered to the authorities and the Court. It was a nice way to make sure I complied and kept my ass in town.

Dealing with the hellhound and Eva Blackstone's attitude became a bit much. So I moved out of NamaStays Inn and checked into Whisper Falls Inn. The owner, an attractive vampire, put me in one of the empty cottages at the edge of the property. It was slightly larger than the bed-and-breakfast.

But the change of address didn't get rid of the aching need I had. I wasn't hungry anymore. After eating two bodies so close together, I could probably go another month before indulging again. No. This hunger spoke to a different need—one that only a night of mad, passionate sex would quell. I was as horny as a sequestered new bride. It was another reason why I either hid in my room or at Izzie and Hunter's place—well, tried to. That damned dog of hers freaked out every time I entered the house. If I didn't love Izzie, I would have made the animal a midnight snack.

Despite my intimate issues, I had work to do. At least that was what the Collector promised. He assured me that my meal was simply a test of my loyalty and my ability. He had his sights on more individuals and thought my unique talent could expedite assembling his *assets*. As long as I ate no one else, my normal pay for each one would be tripled.

It was the only reason I was standing out in the cold, keeping an eye on the tattoo artist. Personally, I didn't get why the Collector wanted this particular Seelie fae, when last time he hadn't been so picky. I'd been observing the female for nearly a week. Her routine was fairly simple—get up and go to work. I assumed she must have one of those apartments above her studio, but then I noticed she was spending a lot of time at a Victorian house on the outskirts of town. I did some snooping around and learned that she'd moved into it earlier this year. Some nights she hung out at the Dirty Knuckle before returning to the house on the outskirts of town. I hadn't noticed her with any friends—female or male. Personally, there was nothing remarkable about the tattoo-covered blonde.

Before I agreed to this job, the Collector repeatedly emphasized that I was not to eat the merchandise.

"Have I made myself clear, Miss Graves?" The Collector strummed his glove-clad fingers on the chair arm. "You are not to eat the asset."

I rolled my eyes as I folded my arms across my chest. "It's understood. No eating the merchandise. I'm not a child. I do practice self-control."

Keeping my mouth off Gwen Facharro wasn't a problem. Empusai didn't eat anyone with piercings or a lot of ink unless we had a death wish. Metal didn't digest. Eventually, it would rot out our insides and kill us. And as much ink as Gwen had? Well, we might as well drink bleach. We'd get the same effect.

"Can you tell me anything about this latest . . ." I didn't know what to call kidnapping people—assets? Acquisitions?

The Collector clarified things, though. "Gwen is valuable merchandise."

Rachelle sashayed into the room and added her two cents. "All you need to know is that Gwen is a fae. Maybe you should watch her for a while and figure out a plan. Or do you need me to walk you through it? I know empusai prefer action over thought."

I wanted to claw her fucking eyes out, but I thought it might not be a wise idea in our employer's presence. She reminded me of someone I knew decades ago. The woman was also a hellhound. We butted heads every time we saw each other. Eventually her crazy antics got me kicked out of the village we lived in. I left everything behind, including my one chance at happiness.

. . .

NEEDLESS TO SAY, I got no worthwhile information from The Collector nor his beach bunny sidekick.

Anyway . . . Back to my target . . .

The girl had a definite routine that she rarely deviated from. The lights went out in her shop and then she disappeared. Not literally, but I saw no sign of her until she arrived back at her house.

My phone pinged just as I was about to walk away from my post.

HellWitch: Have you acquired the merchandise?

SG: Don't you have souls to squash or something?

HellWitch: Our employer wants an update.

SG: I'm working. I'll check in when I have something.

I turned off my phone and tucked it into my rear pocket. Enough with the surveillance for one night. I needed a stiff drink or a man now.

THANKFULLY, it was a busy night at the Dirty Knuckle, allowing me to slip in, place my order, and sit in a booth. Lucky for me, the booth I'd chosen gave me a view of the whole bar.

As I sipped on my drink, trying to formulate a plan of attack, I noticed the boy toy with little miss tattoo. Damn, he was one hot man. The kind I should have servicing me regularly. I was a little shocked to see him kiss Gwen openly. After watching her for a few days, I got the impression she wasn't too fond of PDA. Actually, it was one of the few impressions I got. The girl was mysterious, but I didn't know what her gifts were.

But watching these two together gave me a hell of an idea. I smiled to myself thinking of how brilliant I was. Since no one was paying attention to me, I tapped my glass and gave myself a refill. I planned on sticking around for a moment and soaking up the atmosphere— amongst other things.

I STAYED at the Dirty Knuckle long enough to plan my attack. The crowd had thinned out, and the owner ambled over to my table.

"I don't mean to rush you, but . . ."

My eyes trailed up his body and stopped at his gorgeous face. I'd opened my mouth to speak when Gwen popped up.

"Rhys, I'm ready." She finally noticed me sitting there. "I'm sorry. Am I interrupting?"

He smiled lovingly at her. "Just closing up."

That was my cue. I stood and held out my hand. "My name is Senora. Forgive me for keeping you open so late."

Gwen glanced down at my hand and then at her man. When her eyes met mine, they were hard like stones. Did she pick up on something about me? I couldn't be sure, so I dropped my hand.

"Let me pay my tab so that you two can get home." I reached inside my jacket for my wallet. Purposely, I let it fall from my hands. "Oops! How clumsy am I?"

Rhys chuckled and bent down to retrieve the item. I reached for it and let my hand stroke his palm. That maneuver earned me an eye roll from Gwen. She tugged on his sleeve and cleared her throat.

Time to go. I took out a twenty, placed it on the table, and said goodnight. As I stepped out the door, I noticed Gwen's glare. I hoped it was just jealousy on her part and not a warning I needed to heed.

IN ORDER for my plan to work, details had to be exact. Any deviation, and Gwen would see through my charade. It all boiled down to patience. I wanted to act quickly and get the job done, but my target wasn't making it easy.

Ever since my night at the bar, Gwen's routine had changed. She stopped working late and just going home. For the past two nights, she closed up and then headed to the Dirty Knuckle. Gwen remained there until Rhys closed the joint down, then they would go straight back to her house.

Once again, I sat in the dark, watching the back door of the Dirty

Knuckle. I was ready to call it a night when the door swung open and my mark walked out. She rushed from the building and hopped into her truck. I lingered for another minute to make sure her boyfriend wasn't coming. When he didn't leave the joint, I went into action.

Empusai were great impersonators. Not only could we create our own doppelgängers, but we could become anyone we chose as long as we'd touched them. It had been awhile since I mimicked a male, and the fit was snug, not to mention the uncomfortable extra appendage.

The key with impersonation was getting all the tiny details correct. While mimicking Rhys, I had to make sure he couldn't easily get to Gwen's house. So I created a distraction. I'd done my research and learned that Rhys frequented an industrial part of town. When I checked it out, I discovered Elsmed, a fae on the Court, worked out of a warehouse in the area. I contacted a lesser demon I knew and had him deliver a message for Rhys. Next, I transported into the Dirty Knuckle.

I stood in the shadows, invisible to everyone, and watched Rhys race around the bar's small office. His frenzied state was due to my cryptic, urgent message from Elsmed. Rhys grabbed his jacket and then reached for his phone. Wrong move. I couldn't allow him to contact anyone. I waved my fingers, and the device powered down. Rhys scratched his head and tossed it on his desk. The door slammed as he stormed out of the room.

After he left, I picked up the phone, and it powered up. I accessed his contacts and sent two messages—one to Elsmed telling him to meet Rhys away from the warehouse, and one to Gwen.

Rhys: Hey, babe. I'm leaving early tonight. See you soon.

Within seconds, his phone vibrated.

Gwen: Can't wait.

Time to work a little more magic. Pocketing the device, I stepped out the back door. Thankfully, there was no one outside. I waved my hand and a replica of Rhys's truck appeared at the curb. A necessary evil. I couldn't show up at the house without a vehicle. I hopped in the cab and drove toward my destination.

〜

I PARKED the truck in front of the Victorian house and got out. Something didn't feel right, and it wasn't the skin I was in. The air had taken on an ominous feeling, like it had a pulse. Not good.

Just then, the front door opened and Gwen stepped onto the porch. She waved at me, and I hurried up the walkway. Fake Rhys smiled back at her and gave the girl a quick peck.

Her eyes narrowed as they swept over Fake Rhys. "Why home so early?"

"Wanted to spend some time with my girl. Let's go for a drive."

"Okay . . ." The word trailed off as she angled her body away from Fake Rhys. She lowered her chin and stared for a moment.

For the first time, I really noticed her tattoos, and the gray hawk on Gwen's arm twitched. *Not possible.* I was tired—that was it. I blinked a few times.

"Are you feeling all right, Rhys?" she asked.

I didn't like the way she drew out her man's name—as if she knew something was wrong. "I'm fine. A little tired, that's all."

Gwen brushed a hand over the tattoo, and it moved again. I didn't know about Fake Rhys, but the long hours must have caught up to me. Ink didn't move on its own.

She pursed her lips and walked away slowly. "Give me a minute. I need to grab a jacket."

I strummed my fingers on the counter of the quaint kitchen. Inhaling, I smelled death. A murder took place here. Tilting my head to the side, I sensed it was a woman and her loss was a great one. Footsteps interrupted my reverie. I looked up, and Gwen stood, leaning her shoulder against the doorframe.

"Ready?"

"Yeah, come on."

〜

OTHER THAN THE weird moment back at the house, I was impressed with myself. My copy of Rhys fooled the fae. Honestly, this job was going perfectly. Sitting so close to Gwen, I could read her fear too—being captured by some Unseelie soldier. An inane fear if you asked me. I highly doubted Gwen was that important to anyone other than her boyfriend. The only thing left was knocking her ass out.

Fake Rhys side-glanced and asked, "Babe, any place in particular you care to go?"

She smiled sweetly and said, "Why don't we go to Mt. Alexa? Remember the base I hid in that night?"

Shit. Was she playing me? "Why there?"

"Aw . . . Have you forgotten what we did in the parking lot?"

Fake Rhys was the spitting image of the real one, but when it came down to sex . . . Hell, some things just shouldn't be faked. I chuckled a little nervously. "How could I forget?"

Gwen sat back in the seat with a shit-eating grin on her face. I smelled trouble.

BY THE TIME I pulled into the visitor lot, I was certain that my ass was in deep water, and it was starting to simmer. Fake Rhys opened the door and hopped out of the cab. Behind me, I heard a rustling, then Gwen stepped next to me. She reached for Fake Rhys's hand, but I pulled away.

Wrong move. Gwen eyed me for a moment before crossing her arms. "What's up, Rhys?"

"Nothing." Fake Rhys slid his arm around her slim waist and pulled her close. "I guess I'm more tired than I thought."

She looked at me expectantly. *Was she waiting for a kiss?* Stupid question. Gwen drew me out here with the prospect of making out. I wasn't a prude, but I had yet to kiss a female. It wasn't something on my bucket list. But the prospect presented an opportunity. I could get inside her mind and render her motionless. Instead of moving in for the kill, I'd transport her to the Collector. Job done. Money collected.

"Come here," Fake Rhys said.

When my lips brushed hers, I had to admit it was nice. The girl wasn't a bad kisser—yeah, I remembered she was my first female. Gwen slanted her head and deepened the kiss. I stopped focusing on the kiss and pictured the Collector's lair on the other side of town.

The air changed. Winds howled and snowflakes swirled around us. I expected those things, but not the loud screech. I broke off the kiss, stepped backward, and looked up. A huge ass hawk was swooping for me. I ducked.

"Who the hell are you?"

Gwen's voice forced me upright. Her jacket was on the ground. That's when I noticed the bare spot on her arm. I could have sworn there was a tattoo of a bird there. Said bird was now sitting on a precipice nearby.

"I'll ask again," she said. "Who the hell are you, and what have you done with Rhys?"

It wasn't like she was going any place but inside the mansion, so I lost the glamour. When Fake Rhys faded away, Gwen's jaw dropped.

"The woman from the bar. Senora, right?" She cocked her head. "Not a vampire."

I ignored the insult. "Your boy toy is fine. He might be a little pissed that I sent him on a wild goose chance, but that's not important. I'm here to collect you. There's someone who wants to meet you."

"I'll have to take a raincheck."

"Not an option." I lifted my hand, ready to transport us inside.

Suddenly, the hawk dove for me. My batting at the creature distracted me from the target. I got in a lucky strike and hit a wing. It turned and plucked at my arm. I continued struggling with the bird as strange words surrounded me. Just beyond a dark wing, I saw Gwen's lips moving. I couldn't make out the language.

Another one of her tattoos twitched. This time the tattoo—a length of rope—slipped free from her skin. It slithered like a snake and looped around my wrist. Sorry, nobody tied me up. I waved my hand,

and it disappeared. When I glanced back at the girl, she held a bow and arrow.

Where the fuck did that come from?

While I stood there figuring out my next move, an arrow screamed and spiked my shoulder. Fuck! That shit hurt! I flicked my wrist and launched a swarm of knives—like a throng of bullets—toward her. More ink leaped from her flesh in the form of a metal shield.

"Don't make me hurt you," she yelled out.

"I think you're mistaken. You're the one who needs to worry."

Red hot anger traveled through my veins. My palms glowed with intense energy. I raised my arms and shot flames in the girl's direction. The embers slithered and snaked around her, forming a wall of fire.

I moved closer, satisfied that I had her trapped. When I called my energy back, the girl was gone. *What the fuck?* I scanned the peaks, but she was nowhere to be found. Even that damned bird had disappeared.

The only person I saw was the last one I wanted to see— Supernatural Barbie.

~

"Admit it, you screwed up!" she yelled as we stalked up the stone stairs.

"And you could have done better?" I shot back. "Why didn't you tell me about her damned magical ink?"

Rachelle glanced over her shoulder. "You should have done your homework."

"I did my research. Sorry, is there some fucking manual telling me about the town? If there is, I could use a copy. Got a website I should check out?"

We argued all the way to the front door and beyond. We were so busy shooting insults and accusations that neither of us noticed the Collector standing in the hall—a first.

"What happened?" he rasped.

Rachelle jerked her thumb in my direction. "The mutt lost the fae."

I opened my mouth, but the Collector lifted his finger and cut me off. He didn't speak, just pointed to the drawing room. I felt like a kid waiting to be punished as I dragged my feet to our usual meeting spot.

My employer's robes billowed around him as he sat in his customary seat. "Explain."

I shrugged. "I didn't know about Gwen's magical ink."

"What happened to compelling her?"

Another shrug. "I got it wrong, I guess. I picked up on an Unseelie she was afraid of."

The Collector put a hand up to his hidden face, and his head moved from side to side. "Old news. I will give you another chance."

Pursing my mouth, I shook my head vehemently. "No way. Get Supernatural Barbie to do it." I rubbed my aching arm. The wound was stitching itself closed, but it was a painful process. A meal would expedite the process. "First, you didn't warn me about the fucking tattoos. Nobody said anything about a bird."

"Shall I take it that you want out of my employ?"

Was that what I was saying? "No. Give me another assignment."

The Collector nodded. "Let me discuss the situation with Rachelle. We'll be in touch."

CHAPTER 17

ADDIE

A missing fae. A dead body drained of all blood. Another outbreak of souls from the Infernum with a smartass reaper named Shade StormIron in town to supposedly take care of them. He had shown up right in the middle of the Hot Cocoa & Cookie Crawl last weekend. He still hadn't taken care of them, and unfortunately, they weren't the kind of souls Tasha Young, one of our newest residents, could capture.

Harper was still missing, too. For three fucking weeks now, ever since the last group of souls to escape the Infernum had been rounded up Thanksgiving weekend. We didn't know if she'd disappeared to the Infernum with the souls or if the Collector was behind her disappearance, but I felt in my bones that he was. Especially when Liam and Savage took a trip to the Infernum and found no trace of her. And especially with what Micah had shared after he'd tapped into the divine consciousness.

Oh, and then there was a really pissed off fallen angel on my case. As if Micah wasn't enough, now Elias was freaking the fuck out. He couldn't find Harper or any news on the Collector from his sources. Which reinforced, in my mind, that Harper's case and the Collector had to be related. So I had to wonder if Shade's souls were connected to the Collector, too.

A fucking deity from another realm?

That's what Micah had said about the Collector, and I couldn't even wrap my head around what that meant. He'd said even the angels were scared. We were dealing with a god. From another realm. In my studies and preparation to one day be a High Priestess of the Luna Coven and take the Beaumont seat on the Court, I was highly educated and trained for all supernaturals. I knew a lot about the thousands of deities known or suspected to be in existence. But it'd been centuries, millennia since any had bothered with our world. So why now? And why here, in Havenwood Falls, of all places?

It didn't make sense, making it all too difficult to believe.

Although it did explain why we couldn't find any information about the Collector or traces of his existence. He was a deity. A god. And he was threatening our people.

How in the hell were we supposed to take down a god?

"It's a good thing my wedding is badass and I'm a ninja event planner, because you suck as a maid of honor."

Oh, yeah. And then there was my best friend and her upcoming wedding.

Michaela sat across the table from me at the Dirty Knuckle, a glass of wine in front of each of us, her green-gray eyes narrowed at me. We were supposed to be giving a show like everything was normal while surreptitiously gauging any unusual tension or anxiety among the people of our town, residents and tourists alike. Tase and Xandru were supposed to meet us here, too, but they'd been delayed with something at the ski resort.

"I'm sorry. You know what's going on, though." I grimaced.

She tried to smile, but her lips curved downward instead. "Yeah, I know. In fact, that's what I was just telling you when you spaced out on me. I'm going to put off the wedding. I thought we would have found Harper by now, and the Collector would be long gone—in the Infernum, I hope. But Christmas Eve is less than a week away. Xandru and I have been discussing it for a while, but it's time to make the decision to officially announce that there will be no wedding. Not on the twenty-fourth, anyway."

She pulled in her bottom lip and gnawed at it, her eyes blinking rapidly. I swallowed against the lump in my own throat. I hated that she had to put off her wedding. She and Xandru had been planning this for years. I mean, there was a good five-year gap that she'd been gone from our lives completely, but we'd all known as soon as she came back that the wedding would eventually happen. But then there was the curse on their best man, Tase, so they'd put off any plans until he was cured. And just when we thought their marriage finally might happen, now they'd have to put it off again. It wasn't fair. It made me hate the Collector even more.

I reached across and laid my hand over hers, giving it a squeeze, probably too hard because I really wanted to punch something. Preferably a god. In the throat. Good thing Michaela was a vampire and could easily take my strength.

"This sucks, and I'm really sorry."

Her lips twitched, making another effort at a smile, and she shrugged. Her voice came out raspy. "It's just a party, and we'll still have it sometime. Right now, we need to worry about getting Harper back and protecting our town."

As I pulled my hand back, my eyes drifted over to the bar, and I was surprised to see Gwenn Facharro back there. She and Rhys, owner of the bar, were a serious item, but I couldn't remember ever seeing her behind the bar. She wasn't working it or anything, either. She stood against the wall, near a door, her shoulders hunched in and her eyes constantly darting around. She didn't look herself. Rhys paused to have a few words with her, and they both looked at me. I quickly glanced away, but when I peeked over there again, they seemed to be having a tense conversation.

My hellhound hearing picked up the words "tell the Court." Michaela must have heard it, too, because her eyes lifted to mine, then slid over to them. She looked back at me and tilted her head.

"I don't know," I murmured. "They usually want nothing to do with us, even when I practically begged her to help."

"Maybe they mean Seelie Court?" she whispered, and I nodded, but I wasn't so sure, especially when Gwenn's gaze kept darting back to Michaela and me.

The guys showed up, Tase distracting me, and I forgot about Gwen.

"Weston says whatever you need," Xandru said as he dropped into the seat next to Michaela and turned his full attention to her.

"That's why we're late," Tase explained as he waved at the waitress with two fingers in the air. "We stopped by Everett's office and gave him the rundown, like you asked. He said he's in for whatever the Court needs, but Graysin's not."

I lifted a brow. "Is that her choice or his?"

Tase lifted his hands in defense. "I'm just the messenger. You ask her if you want."

I let it drop. I didn't really *want* to ask her. I didn't want to ask anyone. I hated requesting people to put their lives on the line. But once we found out who this Collector was and how to find him, we'd need an army. Because of that whole deity from another realm thing.

"Did you tell her?" Xandru asked Michaela, and she nodded.

"We'll make the official announcement tomorrow," she said. "We'll pick another date later."

The guys' beers showed up, and our conversation died as we listened to the din around us grow. It was the holiday season, and the tourists and locals alike seemed to be all about the cheer. Good. They had no idea what storm was brewing. I hoped they never would.

I normally walked just about anywhere in town unless the temperature was below zero, I had to haul to something too unwieldy to carry, or I was trying to look somewhat put together and not my usual windblown, au naturel self. But Tase preferred driving since he couldn't use his vampire speed and was too impatient to trek anywhere, even a few blocks away. We were halfway home in his Camaro when my phone dinged with a text message.

"I knew there was something weird going on," I muttered after reading it. Tase glanced over at me, the dash lights illuminating his face. "Gwen wants me to meet her at her shop later, after the Knuckle closes. Says it's important."

"Gwen the Tragic Ink chick? Rhys's girl?"

"Gwen the incredible artist, businesswoman, and Seelie fae," I corrected, giving him the stink eye.

"Do you think she changed her mind about joining Adelaide's Army?"

"We are not calling it that!" I punched him in the bicep, and I didn't know if it hurt him or my knuckles more. He was made of steel. "But no, I don't think she's changed her mind about the task force. Gwen's always kept to herself, and I think she prefers it that way. This probably has something more to do with Rhys. Something was going on between them. I could see him wanting to help us, and maybe she doesn't like the idea."

Who knew Tase was right on this?

"I want to join you," Gwen said a couple hours later when she, Rhys, Tase, and I had gathered in her tattoo studio.

A few years younger than me, the lithe blonde had ushered us inside, her green gaze peering up and down the alley off Eighth Street that ran between Howe's Herbal Shoppe below and Dress Perfect across the way, as if she expected someone to jump us. Normally, that would have been a laughable idea in Havenwood Falls, but these days, one couldn't be too careful.

Rhys brought two tumblers half-filled with a golden liquid and handed one each to Tase and me. He and Gwen already had their own.

"We're both in," he said, his dark gaze locking on mine.

"You want to join us?" My brows rose.

The sides of Gwen's short hair bobbed as she nodded. "I want to kick that bitch Collector's pretty little ass."

"Whoa, whoa, whoa!" I interrupted, nearly dropping my drink before I'd even taken a sip. "You *saw* the Collector?"

"She tried to fucking kidnap me! I heard she took the spiritual writer, and apparently I was next on her list."

I lifted my hand in a stop signal. "Hold on. Back up. First of all, the Collector is a *she*?"

"Beautiful dark skin and eyes, a killer body, about this tall—" Gwen held her hand a few inches higher than her own head.

"She'd probably be a hit in Silk's backrooms," Rhys added.

"You saw her, too?" I was so confused. Why was the Collector coming out now? And like this—why would she suddenly let herself be seen?

Rhys nodded. "She'd been at the Dirty Knuckle earlier in the night. I'd seen her there a couple times, actually, but thought she was somehow involved with the MC."

"SIN?" My jaw dropped.

"Yeah, but I think I was wrong."

Tase rubbed the back of his neck. "Why don't you start from the beginning?"

Gwen drained her bourbon, then proceeded to tell us about the woman who'd made herself look like Rhys to lure Gwen away from home and then used some kind of magic to take her somewhere up in the mountain peaks.

"I don't know exactly where," she said. "I didn't stop to look around, and there was nothing remarkable about where we were—just snow and trees. That could be anywhere. Ethan helped me get away, and once I got a sense of direction, I knew we'd been somewhere on Mount Mae."

"Ethan?" I asked.

She exposed her arm and a tattoo of a hawk.

"And I used this." She pointed to an image of a bow and arrow.

Ah. This was the talent that made me want her on our team in the first place—her ability to bring her tattoos to life. I'd tried it with my own magic, but my results weren't quite so impressive. This was her special fae ability, and could come in very handy.

But I couldn't believe she'd been able to escape the Collector that easily on her own. Well, with the help of a hawk, but pretty much on her own, when we were supposed to be facing a god. Or, perhaps, a goddess. And if the Collector were that easy, after what I'd seen Harper do with spirits recently, I didn't understand why she hadn't escaped yet, too.

Maybe the Collector really didn't have her? Or . . .

"Are you sure it was the Collector?" I asked.

Gwen shrugged. "I'm assuming it was. She said she was collecting me."

"What else did she say?" Tase asked.

Gwen's eyes bounced around the room as she seemed to think about it. "That there was someone who wanted to meet me. I think she was about to do that whole portal or whatever thing again with me when Ethan dive-bombed her."

"The shapeshifter," I said, the word popping out of my mouth even as the idea was still forming. "The one who was trying to get the Eye of Valerian. It said it worked for the Collector. That's who this must have been. Not the Collector, but a minion. You said she made herself look like Rhys?"

"Yeah, and then she morphed in front of my eyes."

My idea immediately got shot down, and my shoulders slumped. "Then not the shapeshifter. The one we know about does a gross explosion thing that sends skin and goo everywhere."

Gwen's nose wrinkled. "Ew. That definitely didn't happen."

"But you could be right about this woman being a minion and not the Collector," Tase said.

I nodded. That made a lot more sense. The Collector didn't do his own dirty work. But at least now we had a lead.

"We need to tell this to the Court," I said, nodding as more ideas started coming to me. I looked up at Gwen and Rhys. "You're definitely in?"

"Definitely," they said in unison like an old married couple, and I couldn't help but notice that Gwen had cringed and Rhys's lips had curved into a small smile.

"So one question," I said. "If this happened two nights ago, why are you just now telling anyone?"

Rhys and Gwen shared a look, and he nodded.

"I didn't make the connection at first," Gwen said. "I thought it was the Unseelie after me again, so Rhys checked in with the Seelie Court. They didn't know anything, but they're still looking into it."

"In the meantime, it occurred to me that it could have been the same person who'd taken Harper Sinclair," Rhys said. "Then it took a little convincing to get Gwen on board with this."

That must have been what they'd been so tensely discussing earlier at the bar. It pissed me off that we'd lost two days—this minion chick could be anywhere by now—but I understood. I just hoped that even if the minion had fled town, that maybe we'd find something on Mount Mae.

But first, I needed to notify the Court, and they'd probably want to discuss and plan.

"I'll be in touch soon," I said, before drinking my bourbon in one long pull. Hell—I wasn't about to leave free booze untouched.

Tase threw his back, and we left. I jogged down the metal stairs, feeling energized despite it being nearly four in the morning. The full moon—the cold moon—was only a few days away, and she was calling to me.

And we had a lead. The first real thing to go on since this all started. Maybe by this time tomorrow, we'd have Harper back, safe and sound, the Collector facing trial, and Michaela and Xandru's wedding back on schedule.

Or maybe I was being an optimistic idiot.

CHAPTER 18

HARPER

I awoke blanketed by shadows, an inky face hovering above mine. No eyes. It took everything I had not to scream.

"What did you do to me?" I whispered, my voice raspy with fear. There was no way I would have fallen asleep on my own. Not here. Not held in captivity by the one person I'd been tasked with helping to find.

My hands pushed at the shadows, surprised to discover that they had some substance to them. Not the way a person would, obviously. They felt different than a person, but I could still *feel* them. Which was more than I'd been able to do before. They felt like a cotton ball dipped in warm water.

Were my abilities with them growing? Had they felt like this before?

"*Harper.*" The shadows' voices were strange, possessive, and yet somewhat affectionate. It was disconcerting but oddly reassuring. The shadows were a moving quilt keeping me warm, from the inside out. As if I was drinking a warm cup of hot cocoa.

"That's because they're drawn to your energy. To anyone else, they'd just feel like walking through a cold spot." From the corner of the room, the creepy ass doll watched me.

I looked everywhere except at her, my heart thudding against my rib cage as my eyes traveled around the room. Ignoring the doll wasn't going to make her disappear, but not seeing her made her presence somewhat easier to deal with. Just like hiding under a blanket when I was a kid didn't really make me invisible, no matter how much I tried convincing myself otherwise. It just made whatever was standing outside the blanket a little less scary.

The blue door the shadows had taken me through led to an empty space, the only piece of furniture inside a bare mattress. The floors were white marble, the walls made of yellow brick. Exactly the way I'd imagine the yellow brick road in the *Wizard of Oz* to look. Such a sunny color for such a bizarre and wretched situation.

"What did you do to me?" I repeated, my question aimed at the doll and the Collector who was controlling it.

"You slept," the doll answered simply, frowning, as if my question offended her somehow.

"Did you drug me?"

She sighed. "Aren't you more interested in your shadow pets, Harper? Ask me about those instead."

I pushed at the wall of blackness covering me like a cloak, and the shadows' embrace loosened. "They aren't pets."

"For you, they could be. Feral, unpredictable pets, but pets nonetheless. Like obedient little shadow puppets." She laughed softly, as if amused by the imagery she'd painted. "They would protect you if you opened yourself up to them. You've only let yourself call on them. But you've never really controlled them. It's a shame. All of that power at your fingertips, and you hold yourself back. Why?"

The doll moved from one corner of the room to the next, so fast she was a green blur on yellow walls. Like grass trying to grow through the cracks in a yellow sidewalk. "Magic, Harper, can be a beautiful thing. Don't limit yourself."

Anger rose in me, a fire that consumed me, and the shadows jumped to attention. They scattered, leaving me and rising, on alert, to a ceiling made of the same brick as the walls. Black on yellow, like an eclipse covering the sun.

"Is that why I'm here? So you can use me?" My powers came from a dark place. Letting myself go completely meant giving the darkness free rein. That wasn't safe or healthy for anybody.

"You're thinking too much," the doll replied, moving to the end of the bed. Only her head cleared the mattress, and I scooted backward, my back sliding up the brick wall behind me, scraping my flesh. "Control them, Harper."

Despite how scary she was—her glowing green eyes watching me as her small doll-like hand appeared on the bed—my anger was too fresh to completely give in to my fear. "I won't do it."

The doll's eyes went black, devoid of all emotion. "You only hurt yourself."

My body grew heavy, so heavy I had trouble lifting my arms and legs. It even hurt to breathe. This was it. The Collector had brought me here to die. Nothing else made any sense.

The doll laughed, practically skipping to the blue door. "Do you think you're the only one I took? If you don't want to use your powers, then someone's going to die." Black eyes found mine. "Isn't that what you're most afraid of, Harper? Losing the ones you love?"

I screamed, but no sound came out. It felt like I was under water, a hard current fighting against me.

Who? I asked, but the question never left my mouth. It echoed inside my head. Who did the Collector have? *Who?*

I didn't think I could live with that kind of guilt. The Collector was right. Losing people I was supposed to protect, especially those I cared about, was my biggest fear.

"I'd learn how to use those powers quickly, Harper Sinclair. Or someone is going to die soon."

I tried throwing myself at her, but I only managed to get my legs off the side of the bed. My feet, which had been sporting boots before I came into this room, were now bare.

Why was it this hard to move? Why had the Collector allowed me to rest and then taken away my energy?

"Life is unpredictable," the doll said suddenly. "It gives you hope, then it takes it away. Just like that. It isn't about how much strength you have. It's about how much trust you have in yourself."

In my head, I summoned the shadows, pleading with them to attack. They rallied, their anger causing the air to heat, their dark forms charging toward the doll in a dive that would make any predatory bird proud. Deafening screeches filled the room.

The doll laughed, cold and unemotional, her hand lifting.

The shadows flew backwards, as if thrown away, their screeches cut short.

"Did you think they would bother me?" the doll asked.

Hopelessness crushed me, the feeling so raw, it made my heart burn. She talked about how big my powers were, but had no trouble stopping me.

"You have to fail to know how to succeed." With one final look, the doll left, leaving me and the shadows shivering on an old mattress in a yellow room.

The Collector was full of ancient advice and cruel intentions.

I wanted nothing more than to give up, to curl up into a ball on the bed and hope for it to swallow me whole. But one look at the shadows, at the shivering mass I knew was acting this way because of me, and I touched my bare feet tentatively against the cold marble floor.

"*Harper,*" the shadows whispered.

I pitied the shadows. They were tortured spirits, their world nothing more than suffering and hurting others based on whoever commanded them to do it. It had made them dangerous, restless, and mean, the kind of darkness you'd expect to find in a poltergeist haunting.

That's essentially what the shadows were. A mass of malevolent energy, most of them the spirits of evil beings who once walked the earth with no chance now of redemption. Others were demons. And no one pitied them. They'd gotten what they deserved, creatures who could never and would never understand what light and love was.

I pitied them. It was hard not to pity something you'd lived your whole life knowing was with you. Rather than guardian angels, I'd had guardian demons I was too afraid to access. Because using them wrong meant I could hurt people. Using them wrong meant I could predict people's deaths.

I'd let the shadows down. I was letting everyone down.

My body wasn't as heavy as it was when the doll was in the room, but it also wasn't normal. It was like I was walking across mud, the ground sucking at my feet, once I left the bed and stumbled toward the door.

My vision blurred, the corners becoming soft and full of illusion, as if even my head was under water, my eyes open beneath the waves. In this alternate blurry-vision world, the shadows glowed. They were colorful rather than dark. Tempting.

"What?" I breathed.

The Collector was doing something to me. I wasn't sure what it was, but I feared what he was making me become and what he planned to use me for.

An image of my mother appeared in my head, the way she'd looked when she'd been pregnant with me and standing before a demoness in New Orleans, Louisiana, begging the demon to save her unborn baby's life. It was the moment before the demoness had shoved a necromancer's athame into my mother's womb, saving me, dooming my mother, and forever complicating my life.

A necromancer's athame.

This wasn't the first time I'd thought of the circumstances of my birth. It wasn't even the first time I'd thought of the athame, but I'd never had a reason to explore it before.

Wrenching open the blue door, I stumbled through, my bare feet and knees hitting wooden floors full of splinters. The hallway stretched out before me, and for the first time, I realized I was wearing the same old-fashioned gown I'd been wearing in a nightmare before coming here. I was inside my dream, but this time there was no escape from it.

"*We told you,*" the shadows whispered.

Reality slammed into me. They *had* been trying to help me. They'd been trying to warn me of my future.

Blood seeped from my hands and my feet, and the weird dollhouse

I was trapped in seemed to breathe in satisfaction. It was feeding off me.

My gaze drifted to the red door, the same one from my dream. "Was that the one where I would have discovered my future?" I asked the shadows. My voice sounded odd even to me, as if it had been pre-recorded and then played back in slow-motion at a deeper pitch.

"*Yes,*" they replied as one.

If the red door had told my future then, would it do the same now? Could I help myself and the people I cared about? Could I actually be someone Addie and the rest of the team could rely on? At the moment, I was closer than any of them to the Collector.

The necromancer's athame.

I'd been told by an angel, a Seraph, what being stabbed by the athame had done to me, what mixing its powers with my natural psychic abilities had done.

I didn't have a clue how to do any of it outside of summoning the shadows and talking with the dead.

I swallowed hard. "The red door?" I asked. Fear crawled like spiders over my skin, nipping my flesh and taunting me.

The shadows circled me. "*The red door,*" they repeated.

Nothing I'd ever learned about myself had been good.

I was getting used to nightmares.

Standing was impossible, the weight of my body too much to lift. I had to crawl toward the red door, the scrapes on my hands, knees, and legs growing worse, the splinters wedging themselves into my flesh. Breathing became an art form. One breath in, one exhale out.

Shadows circled my head, like a crown resting on their fallen queen.

The red door, when I finally reached it, had grown to twice its size.

"*Larger than life,*" the shadows whispered.

It didn't take much deductive reasoning to determine what the words meant. The door appeared the way I saw it: red and larger than life. Not because it was actually red and larger than life. To someone else kneeling before it, it might appear as something else entirely. I would be much more comfortable with someone else's door.

The shadows helped me open it, but I had to give them permission to do so, and the creak it made when it swung open was loud and unforgiving.

On the other side was utter darkness. A black hole I knew I couldn't escape from.

"You were never meant to escape. Embrace it." Out of nowhere, the Collector's voice echoed, sounding giddy. Satisfied. And I wondered if it was because I was giving him what he wanted.

As much as I wanted to leave this place, the only way I could help my team now was to figure out what the Collector truly wanted. No matter the cost to me.

I propelled my heavy body through the door, prepared for the worst and hoping for the lesser evil.

What I found in the darkness was what I least expected: acceptance.

CHAPTER 19

MICAH

I didn't think it was possible to love someone this way. From the moment I'd committed to protecting Holly with my life, I hadn't allowed for anything to distract me from my holiest of missions.

Yet here I was, watching the beautiful brunette add the final touches on her Christmas window display. This year she'd decked out her store with a snowflake theme, snowmen dancing about with the words "some people are worth melting for" hanging above them on a cute blue and white sign.

Sedona had truly outdone herself with her creativity. She'd argue with me, saying that it was another fluke, but I knew better. She took great pride in bringing magic to those passing Shelf Indulgence. The display had already drawn a crowd.

"You ever going to tell me what's going on?" She didn't look away from the snowman whose scarf she was still tweaking so it sat right. "And don't bother coming up with a lie. I know something's wrong. I've just been waiting for you to broach the subject."

There was an underlying tone to her comments that let me know she was done being patient. I didn't blame her. I'd remained quiet about this situation with the Collector and the group of people Addie had brought together. I wasn't used to having someone in my life to share the burden with.

Yet every time I'd gone to talk with my empathic girlfriend, the words didn't quite leave my mouth. All I could see was bringing her into more danger, more ways for me to lose her. The thought of Sedona being involved, being within arm's reach of the Collector, stirred up a different kind of fear within me.

"Everything's fine," I lied, hoping that she'd accept my flimsy response without questioning it.

She didn't. "Liar, liar, pants on fire." This time she did turn to look at me. Her smile dazzled me. "Try again, Micah. This time, how about the truth?"

I took in a deep breath and flashed her my most convincing grin. "No using your gifts, sweetheart." It was a deflection and I didn't care. We were dealing with a deity—one that terrified the angels and had me on edge ever since uncovering the truth. "I'd tell you if there was something to worry about."

Another huge, fat lie. They were beginning to pile up again.

I knew the second she stopped fiddling with her display and leveled me with the full weight of her stare that she wasn't buying any of the bullshit I was dishing out.

"Micah Westbrook," she continued sternly. "Wait, do you have a middle name, because I feel like what I'm about to say requires me to three-name you." Damn, she looked sexy when she was trying to be serious.

"Nothing that you'd be able to pronounce correctly," I teased back. "Enochian can be tricky for those who don't use it as their native tongue." She'd come over to where I was standing, watching her like I did—marveling that such a gorgeous creature could see beyond my defenses and touch my heart.

"Then spill," she demanded as she peered up at me. The earnestness in her gaze all but shattered my resolve to keep her as far away from danger as possible. The Collector had already gotten too close. He'd shown me how easily he could reach her.

But would keeping her in the dark actually keep her safe? It was the voice inside that warred with every decision I made. It was loud and insistent—relentlessly unravelling any argument I answered with.

Cupping her face with my hand, I took a few precious moments to appreciate the softness in her features. She'd finally healed from both attacks, and I'd noticed that she'd stopped looking over her shoulder every time she got spooked. Did I really want to throw her back into those fears again?

"Okay," I began, my fingers tracing over her cheeks. "You're right. Something big is happening, and before you yell at me, I didn't keep it from you because I didn't think you could handle it."

She interrupted me. "You didn't want to burden me." Her gaze drifted over to where the wall between Shelf Indulgence and Coffee Haven had been blasted. We'd fixed the hole as best we could, but it was a bold reminder of how close things had gotten months ago. "I get it. Being in a relationship, though, means that you don't have to face things alone. You know that, right? You don't have to be alone unless you choose to."

Sedona had such a giving heart—the purity of it always reminded me that there was still goodness in the world, despite the chaos.

"The Collector is still in town."

I studied her features, watching to see how she processed my confession.

"I know. What are you doing about it?" She'd shared that revelation so casually that it almost made me double-take.

"You know? For how long?" I shouldn't have doubted her. She was a powerful empath, even though she didn't like to explore the gifts and magic she'd been born with. Even if she hadn't known the details, there'd been a pervasive sense of ominous dread in the air.

"Since you started acting weird and going out alone at night. Whenever I'd ask, you would give me some random excuse." There was that dazzling smile again. "You can't lie to an empath, Micah. You're doubly screwed when that empath is your girlfriend." She gripped the front of my shirt and stepped into my embrace. "How bad is it? Do you need my help?"

The thought of her facing the Collector turned my blood cold.

"Promise me you will stay as far away as possible. This is going to get messy. We're facing a deity from another realm, and I can't do what's necessary if I'm worrying about you. I need you to take care of Holly should something go wrong."

I rubbed my hand up and down the small of her back. Part of me wished that we could stand like this forever and that we were a normal couple with regular problems like bills, long work hours, and the last-minute scrambling to get everything ready for Christmas.

We weren't those people, though.

Havenwood Falls wasn't that town.

"When?" With one word, Sedona had cut through all the lead-up. She understood that the time had come.

"Now." My hand automatically reached for my phone. Addie had texted me earlier about meeting with the Court because, finally, they had a real solid lead. I'd been on my way but had stopped for one last look at the woman who laid claim to my soul. Holly was upstairs visiting with Maxwell, the ghost sharing stories from his past with her.

A steely emotion filled her gaze as she looked up at me again. Standing on her tiptoes, Sedona feathered a tender kiss on my lips. "Be careful. Do whatever you need to do, then come home to me."

I tightened my arms around her. "I love you, Sedona Mathews."

Then, cradling her face between my hands, I sealed my words with a kiss that held every promise I could ever make her. It was fierce, yet gentle. It melted away my fears as I captured her hope and faith. They would buoy me up as I joined the others to face the Collector.

"Be safe," she whispered again.

"Always."

And I would do my best to ensure I kept my word.

ADDIE'S EYES lit up when I arrived at the Court meeting. The session was already underway, and as I glanced up at the dais, I saw Saundra Beaumont, Michaela Petran, Barbie Stuart, Ric Kasun, and the rest sitting there, wearing serious expressions.

A solemn air filled the room.

Gwen stood before them, her back to the small group sitting in the rowed chairs. She was in the middle of sharing the information she'd gathered, so instead of interrupting, I slid into the nearest empty seat.

"Sorry, I'm late," I whispered, leaning forward to see Tase, Elias, and Rhys—members of the group that Addie had assembled. They also wore similar dark countenances.

"You haven't missed too much. Just formalities and Gwen," she answered in hushed tones. "Hopefully after tonight, we'll have a clearer plan of action." Addie's gaze didn't once leave those talking amongst themselves up on the dais. "I'm getting tired of waiting around."

It was a sentiment I was painfully acquainted with as well.

I'd allowed my frustrations over how slow things were going cloud my ability to see reason. After a lifetime of working alone, I was now part of a team. We would face the threat together.

I looked over at the pretty woman who'd started speaking again. She held all our attention.

"I had a run-in with someone who I thought was the Collector. The sneaky bitch tried to fool me by shape-shifting into Rhys so she could take me to her master." She said the last word like it tasted of pure filth.

"Yet you're still standing here," Saundra replied, looking impressed that she'd somehow managed to thwart the attempt. I'd learned the lesson not to ever judge a book by its cover, but that's exactly what I'd done with the young woman. The angels were terrified, yet Gwen had walked away unscathed.

Addie whispered to me, "Gwen has a kickass set of skills, and by skills, I mean wicked tattoos that come to life."

I furrowed my brow, my gaze dropping to study the woman's inkwork. Like Addie, she had many tattoos, but of what I could see peeking from her collar and sleeves, nothing stood out as something that could protect her from the Collector.

"Do I want to know where?" I uttered to the side, just loud enough for Addie to snort, and Rhys to throw me a warning glare. I guess he didn't like me thinking about his girlfriend's body. In my defense, I was only interested in one that may help in my own mission.

"You can't expect a lady to reveal her secrets," Gwen murmured.

Someone from the dais cleared their throat. We were being disruptive.

"Not to shatter anyone's illusions about my abilities, but I'm pretty sure I walked away because I wasn't going up against the Collector. Addie, Tase, and the rest of us decided this chick must be a minion."

That made a lot more sense now. This deity would definitely send out feelers before personally striking. Why risk exposure if they could sacrifice other willing fools?

That sent a ripple through the room as everyone slowly nodded.

"So, we're all in agreement that our next step is to find this lackey and have them lead us to this deity we know as the Collector?" I just wanted to be sure we were all on the same page. We were finally getting somewhere.

Saundra Beaumont answered me, the witch's sharp voice revealing her own impatience. "Yes, Mr. Westbrook."

Her response was clipped, which was partly my fault. I hadn't minced words in the other meetings I'd demanded with them. I'd walked the very thin line between persistent and disrespectful with them, challenging their authority. Hopefully, once this was all over, that damage might be repaired.

That was when another thought surfaced—one that sent chills up my spine.

"Are we prepared to follow the Collector to wherever his home realm is?"

Several Court members answered with a prompt yes.

Elias remained quiet, but his visage explained exactly what he was thinking as his face drained of color. As a fellow angel, even though fallen, he knew what that meant and the logistics it would take to orchestrate such an attack. Judging from his expression, the thought had also chilled him to his core. I wanted to commiserate with him. We could be going to a gunfight with nothing but a finger pointed like a gun.

We had to believe that we were enough to fight and destroy the deity.

"You said *other* realm, right?" Elias repeated.

"We are so screwed," Tase muttered.

Addie stood and turned, to address both the Court and our group in the audience. "Don't whine like you're not excited about fighting this thing. If the Collector is threatening this town, we all stand to lose something or someone we love when it gets messy." Addie's expression went stone-cold serious. "And trust me, this is going to get bad if we don't act now."

"Gwen, can you please give us all a description of the perp?" Sheriff Ric Kasun asked, bringing the discussion and meeting back on topic. There was a lot that we still didn't know, but we did have a solid lead—a reason to hold faith and not give up. "The person who attacked you?"

We all sat up straighter, hoping that whatever she said might stir up something we could all work on. This was another benefit of working with a group—we had a collective knowledge base we could all draw on. Each of us spent time out and about in town. Perhaps we'd also encountered this mystery person.

Gwen closed her eyes, rubbing her temples with her fingers. She began describing the female who'd pretended to be her boyfriend, the way she looked when the charade was finally up.

Ric nodded encouragingly at Gwen, the gesture lost on her because she couldn't see it. "Try to remember mannerisms, sounds, smells can even help trigger memory. No detail is insignificant."

That was something I'd learned rather quickly—that no detail was too small, because it was often the subtle nuances that provided the breakthrough. It wasn't always about fireworks and what made the loudest noise.

Concentrating again, Gwen flicked out her hand as though she was shooing someone away. "She wore a copper bracelet," she finally said. "I got a peek at it when she cast her spell." She bit her bottom lip, her left eye squinting, her eyes still shut. "And there was a stone in the center of it . . . a . . ." This time she scrunched up her mouth.

She didn't need to worry.

I knew who she was talking about. Well, I knew what kind of creature her attacker was, because the angels had been whispering it.

"I know who it is," I blurted, feeling the truth thunder through me. "Or what, anyway. The Collector has an empusa working for them, doing his dirty work."

There was a reaction on the dais as several Court members exchanged curious glances.

Gwen opened her eyes and looked at me with skepticism. "You got all that from me saying she wore a bracelet?"

Everyone stared at me.

I nodded, getting up again and coming to stand beside Gwen. "That stone was a bloodstone." Just to make sure, I quickly scanned the room and grabbed the pen and notebook Addie had been using to scribble down notes from the meeting. I began drawing the bracelet design, stopping only when I was satisfied. "This look familiar?"

"Well, you're no Picasso, but yeah. That's it!" She traced the outline of my drawing before walking forward and handing Saundra the notebook.

Once she'd seen it, Ms. Beaumont passed it along to her fellow court members. "There's one empusa we know of in town. She actually had the gall to request residency not too long ago. How did we not know?"

Barbie was the last to view my sketch. "So we find this creature, and then she leads us to her boss. Simple enough." Her comments earned a round of laughter from everyone. There was nothing easy about this.

"Harper." That one name filled Elias's voice with pain and anger. It was a reminder that so much was at stake here. Not that we needed one.

"Any clue where she's staying?" Rhys asked. He hadn't moved from where he'd been sitting. "If she knows we're on to her, she could skip town before we get the chance to interrogate her."

"Senora Graves—she'd been staying at my inn," Michaela said, her face pale. "She checked out a couple of days ago, but she said she was staying in town, with a friend."

"Wait," Tase chimed in. "Are you telling me this woman has been here all along. Watching. Listening. Pretending to be a part of this town. All while scheming with the Collector?"

It sounded too good to be true . . . too bizarre to accept. Even this had me reeling.

"She can shapeshift," Gwen said. "She could've been anyone."

"Does anybody know who this friend is?" Barbie Stuart asked.

Addie joined me and Gwen before the dais, an excited gleam in her eyes. She also looked as though she was trying to keep up with the thoughts in her head. "I did her paperwork when she applied for residency. Montezuma Tayute vouched for her, but in my dealings with him and SIN on this matter, I don't think he has any idea about her involvement with this, and she's not staying with him. But she's registered, so—"

"So we can find her through her tattoo," Ric finished for her.

Addie nodded. "Yes, we can."

There was so much satisfaction filling that admission.

"And then what?" he continued, leaning forward. I'd heard how formidable he was in a fight, that as a werewolf, he could tear someone limb from limb without breaking a sweat. I'd worked somewhat closely with him when Sedona and Holly had been attacked in Shelf Indulgence. He'd been open to my being involved in the beginning, but I was pretty sure I'd worn that welcome out quickly. Not that I cared. If there was one commonality we did share, it was our belief in justice and protection.

"Do we have the Court's permission to move forward on this new information?" Addie asked, cutting to the chase. "We know who and what Gwen's attacker was. We also know how to find her. Even if we have no proof that she's connected to the Collector, what she did to Gwen is a reason right there to bring her in."

The Court leaders spoke briefly amongst themselves, whispering in hushed tones.

"Please tell me you're honestly not going to wait for their approval should they wish to exercise further caution," I murmured to Addie, careful not to speak too loudly.

"Not a chance in hell," came her rebellious answer. It seemed like we were cut from the same cloth—willing to sacrifice whatever it took to get the job done.

I chuckled beneath my breath. "I like you, Addie Beaumont."

She nudged my shoulder warmly. "Right back atcha, Micah Westbrook."

The clearing of Saundra's throat drew our attention again. "Adelaide, go ahead with bringing this Ms. Graves in for questioning. While I'd like to say use any force necessary to get the task done, please use discretion. Killing her won't bring us any closer to locating Harper or the Collector."

Tase, Rhys, and Elias grunted loudly behind us. I was sure they were each itching to get their hands on the empusa. The difficult part would be reining in the need to retaliate for the assaults and attacks.

The next ten minutes or so were spent finalizing the plan Addie laid out—of our using magic and locating the lackey via the mandatory residency tattoo and then confronting her. We were finally heading in the right direction, and hopefully it wouldn't be too long before we had the answers we sought.

As we filed out of the room, we were one in purpose.

It was time to get ready to battle the threat that had been so elusive until now.

It was time to go confront Senora Graves.

It was time to find the Collector, and silence him forever.

CHAPTER 20

SENORA

*A*fter the fiasco with Gwen Facharro, I'd been keeping a low profile. The girl saw me. If someone pressed her, she could give a fairly accurate description—my first mistake, revealing myself.

So I took precautions. I waited until nightfall before venturing out, and when I did, I transported to locations, shifting into another persona. For the first time, I was grateful that Izzie was close by. With her around, I didn't have to dine on roadkill. She hunted for small animals to keep me fed. Actually, it was part of the bargain I made with her. I'd keep my mouth away from her dog, Zoid, as long as she brought me fresh food.

My days had fallen into this weird routine. I'd take on the persona of a registered tourist and visit the different shops, restaurants, and bars listening for information. Then I'd transport to Izzie and Hunter's place, shifted back to my normal human guise, and entered their house. After two days of this, I was ready to scream.

One spot I didn't dare go was the Dirty Knuckle. Fear kept me out of the bar. I imagined Gwen recognizing me despite my disguise. She probably had another magical tattoo waiting to take out my ass. Or maybe her protector had a gory fate in mind for me. Either way, I needed to stay clear of the pub.

All of this was because of the Collector and his sidekick—two individuals I hadn't heard from since the night I botched the job. Well, that was a lie. Every time I tried to leave town, a message appeared on my phone warning me not to try it. Something told me that Rachelle delighted in sending me the random video clips of me feasting on the dark fae.

It had gotten so bad that the mere thought dispatched the recording. Right now, I was staring at myself, arm deep in the Unseelie's core. Blood dripped from my chin, and my eyes glazed over like a drug addict getting a fix. I'd never realized how gruesome I looked while eating.

"You okay?" Izzie asked as she sat across from me in Hunter's great room. A large fireplace was lit, keeping the space warm against the Colorado chill—another reason I wanted to leave town.

I scowled down at the screen for another minute before tucking it back in my pocket. "Fine. Just dealing with some shit."

"Want to talk about it?" Izzie curled up in the oversized leather armchair with a cup of something that smelled like mint and chocolate.

I wished I could tell Izzie about my situation. She might be able to help me figure out a solution. Despite the lucrative pay, I'd come to regret my affiliation with the Collector. Sadly, I didn't see a positive outcome for me. If I walked away, he'd give me up to the Court of the Sun and the Moon, Havenwood Falls' self-righteous governing body. After our last meeting, I got the sincere impression that none of those beings liked me. It was probably why they were dragging their feet about approving my residency request. With my luck and the shit I'd done—and might do—they'd probably reserved a corner in the Infernum for me. An unsettling thought.

"Senora?"

Izzie's voice snagged my attention. No matter how much I wanted to, I couldn't involve my friend. She didn't deserve to get caught up in evil. She had a bright future with a hot and intelligent shifter. "It's best that I don't talk about it."

Izzie narrowed her eyes. "Really?" She folded her arms over her chest. "Are you in trouble?"

My head jerked up. "No! Why would you ask that?"

She shrugged. "Just a feeling I've been having—a bad vibe or something heinous. And Baba, Hunter's grandfather, said he had an ominous dream the other night. He said it felt like a message."

"Oh?" I'd forgotten about the nagual shaman. The last thing I needed was for him to figure out what I was doing or whom I was associating with. "About?"

"It was cryptic." Izzie set her cup on a nearby end table. "Something about a girl and a red door."

I breathed a little easier. No red doors, that I knew of, in the Collector's estate. "Sounds like nonsense."

Izzie shook her head. "Baba was very insistent about his vision. He mentioned an angel—someone who chose to fall from grace—who was pissed and frustrated because he'd lost somebody. A child he was sworn to protect."

A child? Well, that wasn't anything about me or my business with the Collector. I drew the line with kids. It was the reason I had against stealing the artifact from the Fairchild girl. Youth were innocent. They —whether human or supe—didn't ask to come into this world. They didn't ask to become sacrifices for evil either. As far as I was concerned, whoever this kid was that the shaman saw was safe from me.

Nervously, I pushed to my feet. It was dark and time for me to leave. "Like I said, it's nonsense. I wouldn't read much into it."

But I did. I'd felt that same foreboding. It kept me awake at night. It was time to call in a favor.

I transported to the exterior of the SIN clubhouse. As usual, there were plenty of bikes and a few trucks in the parking lot. Perusing the area, I saw the bike for the person I came to see. I removed my phone and sent him a text message. Within minutes, the door yawned open, and the tall nagual stepped out.

"Senora?" Monte put his hands on his hips and looked side to side.

"I'm here," I said as I left the safety of the shadows. "Is there some place we can talk?"

He looked down his nose and sneered. "Here is good."

I batted my eyelashes. "I was hoping for a little warmth."

He sauntered over to his bike and passed me a helmet. "We can go back to my place."

The shifter lived in a sad little Victorian house on the north side of town. The place was in desperate need of some tender loving care. When he opened the plain wooden door, I couldn't tell whether he was moving in or out. Boxes and tissue paper were scattered around the narrow space. A mattress covered in plastic rested against a wall. Sofa cushions lay on the floor. I glanced at all the mess and then at him.

"Going someplace?"

"Naw. I'm still getting settled. I haven't figured out what I want to do with it yet." Monte weaved around a stack of crates and disappeared through an opening toward the back of the room.

I carefully stepped around an open box and followed behind him into a kitchen. "I need some information."

He faced me and leaned his butt against the sink. "Depends on what it is."

The shifter's voice was flippant.

"Wait just a minute. I helped you and—"

"As I recall, your assistance was paid for, and then I vouched for you with the Court." He folded his arms over his chest and raised a hand to his chin. "I think Hunter and me are all paid up on our debt with you."

I crossed my arms and tapped my foot on his linoleum floor. Nobody pushed me to the side until I was ready to end the relationship. "Perhaps I should tell the Court about how SIN got rid of Kazimir Chekhov. I'm guessing your charter only exists as long as you live like Boy Scouts within town limits."

The shifter glared, silently daring me.

"Maybe the club gets to remain. I seriously doubt if the president will let you or Hunter continue your membership."

Monte's eyes flicked toward the ceiling, and then he exhaled loudly. "What do you want, Senora?"

He was going to get lucky, but not with that attitude. "Know anyone on the Court?"

Monte didn't speak, just bobbed his head.

"My residency hasn't been approved. Do you know why?"

He pursed his lips before shaking his head. "Lately, the Court has gotten pickier. With the disappearance of a few residents, they're being more thorough before granting approval."

What the hell did that mean?

"Like what?" I pressed as my temper flared. "Bank accounts, property records, what? I don't keep a paper trail."

Monte raised an eyebrow. "Maybe that's the problem—nothing to substantiate who you are. Then again, there is the simple fact that you're an empusa."

"And what do you mean by that?" I yelled and fisted my hands. My blood boiled within my veins.

Monte held up a palm. "Calm down. I only meant that you're someone the Court would definitely need to check out more closely." He chuckled. "Can't have you eating up the town's residents."

Ordinarily, that comment would have gotten a swift retaliation, but I couldn't afford to eat someone who would be missed. What if he knew I was responsible for the missing fae? Instead, I plastered a smile on my face. "I don't just randomly feast on people."

Major lie. It was how my kind operated. Most empusai don't act like a supernatural hit woman—devouring marks.

Monte leveled me with a look that said he saw through the untruth. His brow furrowed momentarily. "Tell me something, Senora."

"What?"

"How long have you been *2HecateNBack*?"

I flinched—that was my identity on the dark net. How in the hell did he find out? My mouth opened and closed.

"Don't bother denying it," Monte said calmly. "I stumbled across your signature while checking out something else."

My shoulders slumped. "I haven't done anything."

He grinned slyly.

Fuck! He baited me, and I fell for it. Thanks to the Collector keeping my thoughts occupied, I was slipping. "I give up. What's going on?"

Monte scrubbed a hand over his face. "I'm not sure. All I can say is that someone in the Court is investigating something dark. My suggestion is that you stay off the dark net."

"Why are you telling me this?"

"Because your identity is being used by somebody. If I can figure it out, it won't take long before someone else does."

Rachelle.

"What's the person looking for?"

"Artifacts."

I thanked Monte for his information and left. It was time to pay a visit to a certain supernatural Barbie.

THE DOOR STOOD OPEN, waiting for me to enter the Collector's estate. Anger clouded my judgment, and I stormed in. Wrong move. I hit an invisible wall. When I turned to retrace my steps, I couldn't go forward. I was surrounded by an unseen barrier.

Heels clicked across the floor. I looked up to see Rachelle smiling.

"Let me out of here."

"Not until we have a little discussion."

"About?"

"You haven't completed your job."

I pushed my shoulders back and stood taller. "I don't work for you."

"True, but we do work on the same side. You were told to go after Gwen, and you failed. You were supposed to try again."

I folded my arms. "You want her so bad? You go after her. Maybe you could fight against an angry hawk or magically appearing weapons."

Rachelle tsked. "You really don't . . ."

Her voice trailed off as the Collector swept into the room. "That's enough, Rachelle. Free the empusa."

Rachelle flicked her wrist, and the barrier disappeared. I tested the space in front of me before walking forward. She scowled at me and then walked out the front door. The Collector turned his head in my direction.

"We need to talk," I said.

The Collector nodded and then glided into the drawing room. "I understand your apprehension, not wanting to go after Gwen."

I sighed and collapsed on the chair. "Good. I can't—"

"Problem is," the Collector continued without acknowledging me, "you've been exposed. Not collecting Gwen isn't an option."

"I can't do it," I admitted. My track record of perfection had been shattered with this being, but I no longer cared. I just wanted to be done with it. "Send Rachelle."

My employer lifted a gloved hand and adjusted the cloak hiding his face. In a deeper, raspier voice than usual, he said, "The decision is yours to make. But know this—you owe me merchandise. You will deliver."

Butterflies, moths, or bats—who knows—danced in my stomach as beads of sweat trickled down my back. *Stay strong*, I told myself. *Finish the job and then get the hell out of this town.*

"If you have something—"

"Of course I do." He pointed to the table beside me.

I lifted the large-sized envelope, opened it, and poured the contents into my lap. There were pictures of a girl with long brown hair and hazel eyes. In one photo, she stood outside Shelf Indulgence —a bookstore in town. At her side was a rather stern-looking, attractive man. His signature was apparent even on paper.

I glanced up at the Collector. "You want me to go after a fallen angel?"

He shook his head.

There weren't any other figures in the pictures. I gasped. Surely, this fiend didn't want me to breach my one—my only—rule. My heart sank as he bobbed his head.

"The choice is yours, empusa. Bring me the Seelie fae or bring me the child."

That was where I had to draw the line. I didn't harm children. Never had. Never will. Call it a soft spot. I couldn't have kids—thanks

to that hellhound decades ago. So I looked out for the little ones. I'd
hurt anyone who didn't share my concern.

~

WEARY, I dragged my feet down the stone steps. It took all of my
strength to erect a wall around my thoughts. The effort was necessary
to keep the Collector out of my head. He couldn't know . . . He
wouldn't know.

Those thoughts followed me all the way down the side of Mount
Mae. I'd forgotten about hiding my persona. I'd forgotten that I was
supposed to transport wherever I was going. I didn't notice anything
but the shadows blocking my path. Dread crawled out of my stomach
and over my skin. That spot being saved for me in the Infernum?
Somebody just called my number.

A small group was gathered in front of me—Gwen and her
protector were part of the crowd. I sensed an angelic being, a
hellhound, and another witch. There was something else in the air I
recognized—beings primed for a fight.

My options were limited: fight or flee. Honestly, I'd never run
from a challenge in my life. Why start now? I held out my palms and
let the energy coalesce into fiery balls. The brunette—someone I
recognized—stepped forward, her lips moving in an incantation.

Well, that's just great. The witch wanted to test me. Fine. Time to
skip the dumb shit and fight the best way I could. I called forth one of
the few animals I shifted into—a black bear. Lumbering forward, I was
ready to put an end to whatever battle they offered.

Rhys came close, swinging a knife in each hand. One swipe of my
huge paw sent him sliding backward across the snow. He stopped with
one knee down, ready to come at me again when the angelic being—
incidentally, the man from the picture the Collector had just shown
me—crossed my path.

Seriously? Did they honestly believe an angel would stop me?
When the ground slipped from beneath my feet and my ass hit the

snow, I got my answer. I rose up on all fours and charged. He easily evaded the impact, and I collided with a rock.

Where the hell did that come from?

Looking over my shoulder, I saw the brunette. Undoubtedly, she moved it. Distracted, I didn't notice Gwen, but I did feel the prick of her arrow. In this form, it didn't slow me down.

Take out the protector. End him, and they'll focus on him. You can escape.

He crouched low, as if he heard my thoughts, and inched forward. I barreled toward him, moving so fast that I blurred. Mid-run I morphed back into human form. Energy coursed through my veins. When I stopped, I slung both balls of fire in his direction. Before the flames licked his flesh, a wall of armor separated us.

Gwen!

I was tired of this game. Obviously, so was the angel. He stepped toward me with his own flames.

Laughing out loud, I said, "You've got to be kidding. Do you think that's going to stop me?"

His lips quirked up. "Let's find out."

The angel's hands were engulfed in golden flames. Sparks flew across the distance, and I realized just what he'd used—*holy fire*. Much like the flames of Hell, holy fire was like baptizing a dark soul. It would obliterate me, making me wish I'd gone to the Infernum instead.

I dodged the embers. He mirrored my movements, getting closer. Quickly, I remembered everything I knew about holy fire—he had to touch me. Not happening. I picked up my pace and prepared to move, but couldn't. Tight ropes held me in place. When I glanced up, Gwen had a smug smile on her face.

Game over.

The angel and Gwen's protector grabbed my elbows and led me to a familiar truck—Rhys's truck. I knew exactly where we were going— at least I thought I did. Then Rhys pulled into a spot behind City Hall.

As they dragged me through a metal door, I struggled against the ropes. The angel was close by with the fucking fiery hands—a blatant reminder of what would happen if I broke free. We entered a sparsely decorated room—a dais up front, a few rows of chairs, and a desk in a corner. The brunette—Addie Beaumont, who'd registered me with the Court and done the tattoo—stopped in front of the picture painted on one of the walls. I blinked, and suddenly there was a door.

Somebody opened the cell and tossed me in. The door clanged shut behind me, then the ropes vanished. I stood and reached for the bars.

The angel said, "I wouldn't do that if I were you, unless you want to lose your hands."

I swung my head around, and the tip of my ponytail touched the metal. The smell of burnt hair filled the air. Although the bars surrounding me appeared impenetrable, they held magic just for me. Not good. I moved to the back of my cage and sat on the bench attached to the wall.

"So you're the Collector?" Addie said.

"No."

Gwen approached the bars. "Do you work for him?"

I sighed. "I did."

Rhys slammed his hand into the wall.

"Calm down, Rhys. Breaking your hand won't help us." Addie turned back to me. "Where's Harper?"

"What the hell is a Harper?"

"Who else is working for the Collector besides Rachelle?"

Propping my elbows up on my thighs, I said, "Look, I can tell you everything you want to know . . . for a price."

"How about you tell us what we need to know, empusa, and we won't send your ass straight back to Hell?" barked the fallen angel. His hands lit up with holy fire. "Or we could just end you right now."

Well, that was an interesting proposition. I had no intention of meeting a fiery death or taking a trip to Hell. Maybe money wasn't that important. "Fine. I'll tell you what you want."

When the fallen angel was slow to extinguish his hands, Addie said, "Micah."

The holy fire vanished.

"Okay, empusa. We're listening," she said.

I rubbed a spot on my leather pants and considered what I should say. "I can take you to the Collector, but I need some reassurances."

"Like?" said Rhys.

Lifting my head, I stared back at him. "The Collector is truly evil. He has something dark planned for your town, but don't ask me what, because I don't know."

"Send her to the Infernum," the Micah said. "She knows nothing."

He was starting to work my nerves. Clenching my jaw, I pushed back my anger. "You might want to know who his next target is, angel. She's somebody you've sworn to protect." I glanced over at Gwen. "He wanted me to go after you again. When I refused, he assigned the task to someone else."

Gwen asked, "Who?"

"A supernatural Barbie."

The group exchanged curious glances before Addie said, "She looks like me."

"Yeah, that's Rachelle."

Addie clenched her fists and glanced at the angel before turning back to me. "We'll have to take this to the Court, but I'm sure they'll honor your request—keep you out of the Infernum—as long as you help us."

It wasn't money, but for a change I'd had enough of exchanging services for cash. Maybe it was time to value an unencumbered lifestyle. "Fine. Let me out of this makeshift cage, and I'll take you directly to the Collector's mansion. But I'm telling you, the Magic Marker better have something stronger than a bow and arrow in her bag of tricks."

Addie said, "Not so fast. Is that everything?"

"Yeah. As far as I know. He's planning something evil. Rachelle would know more than I do."

CHAPTER 21

ADDIE

"You're sure about this?" I asked Gwen as several of us gathered in the basement of Soothing Sips.

The Blackstone witch hunters kept a secret armory under the wine-tasting store on the square, their weapons specially crafted and imbued with protection magic. They were the best magical weapons we had at our disposal to use for reasons just like this—to protect our town. Everyone was arming up, preparing to take on this Collector once and for all.

Gwen had volunteered to serve as our bait, since we knew Rachelle was looking for her.

At least, that was according to the empusa. There had been a single sighting of Shelly-slash-Rachelle two nights ago near Tragic Ink. Shelly disappeared as soon as she saw too many people near the tattoo studio and Gwen's apartment above it. They were strategically placed, so she might not have known they were guarding Gwen's place, but Shelly didn't take the chance to find out. This behavior seemed to confirm Senora's claim. It was all we had to go on, so we had to at least try.

Gwen rubbed her hand over her forearm, where Ethan lay quietly, and nodded. "You all better have my back, though."

I handed her the amulet I'd made. "We'll be right on your tail, even if she portals. If she does somehow manage to get away, though, as long as you have this, we'll be able to go right to you."

"And I'll always be right by your side," Rhys added. The Luna Coven would be doing a difficult camouflaging spell so he could be nearby Gwen without being seen or sensed in any way. There was no other way she could do this without us having an extremely pissed off Seelie warrior to deal with on top of everything else.

Gwen bounced on the balls of her feet with nervous energy. "It'll be okay," she muttered, I thought more to herself than to us.

"It will," I confirmed. I hoped. I didn't like the idea of putting her out there like that, but it was the only way we knew how to find the Collector. We hoped Rachelle would take us to him.

Senora claimed the Collector had an estate on the top of Mount Mae, to the east of the ski resort. The sheriff's department and Rusty, the ranger, scoured the whole mountain by land, and Mat, an owl shifter who patrolled the forests as Rusty's assistant, and Lawrence and Tristan Mills, frost dragon shifters, had surveyed from the air. Nobody had seen, smelled, or otherwise sensed a presence there. So either the Collector had an impenetrable cloak or Senora was lying.

It could very well be the latter, but she had a lot to lose, if that were the case. So the plan was to use Rachelle to penetrate that cloak —or take us to wherever the Collector really was. Even if she only took us to where they kept the people they collected, at least we could get Harper. Senora didn't know anything about Harper, but figured the Collector wanted her for a reason and she'd still be alive. Keeping her that way and bringing her home was more important than anything.

I glanced over at Elias, who stood in the corner, rocking on his heels. One fist was pressed into his other palm, his muscles bunched from wrist to neck. A scowl marred his face as he and Micah spoke with Tasha. She and Elias had become quick friends as they both were committed to saving Harper. Senora stood silently near them, magically bound to Elias. Because she knew the Collector's estate better than anyone here and she could shift into the Collector's shape, we were taking the risk of bringing her with us, hoping she could overcome any security challenges. If she tried to run, though, the spell binding her to Elias would stop her heart, and she'd drop dead on the spot.

We'd gathered everyone who'd agreed to help when the time came, and the basement armory was filled with large, muscular bodies and way too much testosterone for my liking.

Tase, Xandru, Liam, Savage, and others perused the available weapons spread out on a table in the center of the wood-paneled room and hanging on four walls. They studied and took swings with various pieces, selecting some and strapping them to their bodies in various ways. I'd already filled all the slots on a leather knife holster that crossed over my chest under my coat, but I planned to use my magic and the boost of strength and senses from my hellhound side.

Sheriff Kasun, Deputy Conall, and Rusty gathered in one corner, making their own plans.

Members of the Luna Coven were upstairs with Lilith Blackstone, who'd be on alert in case the Collector or his minions used any black magic.

Surveying them all and listening to their tense chatter, I had a sudden desire to disappear to my altar room and meditate.

"Deep breaths," Tase said quietly against my ear, suddenly standing behind me and leaning into me. His lips brushed over my lobe as he spoke. "Slow your heart and your breathing. Don't let them see you sweat. Or smell you. Or hear you."

Right. Because just about everyone here had heightened senses, and the last thing I needed was for them to doubt me. I couldn't afford to doubt myself.

His arm slid around my waist, and he pulled me close against him, helping to calm my heart, which he must have heard from across the room.

"We got this, Bean," he said. "We have a plan, and we all know it well. There's nothing more we can do but execute."

He was right, yet so wrong. We did have a plan, one we'd been working on for days, since capturing the empusa. She'd told us what she claimed to be all she knew, although none of it except Rachelle's description checked out. Nothing else could be verified, because the

Collector was just that good in covering his tracks and everything he did. So while we had a plan for finally getting to the Collector's estate—if it even existed—or to the Collector himself, the rest of our so-called plan was just a general strategy because we'd be going in blind.

Even if Senora gave us the truth about the estate, she admitted to only ever being in one room. She couldn't tell us anything else about the rest of the grounds—how big it was, if he actually lived there or not, where he kept the items he collected . . . or the people. We knew nothing about any kind of security system, defensive and offensive weapons at the Collector's disposal, how many others he may have there to protect him, or what the Collector himself was capable of doing. For shit's sake—he was a deity. His power could be potentially endless.

And if we fucked up? Harper's life was at stake. Potentially others' lives. Hell, he could easily wipe out our whole town. And then what? What would be his next target?

"Bean," Tase whispered, his hands moving up to my shoulders to massage them. "Freaking yourself out isn't going to help anything."

I nodded and returned my focus to my breathing. A slow count to five in, and an even slower count to seven out. Five in. Seven out. I mentally recited recent wins for the town and myself—Octavia the necromancer, Infiniti the girl from 2012, the settling in of new mountain lion and wolf shifters, an ice demon, a Marid djinn, and others. The Cold Moon Ball went off the other night with only a few minor hiccups, but nothing like last year, when Heidi Bennett had gone missing. And even Shade StormIron had managed to keep up his end of the bargain. The past several months had been eventful and stressful, but our people were strong, resilient, and determined for love to win. They'd each proven it in their individual stories—their own lives—and many were proving it now.

I looked around again at the people in the basement armory, now with a renewed sense of appreciation. They were all here not only to protect their closest loved ones, but to defend our town as a whole. They all understood just how unique and special Havenwood Falls was, how extraordinary our people were, and they were willing to put their lives on the line to ensure our home, our town, continued on.

They were not going to let some asshole god ruin our sanctuary, and neither was I.

"We got this," I murmured to myself, and I was answered with a loud round of *Hell yeahs* as fisted weapons pumped in the air.

"Adelaide, we're ready." My grandmother's voice floated through the floorboards.

I swallowed and straightened up. Tase turned me around and grasped my chin, tilting my head back to look up at him.

"Be safe," he murmured, before planting his firm but soft lips against mine.

"You too," I said once we separated again.

I looked over at Gwen, and she nodded at me. Rhys went up the stairs first so the coven could do the camo spell. After patting my pocket to ensure the Eye of Valerian was still secure, I leaned up on my toes to give Tase one more kiss.

"See ya on the flip side," I said, before turning for the stairs and heading up, Gwen right behind me.

As we hit the ground floor, a black cat slipped out the back door, then Mathilde Augustine closed and locked it. She led us to the front wine-tasting room, where the other coven members waited, except for Ronya Augustine, who brushed past me and trotted downstairs. I could feel from below us Ronya's magic energy zaps as those down there portaled to their predetermined places outside, scattered around the square.

"The dagger," my grandmother said, handing me a nondescript knife that was supposed to be our saving grace. "The spell's in place. You just need the Collector's blood to touch it, and it will activate." I slipped the dagger under my coat into the one empty slot at the top of the leather holster. She handed me an empty wine bottle with a Stone Falls Winery label on it. "Decoy."

Our eyes locked, hers penetrating mine, making sure I understood. I gave her a slight nod to indicate I did. It was all part of the plan.

"Okay, ready?" I asked Gwen.

"Ready."

Lilith walked us to the front door, we all paused for a beat, and then she opened it for us.

"Now you girls have a good evening. Are you sure you'll be okay getting home?" she said, her voice overly loud to carry across the square as we all stepped outside.

It was late, and the main business district area was pretty dead except for some lively music and laughter that could be heard from Haven Saloon on the far corner from us. Christmas lights lit the square up brightly, though, reflecting off the freshly fallen snow and making it look like a scene from a Hallmark card.

Tomorrow was Christmas Eve.

"I live right over there," Gwen said, her words also loud and slurring just a tad as she pointed a seemingly unsteady finger toward her apartment on the other side of Town Square Park. "I think I can handle it."

"I'm walking, too. As always," I said, also purposely slurring my words. "Thanks for all the yummy samples! They were dee-lish-shussss. And for this!" I waved the empty bottle in the air.

"And thanks for staying open so late for us," Gwen added, extra cheery. Our acting abilities were horrible, but hopefully they passed as drunken behavior.

"Merry Christmas," Lilith called out before closing the door.

"Thank you for inviting me out," Gwen said. "I needed that."

"You should join our girls' night sometime."

We said our goodbyes and holiday greetings, then I gave her a wave and turned to my right as though to head home as Gwen began to cross the street. A black cat slinked from out of the shadows of a bush on the far side of the street, at the entrance to the park—Rhys ready to join Gwen.

I walked down Eleventh Street, toward Weston Designs and the police station across from it, Tase striding toward me. It wasn't unusual for him to meet me in town and walk home with me these days. What was unusual was how the square wasn't nearly as empty as it seemed. Even someone with magical abilities like Rachelle's wouldn't be able to sense their presences, but I knew they were there.

At least, they all better be.

I kept my awareness completely on Gwen, sensing as she approached the fountain in the middle of the square. *Any second now.* If Rachelle was watching, she'd make her move at any moment. Gwen appeared to be ripe for the taking, an opportunity Rachelle couldn't possibly pass up.

Tase and I had just approached the end of the block, about to cross Stuart Street, when several things happened in quick succession.

Sedona came running around the corner and slammed into me, nearly knocking me on my ass.

A loud cracking sound came from the center of town square, followed by a cat's hiss.

Gwen screamed, and I spun toward her to see Rachelle grab her wrist.

Sedona gripped my upper arms, spinning me back to face her, her eyes wild with panic. "Addie! Where's Micah? I can't find Micah! I need Micah."

Rachelle laughed.

Micah suddenly appeared, blowing our cover. "Sedona, what's wrong?"

"It's Holly! Micah, I'm so sorry. So, so sorry."

"What about Holly?" he gritted out from a clenched jaw, his dark eyes piercing hers as if he could see the answer in her brain.

Tears filled Sedona's eyes. Her voice came out in a whisper. "She's . . . she's gone, Micah."

Rachelle let out another guffaw, and my head snapped toward her. She winked at me, then she and Gwen disappeared.

CHAPTER 22

HARPER

a sense of calm settled over me, every trouble and worry I'd ever had simply disappearing. The room behind the red door was a black hole, as if I had literally stepped from the dollhouse into outer space with nothing around me except darkness and time.

My head cleared, my heavy body relaxing, and yet despite suddenly feeling normal again, I had never been so disoriented.

Or warm.

Or happy.

In the vast nothingness, the shadows that followed me glided through the air, their glowing bodies the only source of light. They'd transformed from dark shadows to illuminating constellations. They were magnificent. The photographer in me wanted a picture of their floating beauty, but the realist in me was afraid of what that beauty meant. Sometimes the most alluring things in life are also the most dangerous.

Voices rose from the blackness, whispered and unintelligible.

I was inside the shadows. I didn't know how I knew that, but deep down, I just knew. I'd always imagined being a shadow was cold and terrifying. But all I felt around them since I entered this freaky dollhouse was warmth.

"This is how they've always felt toward you." The Collector's voice

was confident and happy. *"Why would demons be attracted to spirits and souls if they weren't warm, tempting, vibrant, and alive?"*

"Are you calling me a demon?" I asked aloud, voice trembling. I hated that it shook, but I was proud of myself for not shrinking away from the sound.

"You're essentially the child of one."

"My parents were not demons," I argued.

"No, but your body was reanimated inside your mother's womb by a demon. A necromancer's athame raises the dead, Harper."

My body went cold. "Are you saying I'm a walking corpse?"

"You were still alive when you were stabbed, so you aren't a reanimated corpse. You're special. A demon without being a demon. You straddle the line between light and dark."

Tears welled up behind my eyes, and I wanted to rub at them angrily because I knew why they were trying to fall. The Collector called me special—even emphasized the word—and as much as I wanted to hate him, I found myself drawn to the compliment. I'd always been someone to be afraid of. Not many people called me special. And even when they did, I heard a healthy amount of fear in their voices.

The Collector sounded happy. *You straddle the line between light and darkness differently than others do.*

What did he mean by that? My head spun. I was darkness, and I was light. Wasn't everyone? Was it because the darkness within me was more dangerous to mankind? I had, after all, written a prophetic letter to a person as a child only to have him die shortly thereafter. It was then I'd become afraid of myself. It was the darkness within me that worried me. The Collector was only happy because he wanted to use the dark side of me. He wanted to hurt the people I cared about, and I wanted no part in that.

"Let them go," I begged. "Let them go, and we'll talk about what you need me for."

"Let who go?"

"The people you told me you were holding captive."

Silence fell.

"What fun would there be in that?" the Collector finally asked. *"You've lost time here, Harper. While you were sleeping, a week passed. The length of time it took you to get to this door . . . Well, days sped by. Even now, while you stand here inside this room, even more time cheats you. A lot of things have happened during that time."*

The more he talked, the harder I found it to breathe. There was no way that much time had passed. No way I'd spent that long inside this place.

What kind of place was this? What kind of artifact was I trapped in?

I started to walk forward and winced, my knees stiff from the wounds I'd received in the hallway, my hand sliding down my thigh to my leg, my fingers playing over scabs.

My body froze.

It took time for scabs to form over wounds. The Collector wasn't lying. I wasn't sure how much time had passed, but time moved swiftly here.

My breath escaped me in one long, startled whoosh. "Why are you doing this?"

"Because I need you. I need you, and I need them."

I was afraid to ask who *them* was. The Collector was insane. A true psychopath with power issues, and I'd been drawn into his creepy game inside a freaky funhouse of horror.

"What have you done with my friends?" I asked.

Familiar voices rose out of the darkness. All of them calling my name.

"Harper. Harper. Harper." Desperate voices that echoed, as if this room had walls despite looking like we were standing in the middle of outer space.

The voices brought me to my knees, my wounds forgotten. Aunt Eloise. Elias. Addie. Tasha. Micah. Voices I knew as well as I knew my own, even if Micah was a newer acquaintance.

My heart was beating too fast, and I grabbed for my chest, my palms flattening against the pounding rhythm. There was no way they were all trapped here. Especially the angels. Could the Collector really be that powerful?

"You're bluffing." My voice should have come out strong and certain. Instead, the words sounded shaky and unsure.

"*You don't sound confident,*" the Collector replied. "*Maybe the better question is: can you be certain I'm lying?*"

I hated the Collector. Hated him. It was a strong emotion, and it made my insides burn, as if a fire had been lit inside my belly, waiting for the fuel it needed to burn out of control.

"You *are* bluffing?" I repeated, the words firmer. Shadows rallied around me, their glowing forms circling frantically, my rising anger calling to them.

"*There it is,*" the Collector said, pleased. "*That's what this room is for. Accept yourself, Harper. Anger is what they need from you. Give them your hatred. Feed them.*"

From the darkness, I heard the voices of my loved ones again, their desperation rising. Panic caused me to lurch forward, the shadows so close to my body that their glow blinded me.

"*Harper! Harper!*" It was Aunt Eloise who screamed.

These were the voices and yells of the people I cared about. The screams of all of the people I loved for varying reasons. The people who actually gave a damn about me. The people who needed me.

Please let the Collector be bluffing, I thought, my internal dialogue swallowed by my hollered name, the voices filling the room with the deafening noise of terror and death.

"*You feel it building, don't you?*" the Collector asked, his voice somehow audible over the chaos. "*Don't ignore your power.*"

Past memories flooded me, the time I spent with fallen angel Lucas Fox prominent in my thoughts. He'd explained what I was, and even though I'd accepted it to an extent, I hadn't accepted it the way I should have. Even Lucas accepted he wasn't perfect. Otherwise he wouldn't have been a fallen. A mighty fallen at that—a Seraph. Seraphs were the highest-ranking angels in Heaven.

Why did I have such a hard time admitting I could be as evil as I was good? Why did I have such a hard time admitting I was literally yin and yang in one person?

My anger fed off my frustration, and the shadows wailed.

"*Use it,*" the Collector commanded. "*If you want to save them, use it.*"

I suddenly didn't care if the Collector was bluffing. I suddenly didn't care if he had no captives other than me. All I cared about was the anger I was feeling and how good it was to *feel* it.

Looking back, I realized I had never really allowed myself to be angry at anyone or anything. I'd been calm, steady, shy Harper. Anger fed things in me that I'd been too afraid to feed. It fed the darkness.

In this moment, it felt so incredibly good to be angry. It felt so incredibly good to accept the bad in me, the part of myself that found the sinful dark spirits surrounding me beautiful.

"*You've bottled it all up for too long. Why? Accepting yourself is part of accepting what you're capable of.*"

The Collector's words washed over me, the shadows so close it was hard to tell where they ended and I began. Whispers reached my ears, desperate pleas that sent chills down my spine.

"*Let us in,*" the shadows breathed against my neck.

I fell to my knees, relief engulfing me along with the anger. Who knew giving in could feel so right? My body gave the shadows permission to enter, because it no longer cared that my brain wanted to keep them out.

The shadows' warmth pushed against my skin, seeping into my pores, my mouth, my eyes, and my nose. My flesh glowed, the shadows' luminescence infiltrating my body as they sank into me, the shine turning me into a human lighthouse.

Was this what possession felt like? Because it felt good. Too good.

"*You're not possessed,*" the Collector informed me, his voice amused and content. "*You've absorbed their power and energy, Harper. Now you can channel that. They're letting you use them.*"

If what the Collector was saying was true, then . . . "Am I like the Indrori?"

My mind couldn't comprehend what was happening to me, but

my heart felt loved. I felt full, but not uncomfortably so. As if I'd eaten a good meal and then imbibed a glass of wine. Just enough to make me feel happy, a little sleepy, and whole lot of wonderful.

If this was power, then it was addictive.

"*You can absorb the spirits' energy. The question is, are you willing to use that power to your advantage?*"

This felt like a test somehow, as if who I was meant to be as a person all boiled down to this moment and my decision.

I felt the shadows inside of me, restless and excited, their adrenaline feeding mine. I felt invincible.

No one should feel that way.

I wasn't going to abuse my power. There were other ways to channel the darkness.

"Please help me," I whispered into the darkness, my eyes falling closed. With the shadows inside of me, I could see the back of my own eyelids and the way the delicate veins ran across the thin skin like a road map.

"Please," I begged.

In the distance, a voice called, "Harper!"

It was Elias Jamison's voice, and this version of the fallen angel wasn't in my head or part of some illusion set up by the Collector. It was him.

This seemed to excite the shadows even more, as if me reaching out to Elias somehow made them stronger. Their strength scared me.

"*Control them!*" the Collector ordered. "*Control them so they don't control you.*"

Maybe it was exhaustion, or maybe it was the way time had passed without me realizing it, but I was suddenly too weak to use the shadows.

The darkness that had so captivated me before turned dark and eerie, losing some of its luminescence as the shadows wrestled inside of me. They battled for dominance, like a pack of wolves sensing weakness and blood.

My body hit the floor. I couldn't see it, but I knew the floor was there, my cheek pressed against what felt like cold stone. Thoughts rushed through me.

Demons. Nightmares. Lower caste angels.

I was once told I could summon lower caste angels, but I'd never attempted it. Elias Jamison wasn't a lower caste angel, but maybe I could use that same power to draw him to me. Like a homing beacon.

"You're still fighting it." The Collector's voice echoed, the sound of it growing farther and farther away, as if he realized I was a failure and was abandoning me to be destroyed by the shadows I was supposed to embrace. He sounded disappointed, as if the Collector had *wanted* me to defeat him.

I would not and could not let my friends or the town down.

"Elias." His name came out as little more than a whispered breath, but I could feel the power in my desperation. It shot outward like a shockwave, carried on the sudden screams of the shadows.

Time was passing beyond the dollhouse, time I couldn't control. There was a lot the Collector could do with that time. A lot the Collector could do period. His powers were strong. And ancient. Even I could sense he was on a different level from any supernatural I'd ever met. There was so many people he could hurt, and I was helpless to stop him.

Nothing felt worse than feeling helpless. Even death.

"Quit fighting, or it will tear you in two." The Collector's final words to me felt prophetic and ominous.

Weakened, I lost control of the shadows, and they tore out of me.

I screamed, the pain worse than anything I'd ever felt. Blood trickled somewhere, and I wondered if they had ripped skin when they left me.

"Harper."

I couldn't see Elias, but I could hear his frantic voice.

"Here," I whisper-shouted.

My world tilted, my stomach dropping with it, and right before my whole world went black, I wondered if he'd picked up the dollhouse.

CHAPTER 23

ADDIE

*M*icah's body began to glow, and I knew he was about to go full-out angel on us. The energy called out to my inner hellhound, trying to draw her out, and my own skin began to brighten.

"Dude, control yourself!" I yelled at him, then I turned to Sedona. "Get to safety! Now, Sedona!"

"I got her," someone called out, and a witch from our coven swept Sedona away.

I gave the signal to the others, grabbed Micah's arm so he wouldn't miss the ride since he was so distracted, and focused on the amulet I'd given to Gwen.

The ground dropped away for a moment, then we landed in thick snow on a sharp angle. I worked my jaw against the popping in my ears as more than a dozen of us appeared scattered in a twenty-foot radius, including a few members of the Luna Coven, and even Roman Bishop. Saundra, Mathilde, and others, including Everett and the hellhounds, had stayed behind to protect the town and its people.

The wind whipped snow and ice particles around us, stinging my cheeks and eyes as it howled through the trees and around boulders. I dropped the bottle still in my hand as I did a quick turn and found us above the tree line, our town far below us. Searching out pinpricks of lights of the landmarks I was so familiar with, I quickly gained my bearings. We were near the top of Mount Mae, at its eastern end. At the base, directly down, it formed a corner with Mt. Sousa, where Danzan Park was. But that was over five thousand feet below.

"Huh. The empusa was telling the truth," I muttered as I turned back to find Rachelle with Gwen and Rhys, my twin already tied up with one of the ropes Gwen wore as a tattoo. So far, everything was going according to plan. Well, except the whole Sedona and Holly thing.

"Do you really think she didn't know?" Rachelle sneered as her skin began to light up, her hellhound rising to the surface. The ropes around her began to smoke. "She knows everything! She was waiting for this, you idiots!"

"Who?" Micah and I said at the same time as he advanced on her.

"Who do you think? The Collector, of course."

Micah suddenly crossed the distance between us, appearing in a blink in front of Gwen and Rhys—and Rachelle, except she was gone again, the singed ropes lying on the snow. But she hadn't gone far. Only slightly higher up the mountain, standing with her palm against a monolithic stone that rose out of the snow. A glass structure suddenly appeared, jutting out from the mountain peak as though it were part of it.

A figure in a white cloak stood next to Rachelle, much taller than her, the head hooded. The cloak cinched at the waist and flared out over white pants and boots. The shape was no doubt female. She threw her hood off, revealing a stunning woman with long white hair and sharp eyes, whose color I couldn't really determine from here, but so pale, I wanted to simply call it colorless.

Micah went all-out angel. It almost seemed like he doubled in size as his body began emanating a golden glow. He flew to the two women above us, no more than a streak of light. At the same time, Elias seemed to startle to my left. Tasha and I both looked at him.

"Are you okay?" Tasha asked.

Elias shook his head, as though trying to shake something free. His brows furrowed together for a moment.

"Harper?" he said.

I looked around, listened, and smelled. "She's not here."

"Harper?" he called out louder, though I still heard nothing. "Harper, where are you?"

"She's not here," Tasha repeated.

"She is," he insisted. His eyes squinted. "And I know where."

He started running up the slope, toward the side of the house. Tasha and Senora went with him, as we'd planned if Harper's whereabouts were ever determined.

The rest of us started up the slope, ready to face the Collector.

"You can call me Zandra," the woman next to Rachelle called down. "The Collector is a fun nomenclature, but it's time you know my name."

"Where's Holly?" Micah demanded, not giving two fucks what her name was. Or even that the Collector was a she. So we were dealing with a goddess, not a god. Interesting.

"Safer than you could ever keep her," Zandra replied coolly, and that was the absolute wrong thing to say.

Because all hell broke loose, starting with Micah.

He charged Zandra, and the rest of us did, too, but suddenly there were several dozen of her lined up on either side. She was like a fucking Loki.

"Loki's a relative," one of the Zandras said, as though reading my mind. "Well, a distant one. And adopted, you know."

She laughed at her joke. She was apparently well versed in pop culture of our world.

"I'm well versed in all things of your world," she replied.

And she apparently *could* hear my thoughts.

"Your amulet against Elsmed has nothing on me." She laughed, and all her clones laughed with her.

But it didn't last long as our little army swarmed on them.

I made a beeline for Rachelle, blasting a holding spell on her. She deflected it and shot her own spell at me. Ducking and rolling, I avoided it, letting it hit a boulder down the slope. I shot a curse at her, knocking her off her feet. I crossed the space between us as she immediately jumped back up, her eyes glowing a dark red and her skin a bright orange. Her hair lifted from her shoulders, and yellow sparks danced along her fingertips. I called up my own hellhound, surely making myself a near mirror image of her. Our magic flew. Spell and counterspell. Defensive and offensive measures. I had to admit that she was better trained than I expected her to be, making us a near equal match.

But not quite.

She unleashed a whip of fire at me, catching it on the one I'd thrown at her. We both tugged and jerked the ropes of flames, which kept her nicely distracted. She didn't have anyone on her side, though. Not really. The Collector—Zandra—and all of her clones were busy worrying about themselves.

And I had Tase, Xandru, and Michaela.

Moroi vampires, descendants of a sorcerer, all had a simple form of magic, a distinct ability passed to them through the blood of the one who turned them. The Rocas and Michaela had the ability to manipulate metal, and they put it to use now. Tase directed a thick chain he'd chosen as one of his weapons to wrap around Rachelle's arms, binding her, while at the same time, Xandru and Michaela each tore a metal support from the house's immense windows and created a cage, Rachelle trapped within. With a silent murmur, I extinguished both flaming ropes, then threw another spell at Rachelle that knocked her out.

Then we turned for the next fight. Wolves and witches, hellhounds and dragons fought against the many Zandras. For each one defeated, another one appeared. Our people had their own various and distinct abilities and strengths, but they were each tested to their maximum capacity. Their stamina may have been supernatural, but it wasn't infinite. And Zandra's possibly was.

I had to find the real Zandra and follow through on our plan. But identifying her was easier said than done. So I threw myself at a version of her and hoped somebody would learn the one little identifying characteristic that would distinguish the real goddess from her clones.

∾

MICAH

SAFER THAN YOU could ever keep her. Those words burned like a scalding brand in my head. It was a truth that rankled deep inside me and fueled the rage I was feeling.

This goddess—monster—had taken my Holly, and I would wipe her from the face of the earth. Extinguish her existence. Break her so completely that she would forever remain an empty shell of her former self.

Warrior angels made formidable enemies, and I was ready to embrace every ounce of my divine power to obliterate Zandra.

The goddess splintered into many clones, though, rendering it a painstakingly slow process to figure out the real version.

Fire rippled over my skin as my whole body began to glow, my hands shining from the golden energy emanating from me. Angelic fire. There weren't many things that could stir a true fear of death, but I knew the power I held. I would deliver a smiting that would last throughout the ages.

I had to throw away my fear of revealing my location. There was no time for finesse. The angel sword that had been gifted to me upon my initiation into the higher ranks still remained hidden away in a safe location. In most cases, using my hands to incinerate those who threatened Holly was enough. It would need to be enough now.

Everywhere I looked, people were fighting. Groans and sounds of exertion filled the air. I couldn't quite tell if Zandra was mocking us, fighting with minimal effort to give us a false sense of security, or if we truly were holding our own.

This was a goddess—a being of immeasurable strength and power. As one clone shattered, disappearing into thin air, another two or three appeared to take its place. It was endless. It was tiring.

With a battle cry that came from a far distant memory of my past, I launched myself again at the nearest Zandra, wrapping my arms around its body and squeezing with everything I had. Heat radiated outward, and with a triumphant yell, I felt the precise moment the clone gave up.

Whipping around, my fingers grabbed hold of another, clenching tightly as I reached with my other hand and pulled at the arm I found. I pulled hard. The clone dropped to the floor, both limbs torn from its torso.

The comforting burn that filled my palm began twisting up my arms and into my shoulder blades like an invisible vine does a concrete fence. I welcomed the sensation as though it was a long-lost friend. It had been years since I'd last unleashed this part of myself, and I relished the strength it provided.

Nothing else mattered.

I became an avenging angel.

I became my true self.

One after the other, I smote the clones that attacked.

Side by side, I fought with the others until all I could see was our bodies blurred and moving with purpose.

"We need to find the true Zandra," I hollered out over the chaos. "The clones will keep coming and fighting until we do!"

Addie grunted as she killed her own version of the Collector.

"What do you think I'm doing here?" she countered, already throwing spells and a brutal-looking side kick at the three clones that stepped forward. "Work some of your warrior mojo, Micah. Be the badass I heard you were!"

I was ready for this to be over.

"Then keep up, Addie Beaumont."

With a heightened push of adrenaline and energy, I let out another battle cry.

∼

HARPER

My world turned upside down, an earthquake of massive proportions throwing me against walls and floors I couldn't see. I grabbed at the darkness, my sudden screams echoing around me, the pain in my side a searing fire.

"Harper!" Elias roared, his voice way too loud in the dollhouse, the sound causing my ears to ring.

"Stop!" The back of my head slammed against a hard surface, and my breath whooshed out of me as I rolled, my body flipping. "Don't move the dollhouse!"

I knew Elias could hear me. Otherwise, he never would have come to my rescue.

"Put it down," he ordered.

"How else are we supposed to get her out?" another voice asked, indignant.

"Tasha?" I cried, my body going still on a smooth cold surface as the earthquake stopped.

Everything on me hurt. My breath came in frantic spurts, my heart a galloping horse inside my chest. The back of my head throbbed.

Warmth surrounded me, the glowing shadows a sudden halo in the darkness, as if they were embracing me. Hugging me even. I fell back into them, too spent to fight how good it felt to give in to their comfort.

"Stand back," Elias commanded.

An abrupt blue light flooded the space, blinding me, swallowing the darkness and sending me reeling into a tunnel of brightness. The dark spirits with me shrieked, deafening me, and the ones remaining inside of me struggled. No words could describe how bad the pain that enveloped me was. My screams mingled with the shadows' screams, overwhelming pain and heartache suddenly tearing me apart from the inside out.

This was angelic power, the kind darkness could be destroyed by. The kind *I* could be destroyed by.

"Please," I begged, the word merely a whisper, any strength behind its delivery stolen by the pain.

"Hang on, Harper," Elias begged.

His power tugged on me, and I knew he was using it to pull me out of the dollhouse, but the pain his magic caused me was unbearable. Was I so full of darkness that him saving me also felt like killing me?

I was on fire, as if I was being roasted alive.

"Please." It was the last word I breathed before cold air suddenly rushed at me.

The moment I was yanked from the dollhouse, nausea hit me, so strong and violent that I started to retch and couldn't stop, moist droplets seeping from my eyes and nose from the vomiting. Tears, snot, and pain.

Warm, strong arms embraced me, an equally warm breath stirring the hair next to my ears. "Breathe, sweetheart," Elias begged.

Breathing seemed the least of my concerns.

"Harper?" a voice asked, the sound of it unfamiliar and yet . . . I shot backward, Elias's arms the only thing keeping me upright.

"No!" The word roared out of me. My vision was blurred from tears, distorting the figure standing near Elias. Was this the Collector? "Don't come near us!" I flailed, tears pouring down my cheeks, the nausea stealing the rest of my words, the sound of retching replacing my protests.

"Who?" Elias asked, his arms tightening around me. "Harper, it's okay. This is Senora. You haven't met her yet. She won't hurt you."

"Holy shit, Harper," another voice—Tasha Young's voice—exclaimed. "What did you do in there? Eat spirits?"

I continued to retch, dry heaving with each breath in.

Tasha touched my shoulder, and then inhaled loudly and deeply, each sigh she made making my nausea ease. A pulling sensation came from my skin, causing the gash on my side to throb worse than it had before. Black tendrils rose from my body, the smoky mass exiting from the ripped, blood-soaked white fabric over the wound.

"I've almost got them all," Tasha whispered. "Hang in there, Harper."

Elias swore. "She's bleeding."

I think he'd been too focused on getting me out of the dollhouse, followed by my frantic retching and flailing, to notice the wounds on me until now. One of his large hands came up to cup the back of my head, his fingers playing over a sensitive part in my scalp.

I flinched, but my throbbing side stole most of my attention.

"They're gone," I panted. "The shadows left me, Tasha."

"I can see that." Tasha laughed, the sound blunt and hard, her black hair a curtain against my face as she leaned forward. "They didn't all leave you, but I have them now. How the hell did you manage to have your skin ripped by shadows?"

My heart pounded, hard and unforgiving. "I'm just special, I guess."

Elias pressed a hand against my side, and my skin warmed as the same blue light that had blinded me in the dollhouse emanated from his palm. "I can stop the bleeding, but that will have to be it until we get to safety."

My blurred vision cleared, my gaze landing on an attentive slender woman with dark hair and dark eyes that glinted yellow occasionally. As if she were hungry.

Senora, I mouthed. Tasha and Elias were too preoccupied with my wounds to notice, but Senora smiled, a quick flash of white teeth. She had an odd feel to her. It was hard to tell if she was good or bad.

"We're the same, you and I," she said softly. With that, our semi-private conversation came to an end, but it left me shaken.

Was it hard to tell if I was good or bad? An angel saving me from an artifact had felt like it was destroying me. Maybe that was proof enough I wasn't the uncomplicated Harper Sinclair I—and everyone else—wanted me to be.

It was then the trembling began, as much from pain and fear as the cold beyond the dollhouse. The frigid air in the space was a glacial blast against my blood-soaked skin, despite the fact that we seemed to be inside a house somewhere.

"Been sleeping much?" Tasha asked, her gaze dropping to the gown covering my body.

Elias leaned back, pulling the jacket he wore away from his body before enfolding me with it. It was so large it swallowed me whole, the scent of him invading my nostrils. Comfortable and safe. Blood dotted the gray thermal shirt he wore from where I'd leaned against him, that same blood now staining his hands.

"We're not alone," Elias said suddenly, his gaze sweeping the room, his eyes landing on a multitude of artifacts. Whatever room we were in was most definitely the Collector's hiding spot for treasures.

It was then I heard the voice, distant but afraid. Female.

"Holly?" Tasha breathed, the question directed at Elias.

Rubbing my arms a final time, Elias left me and slowly approached an ancient-looking clay vase before touching it gently. Angels had remarkable powers, the kind I didn't think I'd ever understand, even with the power I possessed to summon lower caste fallen angels. Maybe this was something Elias could teach me.

Elias's hand glowed, and a young girl with wild brown hair and equally wild eyes appeared, her arms and legs flailing, her screams filling the space.

"Let me go!" she cried, tears streaking her reddened face. "Please don't hurt me! Please, please don't hurt me!"

She fell to her knees, her fingers digging at the wooden floor below us. I didn't know what had happened to her inside the artifact she'd been in, but if it was anything like my experience, I could understand her fear and desperation.

Like me, she suddenly began retching, her tears mingling with the awful sound. Being pulled from the artifacts was not gentle on the stomach.

Elias leaned down, gripping her firmly, soothing sounds leaving his lips. "Shhh . . . Holly? It's okay. I'm Elias, and we've come to help you." He waved at Tasha and me. "I'm an angel. Like Micah."

The girl stilled, her desperate hazel eyes snapping to us. "Micah?"

Elias smiled. "He's here, too. He's fighting with the others. Are you okay?"

Holly stared at me, her hazel eyes shining. "Harper?" she whispered.

My brows furrowed as our gazes locked. How did she know my name? She'd been a captive of the Collector, too. Had her voice been one of the many voices I'd heard while inside the dollhouse? Had she been a captive that long?

My eyes narrowed. Something about the girl's gaze, the way she felt, captivated me. This girl was special. I didn't quite know how she was special or exactly what she was, but she was going to be really powerful one day. I could *feel* it.

"He wanted us," I said, mostly to myself. "He wanted us for what we are. He wants all of us." My prophetic words came back to haunt me. *United we stand against the one collecting power.* We were as much treasures as the artifacts the Collector had in this room. Maybe the others already knew this, but talking aloud to myself helped organize my thoughts.

"Who?" Tasha asked.

"The Collector," Holly and I replied together. My gaze slid to the girl, and I smiled gently. She smiled back before her gaze left mine to find Senora. The woman hadn't said much, and Elias and Tasha didn't seem to expect her to. She had a calculating look, the kind of pragmatic stare that observed everything without missing any details.

"He's a she," Elias informed us. "The Collector is a woman and a goddess."

"Oh, that," Tasha waved her hand. "Speaking of, I'm ready to kick some ass. Anyone think now would be a good time to join a fight? Maybe let Micah know we've got Holly?"

Certain details I'd been unable to process with my adrenaline- and pain-pumped brain began to infiltrate my senses. Cold seeped up through my bare feet from a wooden floor that was no longer full of splinters. My skin hurt as bad as the rest of me, the splinters from the dollhouse having been sealed beneath my flesh. They were going to have to be surgically removed.

Elias left Holly and came to me. "You can't go out there, Harper. Look at you."

"He's right," Tasha added. "You should babysit Holly." Guilt filled her voice.

Fury pricked my skin, and Tasha inhaled deeply, the shadows she'd taken from me fighting to return to me, drawn by my anger.

"Holy shit, Harper," she breathed.

Interest flared in Senora's eyes while Elias frowned.

"I need to help," I said flatly.

"And I'm not staying behind," Holly retorted.

In this, the teenager and I were united. I had a sneaking suspicion Holly and I were going to get along just great.

I knew by the stares surrounding me that they all planned to stop me. All of them except the teenage girl. So I broke away, rushing blindly through the artifact-filled space, Holly hot on my heels. We desperately wanted to help those beyond this room.

"Go!" Holly cried.

Easier for her than for me. Pain and exhaustion slowed my steps, but no one stopped us. They followed instead, almost as if they knew this was the only answer. It seemed less safe to leave us alone in this room than to take us with them.

"Wait!" Senora called. She had an authoritative voice. "I think there are more trapped in the artifacts. Can you feel it?"

"I do," Elias replied.

My vision doubled, blurred, and then cleared over and over again, and I wondered if I had a concussion from the blow to my head inside the dollhouse.

Holly and I were almost to the door, the others having stopped behind us following Senora's revelation, when a monster appeared before us, my messed up vision turning it into a jumbled up mess of disfigured skin.

"What—"

My question was cut off by Holly's scream of fright and the others' sudden exclamations. Powerful mini explosions went off behind and around us, the pops coming from the artifacts, and I fell to my knees hard, my hands covering my head, Holly stumbling to her knees next to me before her body fell into mine.

"Who are you?" Senora growled.

I was too busy trying not to vomit again, the energy surrounding us causing my pain to return.

I was beginning to believe we were all going to die.

~

ADDIE

WE HAD WHITTLED our way down to three Zandras. Micah held one up in the air by her throat, thinking she was the real one, but as soon as she fell lifeless in his grasp, another two appeared. Fighting the clones had done nothing to reveal the real Zandra's weakness, but I'd come armed with more bait. What I believed *was* her weakness—artifacts. I reached in my pocket and pulled out the Eye of Valerian, trapped in the metal skull that served as its cage to contain its dark magic. I held the skull up for all the clones to see.

"Isn't this what you want?" I called out.

The clones ignored me. I glanced around, my gaze landing on a new figure that had appeared in the doorway to the damaged house. She looked just like the others, of course, but I could feel the power waving off of her. And the realization hit me. The real Collector had never even been out here with us. She'd never been part of the fight. She'd been hiding safely inside, like a coward.

"Very good, Adelaide," she said, her voice just as much in my head as outside it, a reverberation through my mind. "Although I'm not a coward. I'm a goddess, my thoughts and plans far beyond what you could ever comprehend. And yes, I've wanted that piece for my collection for a long time, but do you really think I'm stupid enough to come out and get it? Was that really your plan, Adelaide? I have other means to get what I want."

Her hand flicked, but so had mine. Already prepared, I transported the artifact far away from here. The bait hadn't quite worked the way we'd hoped, but it had served a great purpose—it drew the real Zandra out to us.

Knowing she'd be reading my mind, I focused my thoughts on a spell while slipping my hand under my coat and withdrawing the dagger Saundra had given me. While still thinking about my magic and preparing the spell to fly, my inner hellhound zeroed in on the target, aimed, and threw.

The dagger soared through the air.

Everything else seemed to pause.

Silence fell.

All the fighting had stopped.

The blade drove into Zandra's chest before she even realized I'd let go. The clones disappeared.

Shock filled Zandra's face as she grasped at the hilt. It probably filled my face, too. I couldn't believe I had actually done it. *We* had done most of it, of course, but ensuring the knife hit its target had been my biggest worry out of all of this. I'd succeeded. And now we would all succeed in saving our town, our people.

The collective whoosh of relief seemed big enough to clear the snow away.

But then Zandra's bright red mouth turned up at the corners, and she laughed as she easily withdrew the dagger from her chest. I didn't understand. It was spelled. Saundra had said it was done—the Luna Coven enchanted it with the same magic that bound the Hungarian Hunters to the Blue Dragon Dagger, which trapped them in their own part of the Infernum. And that's what was supposed to happen to the Collector. She should have been gone by now in her own special place in Hell.

"Nice thinking, but I'm a Vanaheim goddess," she said. "A whole different beast than your little Hungarian Hunters. You'll have to try a lot harder than this." She shook her head as if disappointed as she tossed the bloody dagger into the snow. She peered at all of us, standing like idiots in shock. "Now, it's time for me to collect."

And without any kind of warning, everyone, even Rachelle, was gone. Vanished. Disappeared without a trace.

There was the wrecked façade of the house, trampled snow, deep gouges in the drifts, and puddles of red against white. But not a soul around.

Except the Collector.

And me.

One corner of Zandra's mouth turned up, and she tilted her head. "They abandoned you, Adelaide. What do you think about that?"

I shook my head. "No. They would never. You did this."

"How can you be so sure?"

"Because they're my friends. My family. My people. They wouldn't abandon me."

"Wouldn't they, though?" She took several steps forward, closing the distance between us.

"No."

Her smile grew. "You didn't sound so certain that time. Do you truly believe with every fiber of your heart and soul that they would sacrifice their own lives for you?"

I shook my head. "Not for me. For all of us. For our town."

"Oh, Adelaide, I hate to break it to you, but you're wrong. Not everyone is like you. Not everyone is willing to go to the same lengths you are for the greater good. People are much more selfish than that. They only care about themselves. About their immediate loved ones. But I think you know that, deep down, don't you?"

My jaw clenched. My hands fisted. My nostrils flared.

I didn't want to listen to her anymore. I didn't want to hear the words she spewed. I didn't want to acknowledge that there might be truth in them.

"Look at Micah. He only cares about Holly and Sedona, right?"

I shook my head.

"Elias? He went straight after Harper."

I bit my trembling lip.

"And then there's Gwen and Rhys." Her hand swept toward one of those red pools of blood in the snow. "You brought Gwen into this, but it didn't turn out so well for her. And what did Rhys do, as soon as he saw her lifeless body? I don't see him here by *your* side."

Tears sprang to my eyes as a lump lodged in my throat. *No.* I just saw them fighting minutes ago. That couldn't be real. My chin shook even as my teeth dug deeper into my lip.

And Zandra continued on.

"You can't be surprised Roman Bishop and Senora bailed—that's par for the course for both of them. But what about your closest friends—Xandru and Michaela? Tase?"

"They didn't leave! Not on their own! What did you do to them?" I yelled.

She threw her hands in the air and looked around with exaggerated motions. "But I don't see them here. Perhaps they rushed home to their siblings, to try to protect them from my wrath when I'm done here. Perhaps they realized they had no chance against me. *You* have no chance against me, Adelaide. Your friends, your family, your beloved Court of the Sun and the Moon . . . they're not here, are they? Only you are. You've been groomed to lead, but what about when there's nobody to lead? Nobody to help? Can you do this on your own?"

She advanced on me. I couldn't help it. I took a step back, inhaling as I glanced around, as though hoping to see somebody else here. Somebody to fight with me. But I already knew there was nobody.

A small part of me, deep down inside, couldn't help but wonder if she was telling the truth. Had they all somehow ported away, running scared? Had they truly abandoned me to protect themselves and their own loved ones? Did they really not care about our town, our people as a collective? I couldn't be the only one who loved this place . . . who would do anything for it . . . could I?

But she'd really nailed my biggest, most secret fear, the one I'd kept buried deep inside since I was a child, with that last question.

"Can you do this on your own?" she repeated as she continued to close in on me. "*Will* you?"

I'd been groomed from a young age to become one of our town's leaders. For nearly as long as I could remember, I'd been told that I would be a High Priestess of the Luna Coven and take my seat on the Court to lead the town when the time came. And I'd accepted it. I'd never been asked if it was what I wanted, but that was okay, because I did. I'd always wanted to take care of our town, our people, because this was my home. Our home. The place I loved so deeply. The people I loved with all my heart and soul, even the ones I didn't really like.

But there had always been a shard of doubt that I'd pushed way down, ignoring its jabs and scrapes when it was unintentionally jarred out of place: When push came to shove, *could* I protect our town?

Could I be its leader, if it all came down on me? Could I do what needed to be done? I'd always gathered people around me, knowing that together, we could defeat anything.

But the Collector was right. Nobody was here now. Whether by their choice or not, I was here alone to face her. To defend my town, my people, my home against her.

By myself.

Against a goddess.

My biggest fear right here in front of me.

Did I dare try? Was it all worth it?

Of course it was.

And I didn't care if I was the only fool who'd go this far for this town. Somebody had to. Otherwise . . . I refused to think about an otherwise.

I inhaled deeply, then tilted my head from side to side, stretching my neck. I lifted my hands, magic dancing along my fingers.

"I don't know if I *can*," I said, "but I'll fucking die trying."

With a flick of my wrist, my magic flew, and so did hers.

CHAPTER 24

SENORA

"Wait!" I called as Harper and Holly reached the door of the artifact room, making a run for it, Elias on their heels. "I think there are more trapped in the artifacts. Can you feel it?"

"I do," Elias replied. "The artifacts!"

We spun back around and quickly surveyed the space. It was full of trinkets—many of which I had collected over the past few months. Realization that I helped the Collector snare innocent people sickened me. I searched my memory, remembering which ones I'd brought in.

I pointed to a gold vase on a shelf. "Start there."

At the same time I said this, a commotion came from the hallway. Harper and Holly both fell to their knees, as though overcome with illness. A figure stood in the doorway.

"Not so fast," Supernatural Barbie said. "I can't allow you to walk out of here with the Collector's property."

"Free them!" I barked at Elias and Tasha, forgetting who was in charge. "This one's mine."

Her lips curled up, and white sparks flew from her fingers. There was something different about her that I couldn't place. Something the Collector had done to her, maybe. Or maybe I'd overestimated her, because she didn't fight the way I'd expected her to. I was able to hold my own as Elias freed someone from the gold vase.

"What the——?" Elias began. "I thought you were outside, Micah!"

"The Collector did something out there. I think she trapped all of us."

Rachelle laughed. "She has many tricks up her sleeve. As do I."

I charged at her, and she shoved me backward, into a shelf of artifacts that clattered to the ground on impact. I had no idea why she didn't use her magic, but she seemed to be relying more on her hellhound side, fighting me physically. I pounced again, my hands aimed for her throat, latching on and squeezing. She could have burned me with her skin, if she wanted to, or she could have used her magic. Instead, a black mist rose from around her feet upward—the hellhound mist, I thought, used to blind their opponents—and I thought I was done for. But then . . .

She fucking exploded.

Bits of plasma-like goo rained down, splattering my face and the area around me. But I saw it just in time—one last blast the HellWitch had managed to shoot off before she disappeared. Probably aimed at me, it went too wide, to my left, directly at Holly.

No! Not the child! I jumped in front of the girl, and the white-hot bolt pierced my chest.

My breath hitched as my heart slowed.

I dropped to my knees.

This was not quite how I saw myself going out.

～

MICAH

I EXPLODED out of the artifact where Zandra had blasted me. Righteous rage sizzled through my veins as my gaze swept through the room, looking for my enemy. She'd managed to incapacitate me, and with Holly still missing, that was a sin I would never forgive.

"I thought you were outside, Micah!" Elias said with surprise.

"The Collector did something out there. I think she trapped all of us."

"You okay?" he called out over his shoulder as he placed a hand on another artifact, setting Rhys free, and then Gwen.

"Yes," I nodded, trying to gain my bearings. "Have you found—"

That's when I saw her—my beautiful charge. She was incredibly shaken, but it didn't take more than a second to see something that made my heart swell with pride. My Holly was standing there alongside Harper and others—anger blazing in her eyes.

She reminded me so much of her mother, with her back straight, shoulders set, and an expression that screamed she would fight to the death if she had to. There was also a whisper of a hint blazing from her determined stance that reminded me exactly who her father was. I saw him in the way her jaw jutted out a little, like she didn't care how scared she was—she would never back down.

She wasn't ready to be involved in this kind of battle. She was never meant to witness violence, the task of fighting off all threats and attackers solely my responsibility. I was meant to keep her somewhat oblivious to how truly dangerous the world could be.

Yet it was all around us, the empusa and Rachelle in a fight for their lives right in this room.

That's when it hit me.

I wasn't ready for this . . . for her help to shoulder the burden.

"Holly," I called out, my voice a little hoarse from yelling within the artifact. I raced to reach her, to throw her over my shoulder, and get her out of here. She could face the next threat, or perhaps the one after that. Just not this. Just not now.

I wasn't that evolved.

"Micah!" she replied, relief flooding her cheeks.

I caught the flicker of movement from the corner of my eye. Black mist and then a flash of white. My thoughts slowed down until all I could see were the events unfolding before me.

Rachelle had sent a spark of magic flying just before she burst into pieces.

Holly's mouth formed in the shape of an O as she turned to see what held my focus.

I stretched out my hand, already prepared to throw myself in her direction. I screamed for Holly to watch out.

I wouldn't make it in time. Holly wouldn't drop to the ground in time.

Then Senora Graves—of all people—did the unthinkable . . . something I wouldn't believe she was capable of.

She saved Holly, and with a loud agonizing holler, Senora fell to the ground.

I threw myself at Holly and wrapped my arms around her, kissing the top of her head. We'd come so close this time—too close.

"Where's Addie?" Tase yelled with panic in his voice, the last of the group that had been fighting to be freed.

"I hear her outside," Xandru replied.

"I'm going to kill that bitch," Roman muttered, rushing out of the room, leaving us all to wonder if he meant Addie or Zandra.

Most everyone followed, headed back out to the fight, without another glance around. I understood the feeling. Now that I could see Holly was here and in one piece, I needed to join them and end this once and for all.

"Micah, I need your help." Elias was crouched down beside the still empusa. She hadn't moved since taking the blow. "My energy is low after freeing everyone, and I can't heal her."

I grunted. "Are you sure you even want to?" I'd always tried to act with honor, but showing any kind of sympathy for this creature felt like a stretch.

It wasn't Harper's sharp gasp that softened my heart. Nor was it Tasha's insistence that perhaps Senora could still be of some help to the Court—something about uncovering how wide the Collector's organization was, if Senora even knew.

It was Holly, who placed her hand on my arm, and I knew what I had to do. I might not have liked it, but Holly helped me see the truth.

Kneeling beside the fallen woman, I made sure she could see my face when I spoke with her. Senora was weakening, each second taking her closer to death. She must've sensed me staring at her, because she opened her eyes, dark and filled with pain and—was that remorse?

"You threatened my friends. You're an accomplice to the one who hurt my family. You deserve no mercy, except—" I paused to make sure she understood with perfect clarity my next words. "You saved Holly. I don't care what your motivation was. A life debt is owed. Do you accept my offer to repay it?" I reached for my angelic gifts as I watched her lips part.

"Yes."

"Then so be it." Golden light enveloped my hands and inched up my arms. I searched for the Enochian words to anoint the healing, then let my energy enter Senora. Slowly at first, her skin began to grow from gray to a healthy dark brown, her breathing becoming steadier.

That's when I stopped. "You'll live."

And she would. I hadn't completely healed her, only enough that she could walk out of here on her own.

Holly stood waiting for me when I rose, gratitude in her eyes. She had such a pure heart—another thing I would fiercely guard and protect.

"I need to go, sweetheart. I need to help our friends." There was a rightness about those words that resonated within me.

"I know."

Kissing the top of her head again, I let her go and ran through the doorway to where the others had gone.

~

ADDIE

THIS BITCH WAS TEARING me up. Blood flowed in various places on my body, including from a gash in my temple and another long one down my forearm. My bones and muscles ached from the tension— and more than a few bruises, I was sure. But I wasn't dead, and I counted that as a win.

Fighting her had taken every ounce of focus, though. She was powerful, yet I had a feeling she was holding back for some reason, and I didn't know how long that would last.

At some point, my familiars had arrived. I hadn't called them. They were all still young, and I hadn't wanted to bring them into this, what I knew would be a fight to the death. But they'd come anyway. They must have sensed my need. Princess Leia flew in circles around Zandra's head, blasting her with fire, but the goddess easily shielded herself against the flames. I'd already learned with my own fire magic that she couldn't be taken down that way. Chewie charged at her legs, sinking his fangs into Zandra's calf once before she threw him off, sending him flying into the snow. He didn't give up, though. He kept trying to attack, though never able to get close enough again. Kylo and Skywalker stayed down in the trees, feeding me their magical energy. When Zandra, obviously annoyed with their antics, whirled on Leia and Chewie, I ordered them to retreat. I could feel their desire to rebel, but they didn't. They joined the others down in the woods, boosting my magic instead.

With their help, I'd been holding my own against the goddess surprisingly well before the others surged back onto the battlefield, but I couldn't deny being glad to see them. I'd known in my heart they hadn't abandoned me. I didn't know where they'd gone to, but I didn't care. They were here now.

We could do what needed to be done and finally end this.

"Stop her from cloning!" I yelled at Roman while simultaneously turning to summon the object I'd discarded when we first arrived.

The Stone Falls Winery bottle flew into my hand. As everyone fought to contain Zandra, the Luna Coven members formed a circle around her, my beasts joined us, and we began the ritual.

What had appeared to be nothing more than a prop for my ruse with Gwen when we'd left Soothing Sips was another trap, in case the first one hadn't worked. Saundra and Mathilde were sure the knife would have been enough, but it had been Roman who'd suggested the backup plan, reminding them that we'd be facing a powerful deity, not supernatural hunters from our own realm. Thank Goddess he had.

Our chant rose in volume and speed, and Zandra laughed at us, a shrill sound echoing off the mountains. Our magical energy continued to build, though, swirling around the circle and blowing the snow in a tornadic wind around us, silencing everything else, even Zandra. As though controlled by one force, our hands lifted to the air as we yelled the final line of the spell one more time. At the last moment, Zandra gave me a wink before she was sucked into the bottle. Roman slammed the cork into it.

And finally, as the sun began to peek over Mt. Sousa, Christmas Eve dawning, I could breathe.

CHAPTER 25

MICAH

*W*e'd won. That was still sinking in.

I didn't know whether that meant I could relax somewhat and enjoy the rest of the holiday festivities. Part of me knew I would always be vigilant—it came as part of a very long life of habits and sacrifices.

Returning back to the house after everything went down with Zandra last night, no one complained as we crawled into bed. I held Sedona a little tighter, content to listen to her soft breaths while I stared up at the ceiling. We'd talked about whether we should hold a family meeting to process the attack and Holly being taken, but neither of us could find the right words yet. That, and both Sedona and Holly couldn't stop yawning.

We ended up deciding to put the needed discussion on hold—at least until after Christmas.

Christmas . . . it seemed surreal that it was only tomorrow, that after all the darkness and danger, one of the most magical days of the year was already upon us. I'd been so caught up in searching for the Collector that I'd forgotten.

One thing I did know was that life couldn't go back to the way it was before, even though I wanted to reclaim some of that innocence and naïveté for Sedona and Holly both. The attack had worn them out, the adrenaline crash stripping away what energy they had left and leading them straight into complete exhaustion.

I was bone-weary.

Slipping my arm out from under Sedona, I waited a few moments to see if she'd resettle back to sleep. I hadn't needed to worry—she was out for the count. I could only hope that her dreams held her gently while she rested.

I padded through the still house with bare feet, checking to make sure all the doors and windows were locked and secured. The Collector may have gone, and Senora Graves was recovering from her wounds, but that didn't mean I could neglect my duty.

"I thought I heard you out here." Holly's voice reached me from the kitchen, where she was currently sitting at the island. There was a bowl of ice cream in front of her, and she tapped the chair beside her. "Can't sleep either, or are you waiting up for Santa?"

I quickly grabbed my own bowl and spoon, then helped myself to the Wonder Woman–themed ice cream she'd convinced me to buy. The first mouthful all but made me groan out loud, the sweet flavor of toffee and vanilla tantalizing my taste buds.

"You do know I don't sleep a lot," I answered, tapping my spoon to hers. It was a tradition we had and our corny way of toasting each other.

Holly smiled, and I swore she aged before my eyes. I definitely wasn't ready for the teenager—the young woman—she was becoming. "I know, but I figured it would be a way of easing into the conversation. We haven't really discussed what happened."

She was always so thoughtful . . . and straight to the point.

"You're right. We needed a moment to catch our breaths today so we can celebrate Christmas tomorrow."

Her groan rivaled my own as she rubbed her eyes, brushing away a strand of her hair that had escaped her ponytail. "And eat way too much turkey and stuffing and everything!" She looked at her ice cream and pushed the bowl away. "Maybe I shouldn't eat this so I don't ruin my appetite."

I winked at her as I swallowed another bite of my late-night treat. "Sedona's a great cook."

Holly nodded in agreement. "She says it's from all the Gordon Ramsay she watches. Somehow it rubbed off on her." Shrugging, she began fiddling with her spoon. "I know you wanted to wait, but can I ask you a question? There's something I can't stop thinking about."

I knew there was a reason she was up like I was. She evidently had a lot to process as well.

My first reaction was to ask her to wait until Sedona was up. I'd always encouraged her to ask questions, no matter the time or place, but I had a rough idea what she might want to ask. "Sure, sweetheart. You know you can." I braced myself for what she might say. There was definitely much to discuss.

"Would you really have refused to heal Senora?"

Her question surprised me. Not because that was what she picked as her first one, but because it was the very thing that kept me awake.

How honorable of a man—an angel—was I if I had been willing to let her die . . . all because I'd wanted revenge. I'd wanted to make her pay for everything she'd done.

"Honestly?" I replied, watching her as she nodded. "I don't know, Holly. There was a really strong part of me that was afraid, and I didn't want to help her."

That made her sit back, her eyes wide. "You afraid? I didn't even know you could feel that way."

Her shock made me chuckle. Did I really portray that to her? That I feared nothing?

I looked around, as though someone might overhear my next confession. "I was terrified. Someone tried to steal you away and hurt you. Then I found out that others had been attacked."

My revelation seemed to have settled well with her because she'd lost that wide-eyed wonder. "Harper. I don't know what I would've done without her, Micah. Her, Elias, and Tasha. I like Harper a lot. I'm glad she's going to be okay, as well."

I'd noticed this morning, when it was all over, that the two had already formed a bond, and unlike in the past, it didn't set my nerves on edge. I actually liked knowing my niece was establishing relationships with people she was learning to trust.

My gaze caught the clock on the microwave. It was late.

"Okay, you need to get to bed, but let me answer you first, and then I'll ask one of my own questions." I had her full attention. "I didn't know what I'd do with Senora until I looked at you. You helped remind me who I was and what I was truly fighting for. I can't keep you safe if I lose myself to vengeance and anger."

"So, you listened to Yoda when he said that fear leads to hate and hate was the dark side of the Force." A soft smirk curled her lips. Thankfully, I understood her pop-culture reference to Star Wars. Maybe she should have a movie marathon with Addie sometime—let them fangirl together.

"Something like that," I replied, reaching out to squeeze her hand affectionately. "I want you to know that you saved me. We're a team— you and me—so thank you." I pulled her into me and wrapped my arms around her.

We sat like that for a few moments. I was just so damned grateful that I could still do it—that the Collector hadn't robbed me of the ability by taking her . . . or killing her.

"So, what was your question?" she asked. We were back to finishing our ice cream before it was a complete melted mess.

"How do you feel about enrolling in Havenwood Falls High?"

Her loud squeal of delight was the answer. "Are you serious?" She couldn't smile big enough if she tried. Then it finally dawned on her what my question meant. "We're staying?" There was that shock again.

I couldn't pretend that this wasn't big news. We'd had this discussion after every attack, but this time had been different. Holly had actually been taken, and I had been blasted away into an artifact where I was helpless to break free. It was a huge breach in the security I had worked tirelessly to maintain.

I nodded. "We still have a lot to discuss and things will definitely change, but yes. We have friends here. Friends we can trust so we don't need to be alone anymore." It was a big admission to make. I'd never expected to utter these words, but they were true nevertheless. "Havenwood Falls is our home."

And it was.

We'd found our very own family of friends.

~

HARPER

I STARED out my aunt's shop window, my back against a purple chair cushion and my feet up on a footrest, my thoughts lost to the afternoon. Christmas had passed, and New Year's was approaching, the lights and decorations from the holidays still present on the streets beyond. It was ironic really, how everything significant always seemed to happen to me around the holidays. The shadows had come to me for the first time during the New Year's, and they'd been with me ever since.

Now, here I was.

The battle we'd fought with the Collector was over, and each of us had left it scarred and full of resolutions for the future. I'd spent the aftermath of the fight in the medical center being stitched and cared for, my Aunt Eloise hovering over me before she carted me back to her home and shop.

Members of the Court had met us at the door, asking questions I didn't want to answer, but I did anyway, all while Aunt Eloise berated them for interrogating a wounded victim.

I wasn't a victim, but I didn't tell her that. I was stronger. Scarily so.

The Court knew more about what I could do now. They had a record of it. What they did with it and what it would mean for me later, only time would tell. I was safe in Havenwood Falls as long as I never used my gifts for evil. I intended to never go down that road.

Aunt Eloise bustled to and from the shop to her basement apartment and back again, a too-bright smile plastered on her face as she appeared before me, a steaming mug of tea in her hands.

"Chamomile. You need to sleep," she said gently.

"I'm a little afraid to," I admitted.

I was scared of the dreams I'd have, the memories I didn't want to relive. Desi, my sentient pet weapon, bounced from his place on the floor next to the chair. He'd been kept away from the battle, ordered to remain as a backup in case we'd needed reinforcements. It didn't help that, despite being sentient, he was essentially an artifact himself and too useful to the Collector for the Court's peace of mind. The Court also needed supernatural beings that could fight if something happened to the town while some of us were weakened.

"You're a little upset, too," he insisted. "Don't even try to hide it."

Desi was right, but I wasn't saying it out loud. Putting the words out there meant admitting something I wasn't prepared to admit.

My heart was hurting over Elias Jamison. My best friend.

Once he'd been assured I was safe and being taken care of, he'd left town abruptly. There'd been no time to ask questions or find out why. He'd snuck away when I was being stitched up, having left a message with my aunt.

"I'm sorry. I have to take care of some business. I promise I'll be back soon." That was the message he'd left with Eloise. It was an understandable message. He'd done nothing wrong, so why did it hurt so much? We were friends, not lovers.

"Are you hurting?" Aunt Eloise asked.

I was, emotionally as much as physically, but I didn't tell her that. I shook my head instead, lifting the mug she'd handed me to cover most of my face.

Eloise wasn't the least bit convinced, but she left me anyway, disappearing into her reading room to prepare for an appointment.

My gaze slid to the ceiling, gliding from it to the walls on the opposite side of the room.

"When did it become so many?" Desi asked, awed, and I knew it was because he saw them too. Desi had abilities and gifts I'd never even tried to discern. He was an ancient weapon, after all.

Dark shadows stared at us from every part of the room, watching and waiting, as if prepared to come to me at a moment's notice.

It made me feel like a queen, their power a strong force, their energy pulling at me.

If I crooked my fingers, would they come? Just like that?

Memories of my time with the Collector assaulted me, her advice and words playing over and over in my head, and I gasped, my fists clenching around my cup. My head snapped back against the chair, and my lips pressed together, a steely resolve enveloping me.

I would *not* abuse my power.

"You look pale," Desi said from the floor.

I lifted the mug of tea to my lips, my gaze peering over the rim at the shadows.

"I'm fine," I muttered before drinking.

The liquid slid down my throat, soothing me, the sigh that escaped my mouth mirrored by the spirits watching me. As if we were breathing as one.

I felt like a queen.

~

SENORA

STANDING before the Court was probably the most daunting thing I'd ever done. Would they give me credit for what I tried to do? Or would they simply banish me to the Infernum?

A well-dressed witch with silvery-white hair stared down at me from the dais. I recognized Roman Bishop and the moroi vampire, Michaela Petran, seated on the panel as well. Surely, they'd vouch for me.

The witch cleared her throat. "Senora Graves, do you understand why you're here?"

That small voice of reason instructed me to lower my head and appear contrite. "Yes."

"Your actions require punishment befitting your crimes."

My stomach roiled.

"However," she continued, "because you helped Adelaide and the others save Holly and Harper, and defended Havenwood Falls against the Collector . . ." Her voice trailed off. It was obvious that whatever the decision was didn't sit well with her. It seemed almost painful for her to say it. "The Court has decided that you will be granted a provisional residency."

My head whipped up.

"You will be allowed to stay in Havenwood Falls."

"You're giving me a chance?"

For the first time, the stately witch smiled. "Yes. But there is a caveat."

"What?" I asked a little too eagerly.

"We cannot allow an empusa to stay here unchecked. That would be much too dangerous." She paused, as if waiting for me to pitch a fit. When I didn't, she continued, "There is a spell that will harness your cravings. You can keep your other powers."

"But—"

Roman spoke up. "If you want to stay, I would think the sacrifice would be worth it."

"Before you decide," the witch said, "know that your residency is probationary. We will be watching you. If we find reason, we will withdraw our decision."

I nodded.

Addie stepped up to me. "It's over. You're free to go."

Free to go? When they captured me and tossed me in jail, I truly didn't think I'd ever be free again. Working with the Collector had to be the dumbest thing I'd ever done. For what? Power? Glory? Status? None of those things. I did it for something fleeting— financial gain.

Slowly, I turned and left the meeting room with Addie by my side. Outside, I breathed in the fresh air. "How long do I have before you enact the spell?"

"It's done. My grandmother cast it as soon as you agreed. We'll need to upgrade your tattoo into a permanent one."

"Oh? I thought my residency was temporary."

"As long as you follow the rules, you'll be here for years."

ADDIE

TASE and I sat in a diner booth in Colorado Springs, not exactly how I'd imagined spending New Year's Eve, but definitely better than last year's. This year had started with two very big, very ominous challenges set before us. We'd faced them together and both times came out on the winning side. Something niggled at the back of my mind that our luck wouldn't hold out much longer, though. I tried to chalk it up to aftershock or even a bit of PTSD, but this mysterious meeting had me wigged out.

Some woman claiming to know Shelly had called Tase yesterday, asking to meet with both of us. We'd decided to take the request to the Court, because Zandra may have been safely trapped in the bottle—a taste of her own medicine—but we didn't know how far her organization reached and how loyal her minions would still be to her. We had to come, guarded as we were, if anything, to find out more information about Shelly, or Rachelle.

She had disappeared from the battle when the Collector had trapped everyone else, and nobody had seen her since. Not the real Rachelle, anyway. When Senora and Harper had described to the Court the fight in the artifact room and how "Rachelle" had disappeared—in an explosion of goo—Michaela and I instantly knew that hadn't been her. That had been the shapeshifter, posing as my twin. And nobody knew how this particular type of shapeshifter worked—if she needed to kill the people whose skin she wore. Our evidence pointed to yes, she did, which meant Rachelle, my twin and Tase's baby mama, was dead.

"Tase? Addie?" a female voice asked from behind as she approached our booth.

We both looked up to find a young redhead standing at our table now, dressed for the wintry weather in a puffy parka, beanie hat, and boots. Beside her stood a young boy wearing a gray coat and a child's backpack, clutching a stuffed Yoda doll in his arm.

"Carter?" Tase choked. The boy looked at him, confusion and wariness in his eyes. He didn't know us. That day that Shelly was supposed to meet with Tase to discuss him becoming a part of Carter's life now seemed like a lifetime ago.

The woman directed Carter into the seat across the table, then slid in herself. "I'm a friend of Shelly's. She left Carter with me. She does quite often, since she travels so much for business."

"Where is she now?" Tase asked.

Her eyes widened for a moment, then her throat moved as though it took effort to swallow. Her voice dropped to a whisper as she leaned forward. "I don't know. She hasn't come home in weeks. I haven't heard from her since before Christmas." She looked over at Carter, who was playing with his Yoda doll. "She didn't even call him!"

"Is that normal for her?"

She shook her head, her eyes watery. "No. She's always been a good mom, as long as I've known her, anyway. She always warned me, though, that her job was dangerous. I mean, she never told me what she did—she'd freeze up and then change the subject whenever I asked. But she told me every time that if I didn't hear from her for more than a few days, to contact you." She focused on Tase. "You're his . . ." She trailed off, tilting her head toward Carter, and Tase nodded.

"My what?" the boy's small, shaky voice piped up. He hadn't missed a thing.

The woman, whose name still hadn't been given, turned toward him. "Carter, buddy, this is your daddy. Your mommy wanted me to bring you to him."

He looked at Tase with narrowed eyes, then at me. "You look like her. Like my mom."

I nodded. "I'm her sister. That makes me your aunt."

"Where is she?" His eyes filled with tears, and his chin began to tremble, as though he already knew. "Where's my m-mom?"

"She's still away right now," the girl said, smoothing a hand over the back of his head, "but she told me to introduce you to your dad."

She turned back toward us. "Um, it was a long drive, and I really need to use the girls' room. Do you mind?"

We both shook our heads as she slipped out of the booth.

And never returned.

We waited for a ridiculous amount of time. I checked the bathroom, of course, but doubted she'd ever gone in. Hoping she'd eventually return, we ordered a burger, fries, and a shake for Carter. As dusk began to set in, though, and Savage and Liam, who'd been guarding us just in case, came in and said her trail went cold, we knew we couldn't deny the obvious any longer.

"Oh, I forgot," Carter said as he rummaged through his backpack. "I think I have to give this to you."

He handed a piece of folded paper to Tase. He opened it in front of me, and scrawled on it was one line:

"Please take care of him—I can't anymore."

Tase and I looked at each other. Fear shone clearly in his eyes, and I placed my hand over his.

"After everything we've been through, we got this," I said.

Hours later, the three of us stood outside the inn back in Havenwood Falls with Michaela and Xandru, counting down the last seconds of the year. I didn't know what the new year would bring. I'd done all the rituals I knew to ensure it was a good one, and so far, it was looking up. The curse had been broken, and the Collector was no longer a threat to our town and our friends. Michaela and Xandru were already discussing alternative dates for their wedding, and Tase and I had the beginnings of a family together. With friends, family, and our lovely town at my side, I felt confident in saying to any threat or challenge thrown at me: "Bring it on." I knew we could handle anything together.

As the fireworks blasted at midnight, Tase swept me into his arms and delivered a mind-blowing kiss. I gasped for breath when he finally pulled away.

"Marry me, Bean."

EPILOGUE

*C*amellia passed through the portal created for her, arriving right next to the monolith at the top of the mountain, another snow storm blowing around her. She pressed her hand to the stone, and the estate appeared before her, perfectly intact, as though there had been no battle here barely more than a week ago. She crossed the grounds without escort and entered, going straight to the sitting room and the fire.

"The child is delivered," she said, removing the beanie hat and shaking out her hair, which was currently red in the young woman's skin she wore at the moment.

"Very good."

"Is your time here over then?" she asked the cloaked figure in the high-back chair.

A chuckle issued forth. "Not even close. And neither is yours."

Camellia tried not to let her disappointment show. She was so done with this town. She'd come too close too many times to being killed, or worse—being discovered. She knew that would result in her being sent to the Infernum.

"I will always protect you," the other being said.

"Oh? Like the others you 'protect'?" The words came out before she could censor them, and she tried to hide the quotes she put around *protect*.

"There's only one now," the other said, knowing full well what Camellia meant. "And it *is* for their own protection. You will see. But my plans for you are different. And you *will* be rewarded—with your life."

Camellia heard the threat quite clearly. She looked at her booted feet, calculating whether to trust this being or not, wondering if she had the ability to escape even now.

"On one condition, though."

Her head lifting, Camellia peered over at the figure in the chair. "And what is that?"

"You've been holding out on me. I need you to tell me everything. This town—the people of Havenwood Falls—they have no idea what's coming for them. They thought they could trap a deity in a bottle, like fools. They are so ill prepared for what has been awakened."

"And what is that, master?"

"I will tell you everything, about me and about Hermod, if you tell me all you know. But first, enough with the 'master' bit." The figure leaned forward, out of the shadows, a smile on the beautiful goddess's face. "Call me Zandra."

We hope you enjoyed this story in the Havenwood Falls series featuring a variety of supernatural creatures. The series is a collaborative effort by multiple authors. Want to read more about the characters in this book?

Discover Addie, Tase, Michaela, and Xandru's story in *Forget You Not, Lose You Not,* and *Break Me Not* by Kristie Cook

Read Harper's origin story in *Ink & Fire* by R.K. Ryals and find out what happens to her and Elias from here in *Dark Seduction* by Michele G. Miller & R.K. Ryals

Catch up on Micah and Sedona's story in *Nowhere to Hide* and *Addicted to You* by Belinda Boring

See Senora in Izzie and Hunter's story, *Taming the Beast* by Nadirah Foxx

Read Gwen and Rhys's story in *Tragic Ink* by Heather Hildenbrand

Meet Tasha in *The Lurkers Within* by Danielle Bannister

Learn more about the Elan Chain in *Defying Gravity* by Kallie Ross

Also look for the YA line, Havenwood Falls High; the historical paranormal line, Legends of Havenwood Falls; the sexier side of town, Havenwood Falls Sin & Silk; the local supernatural college, Sun & Moon Academy; and the Havenwood Falls holiday short story anthologies.

Stay up to date at www.HavenwoodFalls.com

ABOUT THE AUTHORS

Kristie Cook is a lifelong, award-winning writer in various genres, primarily New Adult paranormal romance and contemporary fantasy. Her internationally bestselling, award-winning Soul Savers Series includes seven books, as well as several companion novellas and short stories. Over 1.2 million Soul Savers books have been downloaded. She has also written The Book of Phoenix trilogy, a New Adult paranormal romance series. Her books have been featured in *USA Today's* HEA section, on Good Morning America, and in the Emmy's Gifting Suite.

Kristie also created, writes in, and publishes the award-winning Havenwood Falls shared world, a collaborative project with multiple series, dozens of authors, and countless stories.

Besides writing, Kristie enjoys reading, cooking, traveling, getting her hippie on, and feeding her addictions to coffee, chocolate, cheese, The Walking Dead, Game of Thrones, and Supernatural. She has lived in ten states, but currently calls Florida home.

Email: kristie@kristiecook.com
Author's Website & Blog: http://www.KristieCook.com
BookBub: https://www.bookbub.com/authors/kristie-cook
Facebook: http://www.facebook.com/AuthorKristieCook

R.K. Ryals is the author of emotional and gripping young adult and new adult paranormal romance, contemporary romance, and fantasy.

With a strong passion for charity and literacy, she works as a full-time writer encouraging people to "share the love of reading one book at a time." An avid animal lover and self-proclaimed coffee-holic, R.K. Ryals was born in Jackson, Mississippi, and makes her home in the Southern United States with her husband, her three daughters, two playful cats named Delphi and Paris, and a coffeepot she honestly couldn't live without. Should she ever become the owner of a fire-breathing dragon (tame of course), her life would be complete. Visit her at www.authorrkryals.com.

~

International and #1 Multi-Genre Bestselling Author Belinda Boring is known to many readers as the Queen of Swoon and also the Queen of Cliffhangers. Her Mystic Wolves series has topped many charts, along with receiving several awards and nominations such as Paranormal Book of the Year, Best Debut Book, as well as being in the Top 3 Best Rated on Amazon. With additional titles like *Wanderlust*, *Enchanted Hearts*, *Loving Liberty*, and *Broken Promises*, it's easy to see why readers are captivated by this swoon-worthy author!

A homesick Aussie living amongst the cactus and mountains of Arizona, Belinda Boring is a self-proclaimed addict of romance and all things swoon-worthy. It wasn't long before she began writing, pouring her imagination and creativity into the stories she dreams. Whether urban fantasy, paranormal romance, or romance in general, Belinda strives to share great plots with heart and characters that you can't help but connect with. Of course, she wouldn't be Belinda without adding heroes she hopes will curl your toes. Surrounded by a supportive cast of family, friends, and the man she gives her heart and soul to, Belinda is living the good life.

~

Nadirah Foxx, the alter ego for SF Benson, has a fondness for dark, twisted romance featuring suspense and adventure. Her characters are flawed, but they always find a way around their obstacles and demons.

Connect with Author Nadirah Foxx

Facebook: https://www.facebook.com/NadirahFoxx/

Twitter: @nadirahfoxx

Blog: https://nadirahfoxx.wordpress.com/blog/

ACKNOWLEDGMENTS

Thank you first to the Creator, who has blessed us with our abilities, our friendships, and our readers. A huge hug of appreciation goes to all of the Havenwood Falls authors who have in one way or another contributed to the making of this collaboration. It wouldn't exist if not for all the individual stories that make up the Havenwood Falls world and the characters that populate our favorite fictional town.

Written by four of us—a first for all of us—this book was definitely a team effort. It has been a fun, interesting, and learning-filled ride. Beyond each other, we are so grateful for Liz Ferry, who cleans up our insides nicely with her editing expertise, and Regina Wamba, who creates our stunning outsides. This particular cover couldn't have been more perfect.

Thank you most of all to the #HWF Junkies and everyone who has read a Havenwood Falls story, even if this is your first. We're pretty sure it won't be your last. Welcome to our town! Be sure to get registered—the people here are a little protective of each other.

AN EXCERPT

Addicted to You (A Havenwood Falls Novella) by Belinda Boring

As Havenwood Falls' resident bookstore owner, empath Sedona Mathews is surrounded by a swirling mess of feelings—both fictional and real. But until now, they'd always belonged to others. Then sexy angel Micah Westbrook walked into her bookstore and her life. After a surprising twist of events, she finds herself head over heels in love with him, and no longer vicariously living through the romance novels she reads and sells. Sedona's deeply embroiled in her very own story, with strong, intense, passionate desires erupting from inside her and throwing her world into chaos and mischief.

Love.

Infatuation.

Lust.

Addiction.

The trouble with emotions, however, is that in the space of a minute, they can twist and change—complicating life in a heartbeat. When Sedona's hunger for Micah pushes her over the edge, she soon realizes just how much she's neglected her abilities. But after the recent betrayal and attack in Shelf Indulgence and rumors circulating about the mysterious Collector, Sedona must figure out if her new attitude toward Micah is really part of the journey, or if there's something more sinister at work.

ADDICTED TO YOU

BY BELINDA BORING

APRIL 2018

"The sooner you hire someone, the sooner things can go back to normal," Maxwell's gruff admonition broke the silence. My ghostly friend had been studying me all morning, and now he was peering around me to the ignored paperwork by the bookstore's computer.

It had been a long, grief-stricken four weeks since the psychic fair and the attack afterwards. Just one short month since I'd been shot and betrayed by someone I'd trusted so completely that I hadn't seen it coming.

I still hadn't brought myself to enter the storage area.

I still hadn't found the courage to sort through the pile of applications stacked on the counter beside me. I wasn't going to rush it. I prayed that my faith could be bigger than my fear, and so far, it was working. One step at a time.

Micah was the one who put away orders as they came in, and he was the one who worked on the to-do list I created each morning. I saw the worry in his eyes whenever I handed it to him, the way his lips kind of parted as though he was about to speak but thought better of it. He understood that I was processing things in my own way, in my own time. The consideration made me love him just that little bit more.

Love could be deadly for an empath.

I knew that painfully well, having lost both my parents to heartbreak. It was a mantra that I'd repeated over and over inside my head, but since meeting Micah Westbrook, there was an even louder voice in my head trying to convince me that it would be one hell of a way to go.

Micah.

The man made it worth the risk.

Maxwell, on the other hand, was not as kind or sympathetic.

I let out a weary sigh and covered the job applications with a magazine.

"Out of sight, out of mind," I countered, not ready to deal with him either today. There was no question that my friendly ghost was struggling as well in the aftermath. His sense of helplessness had been etched across his furrowed brow as he recounted how much he hated not being corporeal. I'd listened to his furious diatribe about Austin, and the only way his temper had been somewhat placated was knowing that Austin had been banished from Havenwood Falls. He'd simply wished for a chance to exact his own justice—the wringing of the traitor's neck.

His words. Not mine.

He'd felt the betrayal keenly because he had stepped in to fill my late grandfather's shoes and watch over me. After I'd discovered the Dunlap Broadside in one of his trunks up in the attic, the truth had come out that not only had my friend been there at the first printing of the Declaration of Independence, but he'd then gone on to fight alongside General George Washington in Yorktown. There was no doubt in my mind that he'd seen all manner of brutality fighting against the English, and had he been able to, he'd have killed Austin with his bare hands.

It had revealed a savagery in him that I'd never witnessed before. I felt like I was meant to be scared of him because of it. Instead, I felt safer. Ghost or not, Maxwell was not a man to be meddled with.

"So you're back to sticking your head in the sand. I see." He didn't bother camouflaging the disappointment in his voice.

My hand hit the top of the counter a little harder than I intended.

"What do you expect me to do?" I asked, my voice filled with exasperation. "I'm not a robot. I can't just experience something . . ." A large lump formed in my throat, making it difficult to swallow and speak. I cleared my throat and tried again. "I can't just bounce back like nothing happened, Maxwell. Why can't you just let me do things in my own time?"

Compassion flooded his gaze, and I could see he desperately wished he could wrap his arms around me in a hug. "Girl, I wish I could. I wish I could say we lived in a world where nothing bad happens and good people live happily ever after. Would you rather I lie to you?"

He peered deeply into my eyes until I could feel him touch my soul. His honesty helped soothe some of the jagged pieces still too raw to mend.

I glanced at the applications again. Here was my opportunity to be equally as candid—to share what was truly at the root of my hesitation.

"What if I make another mistake? What if I don't see the danger and next time it's more . . ." I struggled to finish my sentence.

"Fatal?" The man had read my mind perfectly.

I nodded. "I'm not being morbid or anything, but if it were just me at risk, it wouldn't be too big of an issue. But Holly was there. Micah and I are together now, so she's always going to be around. Micah had tried warning me about the threats he was protecting her from, and I contributed to it." The words came tumbling out with such a force, I was breathless at the end.

Micah's voice surprised me. "Is that what you think?"

Somewhere in the back of my mind, I'd heard the tinkling of the doorbell, but I'd been so wrapped up in my thoughts and conversation with Maxwell that I'd missed Micah entering. The very sight of him made my heart race a bazillion miles an hour, and without thinking, I licked my lips in anticipation.

Kissing was the last thing on his mind, however.

Right now, he pretty much mirrored the exact same expression the ghost did—incredulous shock.

I guess I hadn't confessed that small tidbit to them—my feeling that the attack was my fault and that somehow I should've been able to prevent it.

I shrugged my shoulders, not ready to face both of them about this. "Austin was my employee, my responsibility. It was my store. *I* provided the chance for him and Holly to meet. *I* encouraged their friendship and study dates. How much clearer does it need to be?" I'd gone over the details countless times in my head, often while I lay awake at night, staring up at the ceiling in my apartment. "You know I'm right."

Micah actually scoffed, making a sound that was a cross between a snort and a grunt. "I know you are wrong. One hundred percent, emphatically wrong." He took a step closer, so he could cradle my cheek with his palm. "Sedona, please tell me you don't honestly believe that."

As much as I savored the warmth of his touch, I knew in this moment, with these guilt-riddled feelings churning inside me, it didn't feel right to accept such kindness. Reluctantly, I stepped back and broke the contact.

Micah stared down at where I'd just been standing, a serious look of sadness crossing his handsome features. I hated the fact that I'd been the one to put that expression there. I just didn't know how else to explain what had been bottled up inside me until now.

Maxwell disappeared once he realized this was a private moment. His only parting gift was to mouth the words *listen to him.*

Micah reached for me again, and I skirted away.

"Please don't do that, Sedona. Don't close yourself off from me."

I couldn't help it. I burst into a laugh that bordered on hysterical. "This coming from the man who walked through those doors practically a blank slate, a man with so many secrets that I'm surprised you're not drowning in them all." I could feel my skin heat from the emotional outburst, but I didn't suppress it. "Even now, after everything we've been through, you still keep parts of yourself shielded from me."

There was a hint of frustration in his response. I could feel him trying to be patient and understanding, but like every other man on the planet, he couldn't see it from my perspective.

"This isn't about me, though. We're talking about you." And with all the skill of a ballroom dancer, he sidestepped around my retort, and waltzed me back to where the spotlight was back on me. "Help me comprehend what's going on in that beautiful head of yours." He offered me a gentle smile to try to soften the mood, but it was too late. Everything I'd kept stuffed inside was rushing to the surface, ready to explode.

"Don't flatter me!" I exclaimed. Part of me knew it was unfair to unleash on the man I was dating, the man I was falling in love with. Another part egged my own impatience on, telling me to purge until there was nothing left but the echoes of an empty heart. Surprisingly, there was another voice that had recently emerged. It was that voice that whispered if there was ever a person I could completely confide in and bare my soul to, it would be Micah.

"I'm sorry," he murmured and reached for me again. This time I didn't shrink away.

"Don't you think it's ironic that you expect such transparency from me, yet you keep everything within you tightly wrapped up in some impenetrable fortress?" When he nodded, not speaking a word in response, I took courage. "I may be an empath, but I'm also human, Micah. How else am I meant to feel? Tell me, how am I meant to process this? What must I do so we can all go back to pretending like the world is wonderful and filled with rainbows and butterflies?" I stared up into his deep blue eyes, the challenge thrown. When he didn't reply, I let out a loud, unladylike grunt. "That's what I thought."

Scooping up the damn applications, I gripped them in one hand as I grabbed my keys and threw them at him. "Lock up after yourself. I can't stand being here a second longer."

With one last look over my shoulder, I fled Shelf Indulgence, not waiting to see if he'd follow.

So much for me being okay with what happened and being strong.

Being an empath wasn't as fun as it sounded. It was taxing—both emotionally and physically—and often when I slipped up and invaded someone's feelings (by accident), the consequences resulted in me feeling like an outcast.

Micah had offered to help heal those emotional wounds with his own angelic grace, but I'd politely declined. Every time he used his powers—for whatever reason—it sent out a beacon to those who were hunting for him and Holly. I was grateful that he'd given me a small vial of his divine essence that I wore around my neck, under my clothing. It replaced the black tourmaline pendant I used to wear, but had given to Holly to help ground her after Austin's attack.

Micah's gift was precious to me, and I didn't need to think too hard to know that given time, scars would fade, and it would almost be like my young employee's betrayal had never happened.

Almost.

I could deal with almost.

I'd spent so much time hiding away in my bookstore, sheltering the town from my troublesome gifts, that I'd forgotten just how powerful I could be. Looking down the barrel of the gun Austin had pointed at me, threatening to take Holly away, I'd made a silent vow that should we survive, I would never make myself that vulnerable again.

But that was then and this was now.

It seemed like I was surrounded by lies at the moment, but none bigger than the ones I was telling myself.

I wasn't doing fine.

I was falling apart, and for the life of me, I couldn't stop the tears that finally started to fall.

Purchase *Addicted to You* where books are sold.